THE GRUDGES OF GAJANAN GODBOLE

Salil Desai is the author of the much-acclaimed Inspector Saralkar Mystery Series that includes – *The Kid Killer* (2023), *Murder Milestone* (2020), 3 *and a Half Murders* (2017), *The Murder of Sonia Raikkonen* (2015) and *Killing Ashish Karve* (2014). The books are currently being adapted into a web series by Jio Studios. Titled *Kalsutra*, the first season is based on *Murder Milestone* and is due for release soon. Salil is also the lead writer of the screenplay of *Kalsutra*.

His other popular books are *Murder on a Side Street* (2011), *Lost Libido and Other Gulp Fiction* (2012) and *The Sane Psychopath* (2018). Salil's short story 'Sound Motive' has also appeared in *The Hachette Book of Indian Detective Fiction* (2024), while other short fiction has been published in anthologies by Penguin, Westland and Unisun.

His short story 'The Perfect Day' and novel *The Sane Psychopath* are also in the process of being adapted for screen as feature films.

Salil was also one of the 4 international authors worldwide selected for the HALD International Writers' Residency in Denmark, hosted by the Danish Centre for Writers and Translators in June 2016. He was also invited and spent the month of May 2023 at Gullkistan, Centre for Creativity, Iceland. Know more about him at http://www.salildesai.com/.

'Be ready to be drawn into Salil Desai's terrifically nuanced world of Gajanan Godbole and his middle class Puneri life. Wickedly entertaining and disturbingly relatable, Salil Desai's novel taps into our deepest, most primal urges through Gajanan's journey of revenge. It is the classic underdog story that had me rooting for it like a child. And yet with each act of calculated vengeance, Gajanan's transformation scared me as he went deep into the abyss of the unshackled life that he now had walked into. Local, visceral and funny as hell, this is easily Salil's best!'

SANDEEP MODI, Director of *The Night Manager*
(International Emmy Awards 2024 Nomination) and *Aarya*

THE GRUDGES OF GAJANAN GODBOLE

SALIL DESAI

hachette
INDIA

First published in 2024 by Hachette India
(Registered name: Hachette Book Publishing India Pvt. Ltd)
An Hachette UK Company
www.hachetteindia.com

1

ISBN (Paperback) 978-93-5731-833-4
ISBN (eBook) 978-93-5731-935-5

Hachette Book Publishing India Pvt. Ltd
4th/5th Floors, Corporate Centre,
Plot No. 94, Sector 44, Gurugram 122003, India

Typeset in Electra LT Regular
by Mukul

Printed and bound in India by
Manipal Technologies Limited

MIX
Paper | Supporting responsible forestry
FSC™ C043100
FSC www.fsc.org

In ceremonies of the horsemen
Even the pawn must hold a grudge

'Love Minus Zero/No Limit', Bob Dylan

1

NEAR DEATH

COVID got my wife, Sumitra. In the second wave. I didn't get to see her dead. COVID protocols and all. So, Sumitra got a state-sponsored cremation, and I didn't have to do a thing. Not that I was in any position to, for COVID almost got me too.

But I survived. No one thought I would – not the doctors, not the nurses and ward boys, or even the young patient next to me in the ICU. But then that's the thing about me. I've often pulled through in life pretending to be half-dead.

My name is Gajanan Godbole, and I am sixty-eight. As they say in the Bible or one of those holy books: 'The race is not always to the swift nor the battle to the strong, but time and chance happen to all.'

I don't remember much of my epic life-and-death struggle against COVID. It's all a blur, and I think half the time I wasn't even in my body. My soul however got the uncanny feeling that I wasn't much wanted in heaven either, probably because in life, I wasn't much of the pious God-believing types.

Also, as eerie as it might sound, I seem to remember hearing this whispered conversation, while comatose:

'Do we take him?'

'No,' replied a gruff other voice, 'the one next to him.'

'But isn't he too young?'

'When has that ever stopped us? His purpose is over…' the gruff one remarked.

'And this old man's isn't?'

'You ask too many questions,' the gruff one snapped. 'He's an asset…to be activated soon.'

I can't say for certain whether I was hallucinating or if I really was privy to this purported chat between Yamraj, the god of death, and his assistant Chitragupt. But when I finally recovered, I learnt that the smart aleck next to me had copped it the previous night.

So it set me thinking. I could've died, but I hadn't. That kind of made me feel lucky, even immortal, something I had never ever felt before. In fact, all my life, I had felt much too mortal, as if the slightest cockiness from me would invite divine comeuppance. That is the reason I had remained steadfastly meek, embracing the path of least resistance, since I first started going to school. It made total sense, given my physical size and the size of my heart – avoiding all confrontations whatsoever and waving the white flag, long before even the dim prospect of any battle with anyone could arise.

But COVID did something to me. Something strange. I felt reborn – a different avatar of me, sans my trademark meekness. It was inexplicable, indescribable – that feeling of waking up as an altered Gajanan Godbole – as if my meekness had just been a tight-laced corset which I had worn all my life, conned into believing that the shortness of my breath and the squeezing in my chest were the natural states of my being. And now that it had come undone, I had discovered that my chest could heave freely, and my breathing was no longer constricted.

'Papa,' shrieked my daughter Trupti, as soon as I picked up my ringing mobile.

I frowned. A call from Trupti was always a strain on my nerves. Mercifully, doctors didn't allow patients to receive calls in the ICU, even from kin who were calling from foreign lands, or my recovery would have promptly reversed, if obliged to speak to Trupti. But now that I was home, there was no way of avoiding a conversation.

'Yes, dear…'

'Papa, I was so scared I'd never hear your voice again,' Trupti continued shrilly. 'Thank God you beat COVID!'

'Yes, yes,' I replied, 'it was a narrow escape…'

'But Mum, poor Mum…She wasn't so lucky,' Trupti cut me short, 'Did she suffer a lot, Papa?'

'Ah well, I don't know, dear…I hope not,' I said. I had not really given a thought to whether my wife, Sumitra, had suffered. Normally, anyone or anything that came into contact with Sumitra suffered. But maybe COVID was an exception and had turned the tables on her.

'Didn't the doctors tell you anything?' Trupti asked, dissatisfied with my reply.

'No, no…They thought it better not to tell me the details.'

'But why didn't you ask them?' Trupti demanded indignantly.

'Well…I…I was kind of dying myself…so…'

'Oh Papa, I'm so sorry! I hate myself for not being there when Mum breathed her last.'

I cleared my throat, but stopped myself from comforting her that she wouldn't have been able to be anywhere close to Sumitra, because of COVID protocols. Besides it was a moot point whether anyone would have been comforted by Trupti's presence especially when they were breathing their last. So,

I restricted myself to saying, 'There, there child, don't beat yourself up about it.'

'Was she given a proper funeral, Papa?' Trupti asked.

'I am sure they did, dear.'

'I mean, we have been watching all these horror stories about mass cremations and bodies being disposed in the Ganges,' Trupti said melodramatically. 'I've been having nightmares imagining Mum's fate – visualizing her body floating down the Ganga.'

I could feel the irritation gnawing at my vitals, but I tried not to snap. 'We live in Maharashtra, dear. No Ganga here… the situation isn't all that bad.'

'Thank God, Papa, thank God,' Trupti wailed, 'will you ever forgive me for not being there for you?'

Wasn't she a drama queen, just like her mother! For a moment I wrestled with the idea of hanging up – feigning a call drop or bleating 'hello, hello' as if I couldn't hear her, then ending the call and switching off the mobile. But I just made some appropriate noises that sounded long-sufferingly affectionate. It was a mistake.

Trupti was immediately consoled and encouraged to pile on more suffering. 'Just a minute, Papa, Swanand wants to talk to you.'

I winced and again thought of hanging up. Swanand was my son-in-law, Trupti's husband – a pompous ass and a bore – an IT coolie who acted as if having settled in the USA, he was entitled to be patronizing with every acquaintance back in India. Actually, I ought to have been grateful to him for having taken Trupti off my hands and making her his own problem but there are limits to how grateful one can humanly feel towards an overbearing prick named Swanand, meaning someone who finds happiness within their self.

The ridiculous name only served to disgustingly remind me of masturbation – Swanand. With Trupti as his wife, that might any way have been his only route to happiness, if living with her mother had been any indicator.

'Hi, Baba,' Swanand's voice boomed into my ear from 10,000 miles away. I hated him calling me 'Baba' just because he called his old man the same. I had suggested once or twice that he call me 'Papa' like Trupti did. But no, Swanand stuck to 'Baba'.

'Hello, Swanand,' I replied tolerantly.

'Never thought you would make it when we learnt you had COVID,' Swanand said, as if lamenting my survival. 'You see, of all the people I knew who got hospitalized due to COVID, only three survived, including you! Congratulations!'

It was totally in keeping with his vacuous, insensitive character, and the congratulations sounded more grudging than complimentary. 'Ah thanks,' I replied.

'God's grace, God's grace,' the idiot continued. 'We prayed for you continuously.'

If I hated him, I hated his yuppy spiritualism even more. So he was going to take credit for my survival too.

'Of course, too bad Aai couldn't make it', he said, as if covering up for why their prayers and God's grace could not save Sumitra.

'Hmm…' I responded with malice, calculated to embarrass him. 'Perhaps Sumitra should have been spared and the Almighty could have taken me instead…'

There was a baffled, awkward silence for a second, at the other end. 'No, no,' Swanand finally spluttered, 'God…God… does what's good for each soul.'

Deep, I thought with a silent chuckle and decided to have some fun at his expense. 'If you say so, but I think

Sumitra would disagree that dying would do her soul any good,' I said.

'Of course, of course,' Swanand hastened to reply. 'She lived life with so much…er…gusto…but…but…'

By gusto he was probably referring to Sumitra's unmitigated meanness and spite, which he too had gotten a taste of.

'But like you say, God knows what's best for someone's soul,' I said, completing his sentence for him.

'Yes, yes, Baba! We must seek comfort in that thought,' Swanand said pithily.

'Hmm,' I replied, not done with my fun yet, 'in some cultures I think they celebrate death instead of mourning. Tell me, Swanand, since your spirituality quotient is so high, should we also celebrate Sumitra rather than mourn her?'

Either I really heard or imagined his sharp, vexed intake of breath. 'Er, Baba, well…' he trailed off.

I could almost visualize his pathetic mental calisthenics to answer that question, with Trupti no doubt beside him listening sternly, while making faces.

'Er, I mean mourning and…er…celebrating…are in a way two sides of the same coin, Baba.'

'How?'

Swanand snorted, as if trying hard not to be exasperated. 'Well, we mourn because we miss the person we lost, but that person's soul has attained salvation, which is something to celebrate, right?…*Moksha*…?' he ended lamely.

'Hmm,' I said, suddenly tired of Swanand and his convoluted pretensions. 'Profound and illuminating perspective, Swanand! You should be the Chief Spirituality Officer of your company, not just the CTO,' I added in my most grating, mocking Puneri timbre.

There was a perplexed, offended silence at the other end so probably the shot had hit home, for my son-in-law, after having been sacked from a giant corporation, had begun working for a 7-people company with the pompous designation of 'CTO'.

'Papa,' Trupti's voice took charge again, 'I'll come as soon as it's safe to travel, okay? Maybe in about three to four months, once we've had our second shot. Till then you take care. Don't get infected again.'

'That's virtually impossible, dear. I've got antibodies now,' I said saucily. 'Of course, I might still die of post-COVID complications or just about anything else. But either way, your travel plans needn't change.'

'What are you saying, Papa,' she snapped. 'Don't be morbid. You'll be fine. Ravi and Hema said they'll check on you every alternate day and Sushilabai is coming to cook and clean daily, right?'

'If nothing else kills me, Sushilabai's cooking certainly will,' I remarked.

'Oh, come on, Papa, Sushilabai's not all that bad. What's the alternative? Would you rather order a daily tiffin service?'

'Not a bad idea, but I have a better one,' I said impishly.

'What?'

It was delightfully tempting to shock and awe my daughter by saying that I might consider remarrying, but I decided to save it for a future conversation. 'Never mind,' I replied.

'What, Papa? Tell me.'

I chuckled to myself. It was time to run out of battery. I hollered a frail 'hello, hello', disconnected the call and then switched off the phone, for I knew Trupti would try calling a few times. The BSNL landline was out of order, as usual, so there was no danger of her calling me on it.

It felt so good to hang up on someone. I couldn't recall doing it to anyone in my entire life hitherto. I mean, I had done it a few times but I always hastened to call back again or had taken their call, if they rang back.

This was a new me, who had not only hung up on Trupti, his own daughter – a person who intimidated me as much as her mother had – but had also switched off the mobile phone so that she could not bother me for some time at least. If she wanted to panic, that was her problem not mine.

I hummed a tune I hadn't hummed in over forty-five years. I would've even performed a little jig, if I knew how to. What was happening to me?

2

NEW, AWESOME ME

I sat back for some time, taking in the feeling that was sweeping over me – the realization that I was, at long last, alone and free from the petty tyranny of Sumitra. More importantly perhaps, from the meekness that had yoked me for life, to accepting my lot and the many injustices fellow human beings had heaped on me, without me ever having the nerve to sock them back.

Why did I suddenly feel all that was about to change? What made me think that my system had purged me of fear and inhibition, the two bugbears of my life that had always held me back? It was a delightfully reckless sensation, as if I could dare to do anything. But could I really, or was it just an illusion?

I decided to check it out. I got up and opened the door of my flat and rang the bell of the apartment adjacent to mine. As usual, loud music was blaring from inside, which had frequently bothered me in the past. It grew louder as the door opened and one of the young men, Mobin, I think his name was, stood there and regarded me with a questioning look.

'Arre, Uncle, aap? How are you? Fully recovered now?'

'I'm okay, thank you,' I said evenly.

'Sorry to hear about Aunty…We were shocked. My condolences…' the boy continued.

'Very kind of you,' I replied. 'Can you please turn down the music?'

There, I had done it. And not just done it, but done it calmly; unruffled without being apologetic or obsequious. Something that would have made me a nervous, gibbering wreck earlier, to even ring the bell.

Mobin wasn't exactly taken aback, but I think he was definitely surprised. After the constant badgering by Sumitra, I had in fact, once or twice in the past, made such a request. But it was more like a senior citizen abjectly requesting a favour. This tone was new to the boy.

'Music? But it's not loud, Uncle,' he said.

'It is. I can hear everything, and it disturbs me. That's why I have come.' The words were out of my mouth, with a natural, cool assertiveness that was most unnatural to the 'old' me.

Mobin stared and his shoulders stiffened defensively as he hesitated. On the one hand, I was a frail, old, recently bereaved widower, who had just recovered from a life-threatening illness; on the other, here I was, telling him something that was no less than an affront to people of his ilk and age.

'But, Uncle, some sound is bound to come. Me and my friends are just chilling…'

'By all means, enjoy yourselves but turn down the music,' I replied nonchalantly. 'You are chilling. I am recuperating, and I can't do that with the music blaring.'

He was a little riled now. 'But, Uncle, you can shut your windows.'

'Have you shut yours?' I asked, feeling not even the slightest flutter. Whereas earlier, I would have collapsed by now.

Mobin's eyebrows squished together into a busy frown. 'But no one else is complaining,' he said, falling back on the oldest tactic, by putting the complainant on the defensive. I gave him a steady stare. What I said next, and the way I said it, was so out of character that I felt I had been possessed by someone else. 'Turn down the damn music, or I'll call the police.'

His eyes popped out with anger and bafflement at my demeanour. 'Police?'

I nodded, looking him straight in the eye. Suddenly there were other voices from within the house, and two heads made themselves visible – another young thug and a cute yet pugnacious-looking girl.

'Kya hua, Mobin?' the guy asked, giving me an appraising, cocky look. 'Any problem?'

Rallied by these reinforcements, Mobin said, snarkily, 'Uncle is saying lower the volume or he'll call the cops…'

'Cops?' said the cute girl and gave a little giggle. The other thug joined in with a derisive chuckle of his own. 'Cops won't do anything, Uncle…'

'You stay here?' I asked the two newcomers flanking Mobin.

'No, they are my guests,' Mobin replied.

'Then ask your guests to stay out of this discussion,' I snapped rather curtly. 'And if you also feel that the cops won't do anything, then I'll dial 100 right in front of you and call the beat marshals.'

Mobin's face turned ugly, as if he was about to grab my collar or mouth some abuse, but miraculously I didn't flinch a bit. I just regarded him coolly, as if I were James Bond.

The two guests had also quit mocking and were looking at me anxiously now. The girl put her pretty hand on the boy's arm and whispered, 'Chal jaane de! Let's not spoil the mood…'

I could make out that they were all a little drunk.

'All right,' Mobin said suddenly, then wagging a finger at me, he added, 'I'm doing it only because you've been ill, and because of Aunty's demise...But next time, I won't listen... Okay, Uncle?'

It was his face-saving gambit, but I too, was not done yet. 'There shouldn't be a next time, Son, or I'll directly call the cops.'

He seethed again, his youthful ego egging him on to do something rash. But the girl pulled at him again, 'Let's get back to the party, Mobin...chhod na...' she said in her husky, Usha Uthup–like voice. The shoulder strap of her tank top slipped down to her arm as she tugged at Mobin, and I rather liked what I momentarily saw, for she quickly yanked it back over her shoulder again.

Mobin let himself be dragged in, staring at me with all the hate he could muster. I didn't move an inch till the door shut behind them. The music volume continued to remain defiantly high for a few more minutes before it was turned down abruptly.

A frisson of excitement ran all over me. Wow, I couldn't believe what had just happened! Who the hell had I turned into? I leisurely walked back to my flat and lay down on my bed. Is that what victory felt like? Winning against other mortals – an argument, a fight, a battle of nerves, a confrontation, a combat, the duels of life against bullies; against anyone you needed to stare down or had done you wrong.

Sweet! Mind-blowingly sweet! I couldn't remember the last time I had felt this good. And perhaps, the reason I didn't remember was because I had never felt this good in my life before.

I exhaled.

Somehow, I suddenly wished I'd had a cigarette with me right now and blown smoke rings. I had stopped smoking forty years ago, after Sumitra refused coitus until I did. It wasn't much of a coitus, but it was all I had. That ended my dalliance with cigarettes, although the coitus too ceased a few years later and became a once in two months kind of thing. But my smoking didn't resume, as I couldn't quite gather the nerve to defy Sumitra, although she could no longer dangle coitus denial at me.

But honestly, it wasn't as if the urge to smoke had ever been strong for me. Today, however, I was seized by a sudden celebratory yearning for it. Momentarily, I had the audacious and mischievous urge to go ring Mobin's bell again and ask for a cigarette. How hilarious would it be to see their faces again? I chuckled. The mood I was in, I was sure I could pull it off with sangfroid but then I decided to delay gratification. I had already had enough fun with my new self today.

I was also tired and a little sleepy, so I decided to call it a day. After all, the COVID had been for real. I was about to turn over and sleep, when I heard the doorbell ring. For a minute my old self seemed to spring out suddenly from within. My heart started beating fast. Could it be that after downing a few more pegs, Mobin and his gang had decided to have it out with me? Was I about to get thrashed by a bunch of young louts, if I dared open the door?

But almost immediately, my new self was back in charge. Nothing of the sort was going to happen and even if it did, I could handle it. I was astounded by this self-belief that was sloshing inside me.

I got out of bed, switched on the light in the drawing room, shuffled to the door and peeped out of the eye-hole. Ah well, it wasn't my neighbour at all. It was a hassled-looking Ravi, my nephew. I realized what must've happened and opened the lock wryly.

'Kaka, thank God, you are all right,' Ravi blurted out.

'Let me guess. Trupti called you because my phone wasn't reachable?' I asked.

'Yes, she asked me to come around and check, since she said you got disconnected abruptly and were unreachable thereafter. She thought you collapsed or something…' Ravi said, looking vexed and relieved in equal measure.

'Well, sorry to disappoint you and Trupti, there's no emergency here. I'm hale and hearty, but my mobile ran out of battery and the landline's dead.'

Ravi frowned. 'Haven't you put your mobile for charging? She said it was almost an hour ago.'

'I couldn't find my charger,' I lied brazenly. 'I'll look for it tomorrow morning.'

'Oh, okay,' he said, eyeing me doubtfully. I could read his mind. Ravi had always known me to be neat and fastidious, incapable of such carelessness. 'I'll just call Trupti and tell her you are fine. She may want to hear your voice.'

'Go ahead…call her, but I am going to bed. I'm exhausted, Ravi. Just shut the door behind you,' I said, turning away, playing the convalescing old man, which I really was, but not as much as I made out to be.

'Sure, I'll do that. You want anything else, Kaka?' Ravi asked, looking concerned.

For some reason, this nephew of mine had always had a soft corner for me. At forty-two, Ravi wasn't the least like me or even his own father – my late elder brother, a brain-dead bank employee – who'd promptly kicked the bucket a few days after he'd retired. Ravi had turned out to be more enterprising, and he and his wife, Hema, ran a franchise for a popular sweetmeat brand. His business was badly hit during the first lockdown. But not as much in the second, since his shop could remain open for some hours, most days.

Ravi was perhaps the only one I generally could let my guard down with, although not much for he too tended to get scandalized easily, given the stiff Marathi, middle-class Puneri upbringing he'd had.

'If you can, bring your Kaki back to life,' I said to him, my voice immediately taking on melodramatic pathos. Of course, I didn't mean what I said, but that's the kind of mushy sentiment Ravi would have expected from me.

The poor boy was embarrassed and rattled beyond measure of course and looked at a loss to say anything for a few seconds. He then finally spoke, 'I am so sorry about Kaki. I know what a big void she has left in your life…'

He probably meant every word, but he had only drawn them from the countless Hindi or Marathi films one watched, studded with such corny dialogues in hackneyed scenes of people losing a beloved spouse.

'You must miss her so much…'

'Why would I?' I almost blurted out but didn't. Why did people think old couples were devoted to each other? Or missed each other? I don't know about other countries, but here in India, where arranged marriages were the norm rather than exception, especially in my generation and the previous one, most couples were probably sick of each other. Particularly couples like Sumitra and me, who had nothing in common except equal and mutual disdain. What had held us together was probably her propensity to be a nuisance and my natural talent for being bossed around and henpecked.

What would Ravi know about that of course? He and Hema were one of those rare 'happily married' couples. So, I just gave a pretend-sad nod, as if I was overcome with grief. 'You and Hema are doing so much for me, Ravi…' I mumbled, 'God bless you…' I began staggering to my bedroom.

'You are embarrassing me, Kaka. Sleep well. Call me anytime you need me.'

'Good night,' I replied as I lay down again, brimming with a heady feeling.

Sleep began stealing over me and the last thing I heard was Ravi mumbling silently into his phone, probably assuring Trupti of my well-being and then gently closing the door behind him. I dropped off to sleep wondering how I would wake up feeling – like the new Gajanan Godbole or the old meek one?

3

SPOUSE-FREE BLISS

'What shall I prepare for breakfast, saheb?' Sushilabai asked, a few minutes after supplying me with her special brand of foul-tasting tea. I wondered how I had tolerated this awful brew for almost a decade now. It was watery, it was over-boiled, it hardly had any sugar, too much of ginger and not enough milk. She had mucked up just about every ingredient that one could while making tea.

'Can't you make better tea?' I admonished rather mildly, considering the kind of stuff she'd served.

Sushilabai gave me a surprised stare. 'What's wrong with it?'

'Everything!' I said after putting down the cup.

'Saheb, that COVID seems to have affected your taste buds,' Sushilabai shot back. 'This is the same tea you and madam – bless her soul – have relished for many years…'

'Hmm, well I don't like it,' I said. 'I like my tea milky, with two spoons of sugar, just a tinge of ginger and not over-boiled. From now on, that's how it's got to be.'

She looked at me as if I was telling her to change some ancient royal recipe, bordering on blasphemy.

'Let me see if you can do it. Make me another cup right away,' I added.

Sushilabai didn't like it, yet she nodded. 'Okay. But what about breakfast, saheb?'

I brooded constructively about what in her culinary repertoire I found least offensive to my tastes. I hated her pohe, her shira, her upma, her thalpit, her sabudana khichdi. So, not having breakfast was the best option. But I couldn't do that. I needed to eat something of course.

'Do we have Maggi?' I asked.

'You want noodles for breakfast?' she asked incredulously, as if I had demanded dog food.

'You know how it's made, right?' I asked. 'It's just putting the contents of the packet in boiling water and stirring.'

'Of course I know how to make it, saheb,' she said, scowling, then went to the kitchen, reached for one of the shelves, rummaged through it and found packets of Maggi that Sumitra had probably stocked to feed me and herself on the days Sushilabai would absent herself.

'One or both?' Sushilabai asked holding them up for me to see.

'Let's try your skills with one first.' Without another word, Sushilabai got busy with it as I waited with trepidation.

'Here, saheb!' she said, a few minutes later, placing a bowl full of noodles in front of me. Miraculously, they didn't look soggy or tough to chew or anything like that. 'And here's tea…'

'Bravo, Sushilabai,' I said and thought of blowing a kiss at her, but desisted. My new self couldn't go that far so soon.

'And what for lunch?' the cook asked, disregarding my praise, sticking to her agenda.

'Ah ha!' I said, taking my first mouthful of the noodles, turning her question over in my mind. To the best of my memory, rice and dal were the only two safe bets, but I decided

I had to at least try my best to explore Sushilabai's potential as a cook.

'What is it you cook the best, Sushilabai?'

'What?'

'Tell me some of the finger-licking stuff that you make for your own family?'

She frowned again, as if I had asked her to spill some deep conjugal secret. 'Veg or non-veg?'

'Anything. Veg or non-veg, even beef…' I said recklessly.

She didn't flinch or look as if she was ready to arrange for my lynching, because of hurt religious sentiments. 'Well mutton and bhakri…my kids love it…' she finally said with an unsuspected degree of coyness.

'Oh wow! How about you get some mutton and make it tomorrow's menu,' I responded encouragingly.

'Okay, saheb,' she replied readily.

'So that's settled, but the problem is today's lunch. What can you rustle up?'

She wiggled her nose a bit, then said, 'Well I make really good curried potato, but not the way madam let me cook…'

'Ah, but Sumitra isn't amongst us now,' I pointed out, 'And I am game for potato curry, your style…'

'But, saheb, it's really hot and spicy…' she said doubtfully.

'I like it hot and spicy, Sushilabai,' I replied, raising an eyebrow, and perhaps there was something in my voice and manner that she actually seemed to blush.

'Okay, saheb. And should I make chapatis, rice and dal to go with it?'

I was again filled with misgivings at the mention of chapatis. Sushilabai's chapatis were prison-quality – thick, unevenly baked and many a time, hard to chew and swallow. Sumitra would always take the better ones by design or accident, and I would be left with the cud-grade ones.

'Sushilabai, let's skip the chapatis for today, just rice and dal are fine.'

'And what about dinner, saheb?'

I was exhausted by now. 'I'll manage dinner with eggs and bread.'

The cook seemed disappointed, but then brightened, probably realizing her workload was decidedly lighter. 'I was so sad after hearing about madam,' she said, becoming chatty, deciding to use the time saved on cooking, for dishing out some condolences to me. 'Such a wonderful lady – ever smiling, always considerate.'

I looked up at her, astonished. Chewing my noodles, I was wondering whether she was really talking about Sumitra. All I could remember of their relation was a state of constant verbal spats – Sumitra haranguing and ordering, and Sushilabai grumbling and sulking – the result was an unappetizing fare at every meal for ten long years.

I was sorely tempted to tell Sushilabai about the choicest epithets Sumitra had verbalized and the innumerable grouses she had nursed against her, just to see her reaction. But I let it pass, sipping the second cup of tea, which clearly marked an improvement over the first.

Sushilabai, meanwhile gushed on with her homage to her late mistress. 'She never hesitated to give me advance wages. She used to say, *Sushila feel free to ask if you are in need of money…*'

I nearly spilled my tea at this utterly contrary description of my tight-fisted wife and gave a non-committal grunt. Sushilabai sighed. 'But who can stall God's will. They say God first snatches the sweetest amongst us all…'

Now this was too much and if she'd said one more syrupy word about Sumitra, I would've rolled over with laughter. 'I can see you were quite fond of her, Sushilabai,' I responded wryly.

The irony was lost on her. 'Yes, yes, I was, saheb,' Sushilabai replied hastily. 'You must be so lonely without her…'

'Ah well,' I said, gagging back a giggle. For a moment a roguish visual flashed through my mind, of me suddenly lunging at Sushilabai, hauling her over to the bed like a caveman and…

I hiccoughed, strangely aroused by the thought. How long had it been since I last had intercourse in my life? Twenty years? Twenty-five? Probably more. I couldn't really recollect. Sumitra had downed shutters on that a long, long time ago. Why would I miss my wife or be lonely without her? Oh, what a waste! To have lived like a monk even when married. I bet many monks had a better sex life than I had had. No good fretting of course, but maybe now I could make up for it somehow, although definitely not with Sushilabai, despite the recently concluded momentary wet daydream.

She was awaiting my response to the mournful remarks she had made about Sumitra and my loneliness. 'Well, I have Sumitra's memories to keep me company, Sushilabai,' I said, 'Alas, why didn't she take me along?'

'No, no, saheb. Trupti tai would have been orphaned then. Madam left you behind for a purpose.'

Now that sounded exactly like something Sumitra was capable of doing – making me carry the can. Moreover, I doubt Trupti would really have minded being an orphan. But I couldn't say this to Sushilabai, could I? So instead I gave a half-sob, tucked into my noodles and noisily slurped my tea.

Mercifully, the cook took the hint to end the conversation and went into the kitchen.

4

REWIND AND REBOOT

I finished my breakfast leisurely. The house was still and remarkably peaceful in the absence of Sumitra's voice or movements. By this time, she would usually have been raising hell about something or the other – mostly with me or Sushilabai or the dhobi, the vegetable vendor, the grocer's delivery boy or some other hapless soul who happened to be part of her routine. That's just the way she was and if it hadn't been for this once-in-a-century pandemic, I'm sure she would have easily outlived me and thrived till a ripe old age.

My eyes strayed to her photo on the wall that Ravi had hastily arranged, framed and mounted, keeping up with a custom that God knows who had started. What did they do in the era before photography? I doubt most people could afford portraits 150 years ago. So when and how and who decided that hanging images of the dead should become a hallowed custom?

In fact, where had Ravi gotten Sumitra's photo to blow up for framing? I couldn't even remember where and when this particular photo of hers had been clicked. She had a sly, superior half-smile on her face, as if she had the measure of whichever person she was glancing at. I doubt it was me, because then the expression would have been more of a sneer.

And then I realized with a shock that this was the longest I had ever looked at my wife in the last two decades or so. Most of my life I had spent throwing anxious, momentary half-glances at Sumitra or avoiding her eyes to minimize interaction. When had I last looked at her properly, full in the face? No, I just carried around a mental picture of her, regularly updated in my mind's eye by those quick, anxious half-glances, nevertheless retaining the core image of her meanness, formed and frozen since the time I stopped looking.

Now that she was safely dead, I was surprised to be reminded that she had been plain-looking, and the unpleasantness of her personality was not evident in her facial expressions as such. Ugliness, like beauty, was in the eyes of the beholder. It was my lived experience of Sumitra's spitefulness, which subconsciously superimposed that sour attribute onto her face every time I had regarded her. The face in the photo didn't reflect or foretell her mean temperament, yet she always appeared like that to me.

Sumitra could have been nice, you know, if she had just made an effort but she hadn't. Why? I suddenly wondered. There had always been a sullen, embittered quality to her, as if she was incapable of normal happiness and found a tiny bit of it only in the compulsive need to make others unhappy.

I cackled to myself at the brutally honest insights of my new self. Would my old, stuffed, timid self even have dared to think such thoughts – of bearing ill-will towards the dead?

'Saheb,' Sushilabai said, suddenly popping up like a jane-in-the-box. 'You'll need to sort out madam's things, no? Just let me know and I'll help you with it.'

I couldn't help admiring the cook's chutzpah. No doubt she hoped to get her hands on some of Sumitra's stuff that she could persuade me to part with – a saree here, a purse there, some cosmetics maybe or even a handful of the millions of trinkets and knick-knacks that women bought and hoarded. And all under the pretext of helping an old widower look through his dead wife's belongings.

'It's too soon for it, Sushilabai,' I said, sighing and dashing her hopes just a bit. 'But I'll definitely tell you when I need the help…'

She gave a thin smile, trying to mask her disappointment as I pretended to be the frail old codger and she, the concerned, helpful housekeeper.

'Or perhaps I might leave it for Trupti to sort out,' I said wickedly.

Sushilabai stiffened and frowned. 'Is…is Trupti tai coming? I mean with this COVID and all…'

I shrugged. 'She said she's trying. It would be much more apt, wouldn't it? For a daughter to look through her mother's belongings.'

'Yes, yes,' Sushilabai said, none too pleased and returned to her cooking.

I left it at that. She was right of course. I needed to rummage through Sumitra's stuff – her accumulated stash of jewellery and valuables, and most importantly, documents like the house papers, our joint bank account, fixed deposit receipts and a lot of other such things that had been in her name, which she had guarded like a cobra sitting on treasure. It would have to be done when Sushilabai was not around. But the first question was – where was the key to Sumitra's almirah?

And that was the first time I noticed my complete blankness, I simply couldn't remember her usual hiding place.

'No thief will ever think of looking for it here,' Sumitra had often boasted to me, assuming of course that some thief would bother breaking into our one-bedroom apartment in the first place. While I could clearly remember this assertion of hers, I could not recollect the hiding place, for the life of me, at this moment.

I had of course never bothered to challenge Sumitra's assertion. Nor, for that matter, had any thief. A few times though I had been tempted to displace the key and put it elsewhere just for the heck of it. But I hadn't ever summoned the nerve. Ironic then that now that I could place the key wherever I wanted to with Sumitra in no position to stop me, I had completely forgotten where it was, in order to first retrieve it.

Was it some side effect of COVID – this kind of memory lapse? Or was it Sumitra's way of fingering me from beyond? It was simply infuriating. I shut my eyes, trying to think hard and shine a light down the dark pathways of my memory. My new, powerful self suddenly felt powerless. Then I told myself to relax. Maybe it would come back to me if I let it be.

Meanwhile, what did I want to do with myself now? I was surprised to stare at this existentialist question which had never occurred to me before. My routine, after retirement, had fallen into an unwavering pattern. Wake up at dawn, slip out of bed noiselessly for fear of stirring Sumitra, finish my ablutions and go for my morning walk, looking exactly like the jaded, dull pensioner I was. I had even managed this on most days during the lockdown; of course, only under the cover of a few other senior citizens in the area.

Back home I would have tea with Sumitra, who would be slurping her second cup served by Sushilabai. Her early morning harangues would be lighter than the ones later in the day, but reading the newspaper would help me cope with it. Then, of course, nothing much. I would bathe and have breakfast. Afterwards I would either set out to do some bank work or other work or was sent out on an errand by Sumitra –

to buy some groceries or vegetables or to fetch some medicine from a chemist or to round up some electrician or plumber or handyman to do some repair work in the house, which my wife would claim was long pending.

If it got done, she'd grumble it wasn't satisfactory, and if it didn't, she'd grind her teeth and fret at me. Then came lunch, during which she'd complain I was eating too less of something or too much. Then she'd lecture me on the topic of the day, most of which were about my many personal failings and flaws in life. That took good care of both her digestion and mine.

Thereafter, there would be some peace for two hours, when she retired for an extended siesta while I had a shorter nap, after which I'd read a little as she snored. At 5 p.m., she'd stir and complain about not feeling well – acidity, migraine, feverishness, knee pain, lower back pain, headache, vertigo, nausea, fatigue, you name it.

When I'd offer to make tea, she'd snigger that I didn't know how to make good tea, then stagger to the kitchen and make two cups. I must say, this tea would usually turn out well. Sumitra would then turn on the television and start watching her blasted serials, which would go on till night fell. In the meantime, I would saunter down and sit for a while in the society premises, usually bumping into some other senior citizen at a loose end like myself, exchange some boring and tepid conversation or amuse myself by smiling benignly at whoever happened to pass by.

At 8 p.m., I'd be back home to quickly watch some news, while Sumitra heated up dinner or chatted up Trupti or one of her friends or relatives on the phone. Dinner accompanied by more end-of-the-day harangue from Sumitra followed, about all the things I hadn't fixed, some gossip which I was entirely uninterested in and then off to bed. Mercifully, I would fall asleep the moment my head hit the pillow.

Sometimes, this routine would vary of course when Sumitra would go for her *bhishi* group meetings or other engagements, or when some guest came home or we got invited by someone. During COVID, this too ceased, but all in all such was my dull, insipid existence – a life in which I don't remember wondering what I wanted to do because everything was set and all I had to do was breathe and go through the motions of being alive.

I guess my old self had gotten so used to things that it never expected to be confronted with a change of scenario. So my new self wondered – what did I, a sixty-eight year old survivor of COVID, suddenly imbued with a new unfamiliar spirit, want to do now? Like a man who had been blind all his life, suddenly receiving the gift of sight, I was dazzled and baffled – trying to make sense of a sensibility that I had never known before.

Why did I suddenly want to do something anyway? Where had this question come from? Or was it just because I had no clue how to spend the time of my days now that it wasn't going to be punctuated by Sumitra's overbearing presence? That having been relegated to playing a particular side role, I was now suddenly thrust on to the centre-stage in my own life.

And then, just like that, answers to the question began trickling out of my brain. I wanted to do things I'd never done before, things I hadn't even known I wanted to do. All the things my meek self had been too inhibited to even desire or imagine – to live like I had never lived before – unfazed and unafraid of the consequences. To do whatever took my fancy, to do things simply because I felt like doing them and because they were there to be done!

But most of all I wanted to get even – with life and its oppressive compulsions and with people and things that had harmed me, humiliated me and boxed me into my pathetic meek self. Could I do that? Or was this just a storm in a tea-cup due to some excitable hormones or volatile chemicals in my brain that would soon quieten down? Could I do something right here and now? For instance, could I throw and smash to pieces that stupid ceramic flower pot without flowers that Sumitra insisted on keeping on the window sill of our bedroom, citing Feng Shui or Vaastu or some such tripe? Right here, right now! Spontaneously, without a second thought?

The next moment I picked up the damned vase and simply hurled it across the room. It shattered to pieces, and I experienced a warm, angry glow of satisfaction, totally disproportionate to the inconsequential act.

'What happened, saheb?' Sushilabai's voice came through the kitchen. 'Are you all right? Hope you have not collapsed or something?'

I made no reply, still savouring the rush of pleasure from this seemingly insignificant act of violence that my new self had actually performed.

'Saheb…' Sushilabai's shrill voice rose higher and came nearer as she peeped into my room, having made her way from the kitchen.

'It's nothing, Sushilabai. Just a smashed flowerpot…' I said, grinning at her.

She stared. 'But it used to be kept here by the window. How did it fall and break there?' she asked, looking puzzled.

I just gave her an enigmatic smile. 'I threw it, just clean it up later.'

She goggled, almost unwilling to believe me, but finding it hard to make sense of it. 'You threw it, saheb?'

'Yes.'

'But why?'

'Because I loathed that flowerpot,' I replied.

She stared again, then shrugged. 'Okay, I'll clean it up.' She turned her back, shaking her head as if it was more than she could process.

5

MY GRUDGE LIST

I beamed triumphantly at the pot I had shattered. They often said, many a time people had to pick up and put together the broken pieces of their lives. Well, in my case, the opposite was true. Blowing to smithereens all that formed the architecture of my bondage would do me good. My own brand of creative destruction.

What had been most exciting was the violence in the act. It had been a moment of pure exhilaration – a release, a feeling of physical power, of raw dominance. It had been almost therapeutic. I felt like picking up something else and flinging it at the wall to experience the same kick again. I had never committed an act of violence before, and I had never known how good it felt.

If it felt so wonderful to smash an inanimate object, how much more thrilling would it be to pound someone's face or, better still, kill someone! My thoughts quickly escalated to the realm of bloody fantasy.

Kill someone?

I blinked once, I blinked twice, then thrice and the thought hadn't yet been retracted by my mind – no shock, no fear, no guilt, no bewilderment, no moral rambling.

Instead, a curious stillness had filled my mind, cutting out all the white noise and ambient sounds. And then sprouted a quiet question – If I ever contemplated killing, who would I most likely kill? An imaginary clock began to tick in my mind, like the one we hear on quiz shows while the audience waits for the participant to attempt an answer. The names percolated out of my brain almost effortlessly:

Nandu Khandagale. Sundar Nambiar. Kamal Kishore Puri. Geeta Hirway née Divte. Srinivas Bapat.

Five names. Five people who had harmed or humiliated me so badly that I bore a grudge. One that had lasted long enough for me to remember them instantly with the same bitter intensity. Five people who I had let run roughshod over me, without having a hope in hell of thwarting or hitting back. Five people who I had been too weak and meek against to stop from doing damage that chipped away at my life. Five people who could have let my life be better or happier but had instead robbed me of it.

Five evil people who had committed crimes against me and who needed to be given the punishment they had escaped!

NANDU KHANDAGALE

6

BURPS AND FARTS

1964: That's the year Nandu Khandagale came into my life.
1965: That's the year he ruined it for me.

Nandu Khandagale didn't need to come to school. He didn't want to come to school, certainly not for the purpose he was being sent to school for. His family was rich. Nandu's father owned a cinema theatre, a saree store, a brick kiln, a sand supply agency and an illegal desi liquor outlet that did roaring business. He probably ran other quasi-legal businesses too.

Nandu had been enrolled because he was too much trouble at home and basic schooling was a badge of honour back then for those prosperous but illiterate. To wit, Nandu showed neither inclination nor aptitude for studies. He was anyway two years older than all the other students in my class and spent his time in a state of blissful boredom, nibbling away at the copious amounts of eatables in his school bag – bananas, guavas, raw mango, or dry fruits like cashews and raisins, sometimes biscuits and hard toffees and, of course, the food in his tiffin.

It was as if his school bag was meant for snacks and not books. When Nandu was not munching, he fiddled with marbles or distracted his bench partner or the boys seated in front of or behind him. He chatted away in an undertone that was more like a stage whisper, or cracked jokes or if completely bored, he would constantly produce a burp or yawn at will. At other times, he would let out farts of varying notes that were a veritable sound and smell show.

For a long time, I had nothing to do with him. Neither was my desk anywhere near his, nor did we have anything in common. Also, Nandu wasn't a bully to pick on anyone and everyone, so we were in the same class but quite unacquainted with each other.

But then our class teacher, Sarode Sir, on a sudden whim reshuffled the desk positions and partners of all the students. And as fate would have it, I landed right next to Nandu. As my meek little heart sank and I took my place next to him, Nandu was busy polishing off a dozen cashew nuts. A few minutes passed before he dusted his hands and began a conversation.

'Your name's Gajanan, no?'

'Yes…'

'Where's your elephant head?' he asked, bubbling with mirth; my name being one of the many of the elephant god, Lord Ganesh.

I was too nervous to reply.

'What? Forgot it at home?' he teased again.

I gave a weak smile.

'What's your surname? Godbole?'

'Yes,' I said.

He rumbled with mirth again. 'You a Brahmin?'

I nodded.

'My father says Brahmins are no good. They scare easily,' he observed, but there was no animosity in the way he said it.

I suppose someone else in my place could have at least taken offence, but I saw no reason to stand up for the entire Brahmin community.

'My father says he can beat the shit out of any Brahmin, and they'll run away squealing,' Nandu continued in the same vein. I cast an anxious sideways glance at him, but his face was amiable.

'What…what are you?' I whispered.

'What caste?'

'Yes.'

'We are Marathas,' Nandu replied, some kind of pride creeping into his face, 'Shivaji Maharaj's caste, warriors!'

'I see,' I said, my voice quivering. 'Why does your father want to beat up Brahmins?'

He looked stumped for a few seconds. 'I don't know,' he said finally. 'I'll ask my father.'

Sarode Sir suddenly howled at someone in the classroom, and my first conversation with Nandu Khandagale came to an end, at least from my side, because he resumed talking after a while.

'Do you know how to burp?'

I looked at him quizzically. Nandu grinned, then gave a live demonstration of his burping abilities.

'Like this…'

I tried to shush him, scared to death Sarode Sir might suddenly take notice and decide to wallop me. Times were like that. Teachers could wallop pupils with abandon, no questions asked. Hardly a day went by without at least a couple of us receiving a hiding.

Nandu himself was a habitual delinquent – yelled at or beaten up at least once a week. But of course he was undeterred. 'Or like this…' he continued, burping louder.

I was hit by sheer terror. 'Not so loud…Nandu…' I pleaded.

'Good one, no?' he said triumphantly. 'Want me to teach you?'

'Not now,' I whispered again.

'Okay, later,' he replied, probably taking mercy on me. For a few minutes he remained quiet, then asked, 'You a scholar or what?'

I shook my head.

'I thought all Brahmins are good at studies,' he continued, this time tucking in a black raisin.

'I'm okay…' I said modestly.

'I hate studies,' Nandu remarked with a wink.

'You don't like school?' I hissed, unable to stop myself from getting drawn into a conversation.

'No, I like school. I just hate studies.'

'But school is for studies…'

'Nah! Not for me,' he asserted with a twinkle in his eyes. 'Studies are for Brahmins or folks who need to get a job.'

I gawped at him. 'Then why do you come to school?'

He sighed and suddenly looked grumpy. 'For fun – but a fat lot of fun I can have when my father wants me to be the first matric pass in the family…' he grumbled, then brooded for a few seconds. 'Why me? My father's non-matric, so are my uncles. My grandfather never had to study. So why must I? It's not fair! What do I need to pass matric for, when we are rich?'

It was of course a novel point of view, given my cloistered life in which school and studies were not to be questioned why. I gave Nandu a sympathetic nod, but he had already found solace in a raw mango. Little did I know then that fate had got me in touch with Nandu Khandagale for a much more sinister reason – my first big downfall in life!

7

DARA SINGH @ POOJA TALKIES

Which hero do you like?' Nandu asked me one day, about a month later, when I had more or less settled down to become his bench partner.

It had been a nerve-wracking month; getting used to his incessant munching, his wisecracks, his burps, yawns, hiccups and farts. I had had my ears painfully squeezed twice by Sarode Sir along with a few clips on the head, all courtesy Nandu's antics. He, on the other hand, received a more thorough thrashing once and a few other punishments too – all of which Nandu had borne rather nonchalantly, as if enjoying it all.

He leaned across now, since I had not replied and repeated the question, 'Which heroes do you like, Gajanan?'

My parents didn't take me to the movies often and certainly not for Hindi movies. 'Raja Gosavi,' I whispered back, recollecting the name of the most popular Marathi movie star of the time.

'Tchah…not Marathi heroes,' he said dismissively. 'Hindi film heroes – Dilip Kumar, Dev Anand, Raj Kapoor, Shammi Kapoor?'

I shook my head. 'I…I…My father does not take us to Hindi films…'

Nandu gave me a puzzled look. 'Why? Brahmins don't watch Hindi films or what?'

Why he considered me a spokesperson of all Brahmins, I don't know. But I refused to answer on their behalf.

'My father thinks Hindi films are a bad influence on children,' I replied.

'Why?'

I shrugged, trying to be unobtrusive, not interested in attracting Sarode Sir's attention.

'So, you haven't even seen any Dara Singh movies?' Nandu asked me in a tone that suggested my life hadn't been worth living.

'Dara Singh, the wrestler?' I asked, my curiosity piqued.

'Yes. Who else?'

'He acts in films?'

'Of course he does. You didn't know?' he asked incredulously.

I shook my head, wondering what all had I been missing.

'I have watched all his films – *King Kong*, *Faulad*, *Rustom-e-Baghdad*…total timepass. Dara Singh beats the shit out of all the bad guys,' Nandu said rapturously.

'Shush, Nandu…' I said, realizing his voice was rising with excitement.

'Tchah,' Nandu assured me. 'Sir's done his walloping for this week. He won't do anything today.'

I wasn't buying his optimism. Teachers were unpredictable creatures, and Nandu possessed a rhino's hide, but I didn't.

Nandu was quiet for a while and I heard him munching on peanuts, while also producing one or two full-throated yawns.

'Dara Singh's new movie is releasing next week – *Hercules*! You want to watch it?' I heard Nandu whisper, as he prodded me in the ribs.

'Me?'

'Yes, you with me.'

I glanced at him, perplexed. 'Where?'

'Pooja Talkies, you ass. My father owns it. I thought Brahmins were supposed to be bright.'

It suddenly dawned on me, for I had forgotten Nandu's father owned a cinema theatre.

'But when?'

'Any show, any time.'

'But I can't bunk school…'

'So, after school. How about the 3 p.m. afternoon show?' Nandu asked.

'After school? What will I tell my parents?'

He shrugged. 'Think of something, man. What's the use of that Brahmin brain otherwise?'

I was quiet for a while. The idea of watching a Hindi film, that too a Dara Singh film, was a forbidden fruit and it seemed massively tempting, even to one as timid and mousy as me.

'But where will I get the money?' I said, turning to Nandu.

'Who's asking you for money? You are my guest. I know you are poor,' Nandu replied, but there was no hint of derision in his voice.

Nevertheless, I did feel he was clubbing me with the unwashed masses and slum dwellers by designating me as poor. 'We are not poor,' I remonstrated.

'You father does a government job, no?'

'Yes, he's an assistant postmaster.'

'Well, then you are poor,' Nandu asserted decisively but before I could protest again, our heads were banged together with a thud. Our bête noire, Sarode Sir, had prowled over and caught us talking in class, which was punishable by hideous walloping.

~

True to his word, Nandu smuggled me into Pooja Talkies to watch *Hercules* the following week for the afternoon show. The theatre manager, Baban Chavhanke, a man rendered strong and silent due to a plug of tobacco embedded in his mouth, waved us inside, casting a supremely contemptuous look at me. He had first gestured in my direction, rubbed his thumb and finger together, signalling money.

'He's my friend,' Nandu replied. 'Give us good seats.'

Chavhanke pointed out to the 'House Full' board anointing the entry gate.

Nandu gave him a sly grin in return. 'Chavhanke Kaka, you want me to spill your black secret?'

The manager was unfazed, although the plug of tobacco made his Adam's apple bob up and down. But he was not moved or agitated enough to spit it out. He blinked at Nandu, then gestured to us to follow him up the stairs leading to the balcony and handed us over to the usher. The usher, Banya, turned out to be as garrulous as Chavhanke had been silent.

'Nandu Dada,' he hollered like a long-lost friend as soon as the manager was out of earshot. 'You'll love the movie. What fights, what stunts! Dara Singh is the best! Who's this?'

He looked at me appraisingly. Since most patrons had already been seated and the rest were either relieving themselves in the loo or buying greasy samosas or wafers, Banya wasn't particularly busy.

'That's my friend, Gajanan. He's a Brahmin,' Nandu replied, and both looked at me as if I was some specimen to be pitied.

'Ah ha!' Banya exclaimed and then winked at Nandu. 'But is he old enough to watch Mumtaz?'

Both burst out laughing. Little did I know that they were referring to the buxom heroine of the film, who later went on to become a much sought-after star in the seventies.

'No, he's a *limbu-timbu*,' Nandu answered with a chuckle. '*Limbu-timbu*' was a pretty serious insult, back then, for any boy to be dismissed as underage and therefore, of zero practical value in any enterprise, particularly team games.

'Watch out for his hormones then,' Banya said. 'He might suddenly attain puberty when Mumtaz comes on screen.'

Both of them cackled loudly again, and Nandu slapped me on the back as Banya pointed to our seats in the dimly lit balcony hall.

Awe and bewilderment were the only emotions raging through me. It was such a new experience. It's not that I had never been to a theatre before – my father took us to a Marathi movie every six months or so, and we would sit in the stalls. But the atmosphere of watching a Hindi movie, that too from the balcony, promised to be totally different; and so was the crowd.

This was also the first time I was sitting on cushioned seats and no sooner were we seated than the newsreel playing on screen ended, the hall turned pitch black and suddenly the movie began, accompanied by shrill whistles from the audience.

I have no recollection of the movie at all – perhaps if I underwent hypnosis now, I might – but whatever it was, it simply blew my mind. All I do remember was Dara Singh clobbering half a dozen people every few minutes to earth-shattering music; Mumtaz romancing him between fights and perpetually breaking out into songs, interspersed by close-ups of Dara Singh's macho face and his magnificently sculpted physique.

Every now and then Nandu would nudge me and gush, 'Man, look at that punch! I am going to become like Dara Singh when I grow up.' And so on and so forth. When he wasn't saying that, he'd declare, 'I'm going to marry Mumtaz, just you wait, Gaja…' And then he'd whistle and join the happy hoots.

To me, it was an introduction to a world I'd been totally sheltered from. It was a cultural shock – I'd been abducted from a drab planet and held to heavenly ransom in a new, colourful galaxy.

Who would want to go back?

8

POCKET MONEY

So commenced my forbidden life in Nandu's paradise. I bluffed to my mother that I had been told to stay back and do some work at school. There were a couple of kids from other grades in the tenement we lived, but none of them was old enough to pose a threat even inadvertently. The closest any of my classmates lived was a few houses down the lane, but my parents were unlikely to have any contact with them. My elder brother, four years older than me, went to a different school altogether, so there was no danger that my visit to the cinema would be discovered by him either. And if I was meek, my elder brother was meeker still.

So Nandu and I fell into a pattern. Every fortnight or so, he would propose a movie and off we would go to his father's theatre, scowl at the manager Chavhanke, get regaled by Banya's repartees and, of course, watch a dazzling movie, with evil villains, plenty of fights, ear-splitting music, tuneful songs, lovely damsels and catcalls all around.

It went swimmingly for almost a year or more. Of the movies I do remember watching wide-eyed were Dara Singh's *Samson*, Shammi Kapoor's *Rajkumar* and Kishore Kumar's

Mr. X in Bombay. Nandu continued to fart, burp, eat and pay no attention whatsoever to studies. Life was good but then the first sign of the disaster that was to assail me, struck.

One day, I noticed a bunch of papers lying under our desk. Curious, I picked up the bunch to discover 15–20 movie tickets. 'Nandu,' I said, nudging him, 'why have you brought these tickets to school?'

Without a word, his instant reaction was to snatch the tickets from my hand.

'Where'd you get that?' he growled.

'Below the desk…You must've dropped them,' I replied.

His face broke into a sheepish grin. 'Don't tell anyone.'

'Okay,' I replied, finding it odd but at a loss to understand. Nandu said nothing further, so neither did I. But a little later, curiosity got the better of me. 'Are you taking the whole class to a movie or what?'

He burst out laughing, sending a ripple of anxiety down my spine that Sarode Sir would hear.

'No!'

'Then why so many tickets?'

'It's my pocket money,' he replied and winked.

'Your father gives you movie tickets as pocket money?'

Nandu's rumbling laughter sounded again, followed by an aggressive bellow from Sarode Sir warning us of dire consequences that would leave our backsides permanently etched with foot-ruler marks.

'No, you numbskull,' Nandu whispered once Sarode Sir turned to the blackboard again. 'I got these from Chavhanke.'

I didn't know much about pocket money because my father never gave us any, but it did seem odd even to me that the theatre manager, Chavhanke, should give Nandu pocket money, instead of his father. But then what did I know about the practices followed in rich households?

It was not long before I got to know the secret of Nandu's pocket money. I had often wondered where he disappeared during the tiffin breaks or sometimes even in the short interval between two periods. A few times I had spotted him talking to students of senior grades – older boys who we never went near for fear of being mercilessly bullied. How was Nandu so at ease with them; barging into their strongholds and speaking on equal terms, I wondered?

Somehow, I suddenly had a hunch that it had something to do with the cinema tickets. So, I began watching Nandu closely on these sorties. And sure enough I soon realized what he was up to. The older boys he met would usually hand him a school notebook. Nandu would open it casually, pick up something from it and slip it into his pocket. Then out came his hand from the other pocket, placed something in the book, shut it and handed it back.

Bingo!

'You sell the tickets to those older boys?' I hissed triumphantly, when I had observed him on a few more occasions. He gave a huge grin and gurgled, 'Ah that Brahmin brain of yours is working all right! It's a secret, Gaja…You better not tell anyone.'

I shook my head vociferously. 'But why?'

'Why what?' he asked.

'Why do you have to sell them tickets? Can't they buy it from the counter at the theatre?'

He sniggered. 'Because the shows are always "House full", you bum, and then they'll have to buy in black…'

'Black? What's black?' I asked. I faintly recalled he'd said something to Chavhanke about 'black' that first time he'd taken me to see *Hercules*.

'You don't even know what "black" is?'

'No,' I said.

He sighed and gave a burp, then gobbled a few cashew nuts as I waited for his reply. One thing I'd always noticed was that Nandu would never offer me any eatables, except for that first time.

'Look,' he said, munching away, 'usually some goons buy up many tickets and then they stand outside the theatre and sell them at a higher price. That is called "black", understand?'

'Oh, but can't you stop them?'

He looked at me pityingly as if I were some imbecile. 'No,' he said shortly, 'and don't ask me why not.'

'Okay.'

'Good! Now these boys in our school can't afford black, so I sell them tickets at just a slightly higher price, but much below the black ticket price.'

I gaped at him with new respect in my eyes. I was finally beginning to see what a crooked character Nandu was. 'Does your father know?' I asked innocently.

'Are you mad? He'll wallop me to the end of the world,' Nandu said with a look of amused horror.

'Then how do you get so many tickets?'

Nandu grunted and a cunning yet pleased look lit up his face. 'Chavhanke Kaka! He's my hen that lays golden eggs.'

Then he gave the lowdown on his sordid tale of blackmail. Apparently, Chavhanke was hand-in-glove with some black ticket–sellers. And it was this 'black' secret that Nandu had stumbled upon, courtesy the usher Banya. It hadn't taken long for Nandu to figure out a way to make some additional pocket money on the side by working out an insider deal with Chavhanke.

A thrill passed through me. 'But…but what if your father comes to know?'

'Tchah! How will he know? Nobody knows I've put the squeeze on Chavhanke, not even Banya. And, Chavhanke

Kaka is hardly going to tell my father! He'll find himself thrown out of the job, not to forget he'll earn a thrashing from my father or even the police…' Nandu summarized succinctly.

I was impressed by his daredevilry. The tobacco-chewing manager had looked every bit a villainous character and Nandu suddenly seemed like Dara Singh himself. From then on, I felt an added frisson whenever I watched Nandu skip over with his contraband. It used to happen once or twice a week and Nandu would be considerably busy making multiple trips to different corners of the school – mostly the corridors in front of the senior boys' classes or in some corner of our small playground or near the toilet, wherever the rendezvous had been pre-planned.

It was almost as if I had appointed myself the lookout. Having spilled his secret to me, Nandu would randomly whisper to me every now and then, just how much profit he'd made, whenever there was a bumper sale of tickets. He also boasted about the negotiations he conducted sometimes – tales of arguments and gullibility and his own wiliness.

I listened in awe, sometimes with envy, at his enterprise and abilities. Then one day he casually said, 'Do you get any pocket money, Gaja?'

'Yes,' I lied.

'Then how come I've never seen you spend it on anything?' he challenged me.

'I do…at a shop on the way.'

He gave me a sideways glance and poked me in the ribs. 'How much?'

I let my imagination soar. 'One rupee…' I hazarded a princely sum by my standards.

'Every month?'

'Every week,' I said, emboldened further, 'Five rupees per month actually.'

He burped then cackled. 'You lousy liar,' he teased. 'Unless your father pilfers money orders at his post office, he'd hardly be able to give you that much.'

'I am not a liar!'

He sniggered. 'Then turn your pockets and show me your money.'

'I already spent this week's,' I said defiantly.

'On what?'

I was stumped for a second. Since I had never received any pocket money, how was I to think on my feet what I had spent it on? 'Why should I tell you?' I fumbled.

He threw back his head and laughed, and for a moment I hated him. 'Why must you always make fun of me?' I said. 'Just because you are rich?'

His laughter stopped abruptly, and he was quiet for a while, as if he'd realized he'd done something mean. Ten minutes later he spoke again, his tone very conciliatory. 'You can also earn some pocket money, even if you don't get it from home, Gaja!'

'How?' I said, turning to him eagerly.

He smiled conspiratorially, 'By doing what I do.'

I looked at him quizzically. 'Means?' I asked, trying to decipher his statement. 'Sell tickets like you?'

'No, by selling postal stamps in black,' he said with a poker face.

'What?' I said, scandalized.

Nandu dissolved into a giggle. 'Of course by selling tickets, you idiot! Hand over tickets and collect money for me. I'll give you 10 paise per ticket.'

I stared, dumbstruck, unable to process the offer. 'But…but why…why do you need me?'

He let a beat pass. 'I don't…but you are my friend, so I thought I'll give you the chance to earn some pocket money,' he said with a shrewd expression I could not read then, '…if you want to…'

My heart suddenly began beating harder at the thought of dabbling in something forbidden yet exciting, and visions of earning money for it. But then my timid self sprang back to life. 'No…no…' I said.

He gave me a jeering frown. 'Just like the Brahmin you are…My father's right, I think your ancestors were all rabbits, scooting away from the slightest risk!'

'I am not scared,' I blurted out involuntarily, rising to the bait.

'Then do it once and show me,' Nandu said, 'Afterwards you can decide if you want to continue to earn pocket money…'

And that's how Nandu reeled me in as an accomplice in his nefarious activities. The same day I made my very first delivery, with my heart beating at two hundred strikes per minute. I had earned my first pocket money of thirty paise. The die had been cast for my downfall!

9

FOREBODING

For the next few weeks, life was a breeze. What do they call it these days…Ah yes, mule! I was the mule who smuggled tickets to students of other classes – small consignments of course – two tickets or maybe three. Bigger consignments, were handled by Nandu himself, especially for the seniors. I was the one who catered to students of the fifth, sixth and seventh standards – approximately my age group. My earnings averaged about fifty paise to one rupee a week, and boy was I content!

At first, I would buy coloured hard-boiled sweets or salted peanuts from hawkers outside the school, but then I realized my consumption was simply not keeping pace with my income. I dared not carry my wealth back home. So I started buying ice cream or a pack of biscuits or batata vadas on the trot from school, whenever I was flush with my ill-gotten gains.

Nandu and I still continued to watch movies at his theatre. But now, the visits were marked by some uneasiness every time we encountered the theatre manager, Chavhanke. If he'd looked inscrutable earlier, he appeared undeniably sinister now. He had a way of regarding us that sent shivers down my adolescent spine; as if he would've liked to wring Nandu's neck then and there but was just biding his time.

Nandu, however, seemed to treat him more and more like a worm that he'd crushed under his heel. He would mock the manager often with his tone and impudence. Once or twice, I'd tried to remonstrate with Nandu.

'Nandu, why do you antagonize Chavhanke so much?'

'What's he going to do?' Nandu scoffed.

I shrugged unhappily, not quite sure what grave crimes Chavhanke was capable of.

'He looks like that villain in *Mr. X in Bombay*,' I said lamely, my world now having been populated by assorted bad men of the screen.

Nandu gurgled with amusement and suddenly, a chalk sailed our way and struck me right in my left eye. 'Nandu and Gajanan, you are going to have it from me, you twerps!' I heard Sarode Sir bellow.

As my eye stung, I heard rapid strides and moments later, Sarode Sir's fingers wrapped around my right ear, trying their best to detach it from the rest of my face. If that wasn't enough, a slap landed on my cheek, and then led by the very same ear firmly in Sarode Sir's grip, I was evicted from the class. 'Stand outside on one leg like a stork for the rest of the class,' Sarode Sir roared, his bloodthirst quenched for the moment.

I stood on one leg and rested my other foot on the side of the knee, counting the minutes, which ticked by super slowly. Just as I started cramping up, I saw a man walk out of the school office below, accompanied by a clerk named Rasne.

My heart gave an almighty lurch. Were my eyes playing tricks with my mind? Had I just seen Chavhanke with Rasne? The two men had disappeared from my line of vision within seconds, so I couldn't be certain. But why would Chavhanke be here? What business did he have in school? Could it be that he'd come here to rat about Nandu's black ticket sales? My mind was aflame with anxiety. I had to talk to Nandu right after class.

'Nandu,' I hissed as soon as the period got over and I could become a two-legged creature again, 'I...I think I just saw Chavhanke.'

'What?' Nandu asked with disbelief. 'Where?'

'He...he came out of the school office...about fifteen minutes ago.'

'Tchah! How can you be sure from this distance? Your eyes are not binoculars...' Nandu scoffed.

He had a point. So, I tried to revisualize in my mind's eye the momentary glimpse I had of Rasne and the other man. I had, of course, not had a clear view of the other man's face, so why had I instantly felt it was Chavhanke? I probably thought harder than I'd ever done in my life but could not grasp the reason.

I clicked my tongue sullenly. 'What if it was him? Maybe he has a son who's studying in our school.'

'Gaja...Chavhanke has one daughter! You think he dresses her up as a boy and sends her to our school?'

I blushed, shocked at the very thought of a girl infiltrating a boys' school dressed as a boy. As I said, the times were different.

'Now, are you going to waste time or are you going to deliver these two tickets to Sudhir Bhagwat in 6C?' Nandu continued impatiently.

I gave a shudder. I had totally forgotten I had tickets to deliver today. 'I...I...am not feeling well Nandu...' I stuttered, 'You...only go today...'

Nandu grinned wickedly. 'Don't bluff, Gaja! How come you are suddenly feeling unwell?'

'You saw how Sarode Sir hit me really hard,' I whined. 'My jaw and ear are stinging and…and my leg is paining because I had to stand on one leg.'

Nandu's grin became wider. I braced myself for an inevitable 'Brahmin' barb, which didn't come. 'Rabbit…' he teased instead, 'you are going to lose forty paise if you skip delivering your share of tickets today…'

For a moment, greed almost trumped fear, but eventually the latter prevailed. 'It's okay,' I replied, then pleaded. 'Please, Nandu…you go.'

He shrugged. 'Okay…but get it out of your mind that Chavhanke was here…'

I nodded but somehow, I was sure it had been the theatre manager.

10

DISGRACE

I spent the next few days constantly expecting Chavhanke to suddenly show up at school again. When he didn't, I found myself obsessively watching Rasne, the school clerk, whom I thought I had seen in Chavhanke's company that day. And sure enough, whenever I spotted Rasne, I got an uncanny feeling that his eyes were trained on Nandu's movements, observing him flit to other classes for ticket deliveries. Rasne, however, seemed to have no interest in me, although I thought he did squint at me thoughtfully once or twice. During this time, I avoided making ticket deliveries on one pretext or the other.

'Nandu,' I confided one day, 'that clerk Rasne watches you, I think.'

'Rasne? That guy with a squint?' Nandu enquired, preoccupied with counting his cash stealthily.

'Yes…I told you, he was the one with Chavhanke that day…'

Nandu grunted then burped. 'How many times do I have to tell you that Chavhanke's gone to his village on leave? He couldn't have been there that day unless he's a sorcerer or something! He's gone for a month and you are missing out on your pocket money, you clod!'

He'd told me that twice already, but somehow, I couldn't shake the dread off. Another uneventful week passed and soon I too began to feel it had been a false alarm. The loss of pocket money had also begun hurting, since I'd gotten used to the jingle of coins in my pocket to buy goodies. So, when Nandu taunted me once again about how long I was going to behave like a wimp, I resumed my ticket deliveries.

Everything was back to what it had been earlier. The demand for tickets was good as usual and once or twice I actually earned more than a rupee, sometimes making it a problem of plenty for me. I did wonder where Nandu was getting his tickets from, if Chavhanke was on leave. We hadn't been able to go for a movie for some time, so I didn't even know who was managing the theatre in Chavhanke's absence.

And then, disaster struck.

I had just returned from delivering tickets to some kids in the fifth standard, only to find Nandu missing from our desk. Not only that, but his school bag was also nowhere to be seen.

I was just puzzling over this and was about to ask another classmate if he'd seen Nandu leave, when Rasne, the clerk with a squint, entered the class along with a peon. 'Godbole,' he cackled, 'take your bag and come with me.'

I stared at him, dumbfounded, my legs suddenly rubbery. All the moistness in my mouth was suddenly gone. This had to be bad.

'Sir?' I managed to say, my whole self wanting to flee.

'Come quickly!' Rasne said, gesturing energetically. 'And no tricks, okay? Your goose is cooked.'

The whole class was staring at the scene, fascinated, as if they'd just seen a criminal being nabbed in action.

My heart had stopped, and I felt I had turned into a statue. 'Why, sir?' I asked pitiably.

'Why? You have the gall to ask why!' Rasne rasped, his squint becoming more prominent. 'A medal's waiting for you in the principal's office, Godbole. Come…'

I think that's when I started sobbing. The next thing I remember was standing in the principal's office – being glowered at by the headmaster, a bald, thickset man with fiery green eyes called Chaphekar Sir, who seemed itching to wring my neck. But he was not alone; Sarode Sir, my class teacher, was also present, looking rather ashamed of himself, accompanied by two other stern and grim-looking teachers, the clerk Rasne and of course Nandu Khandagale, standing in the centre with me, just a few feet away.

He gave me a quick glance, then looked down again.

'You searched his bag?' Headmaster Chaphekar barked.

'Doing it now, sir,' Rasne said. He grabbed my bag from me and promptly overturned its contents. My schoolbooks tumbled out, along with my tiffin, which was wrapped in a small cloth bag. Rasne began rummaging through the books, licking and turning pages, shaking them in the hope that something might fall out.

'Where have you stashed them, Godbole?' he asked, looking even more fiercely cockeyed than usual.

'What, sir?' I asked, sniffling, trying not to bawl again.

'Don't act clever, you shameful boy,' Headmaster Chaphekar growled. 'Check his pockets, Rasne.'

I stole a horrified glance at Nandu, who carried a belligerent expression on his face. Rasne had already commenced a body search, as if he was prepared to turn me upside down, like my school bag. He didn't need to, for he found the money he was looking for right away. The two boys, to whom I had just delivered tickets, had paid me in twenty-five paise coins and my pockets had been bulging.

'He's got quite a treasure trove, sir…' Rasne said gleefully, emptying the fistful of coins retrieved from my pocket on the headmaster's table.

Headmaster Chaphekar gave me a ferocious look. 'What's this?'

I began to tremble some more and wailed more tearfully, in response.

'Are you deaf? I asked you a question,' the headmaster said, sounding incensed, his green eyes blazing.

'Gaja, have you been selling cinema tickets in school?' Sarode Sir asked with reproachful softness, totally in contrast to his usual anger.

Oh, the shame of it!

'No, sir,' I bawled, 'no, sir…'

'Don't lie…' the headmaster thundered, 'Nandu has confessed to everything.'

I flinched as I watched his merciless face. 'I…I…was just helping Nandu, sir.'

The moment those words were out of my mouth, Nandu gave an almighty whine. 'No, sir, that's not true! Gaja's lying, I was helping him, sir. I took pity on him, sir, because he told me his father was too poor to afford his school fees…so…so he needed to earn some money. He asked me if…if…I could get him tickets, which he could then sell to students in school at a higher price. He…he kept begging, sir. So, I took pity on him and brought tickets for him to sell from time to time, for earning enough to pay his school fees.'

That's when the world started spinning around me and the last thing I remember was Nandu's face mouthing lie after lie with astonishing ease and, worse, with the fervour of one speaking the truth. No one sounds more convincing than a liar spewing untruths.

When I came to, the same faces were scowling at me, joined by another face which made me want to curl up and die. It was my father's, who looked every bit the hapless, wretched and harried assistant postmaster that he was. There was a look of congealed disgrace on his face, like he'd been found guilty of misappropriating money orders.

'He's regained consciousness,' Rasne announced, as if alerting others to start humiliating me again. He held a tumbler of water in his hand, into which he dipped his fingers one last time and sprinkled water on my face. I blinked with shame and sat up.

'Stand up...' the headmaster snapped at me, 'you have thoroughly shamed your father.'

I stood up, a little wobbly, and wished the earth would open up and swallow me, as it did the characters in mythological stories. My father gave me a sombre, angry look as if he'd like to disown me there and then. He turned to the headmaster, joined his palms together and said, 'Please...please, sir...I know what Gajanan has done is unforgivable...But I beg you to not rusticate him. It's a question of his future...his whole life.'

Rusticate? At this point I should really have fainted again. Rustication was like the death sentence of school life – drilled into our heads as an incomparable ignominy that signalled doom. My eyes searched for Nandu, who was nowhere to be seen. Why was he not here like me? Why was his father not here like mine?

'Mr Godbole, selling cinema tickets in black is a crime...a heinous crime,' Chaphekar Sir said. 'How can a prestigious school like ours keep a student with criminal tendencies? This school's honour is at stake. What will the other parents say?'

He paused, his face puffed up with pomposity, his eyes bulging and flashing with righteous indignation.

He turned to look at me with haughty contempt and continued his denouncement, 'Look at how diabolically your son has plotted everything. He gained the sympathy of that rich boy Nandu, claiming you can't pay his school fees and that he might get thrown out of school. He knew the boy's father owns a theatre, so he asks Nandu to help him earn money by getting tickets, which he can sell! Absolutely sinister, as if he's a born criminal. Not only does he commit a crime but also encourages Nandu to dupe his own father by getting tickets on the sly.'

My father shrunk further into his clothes, cowering under the headmaster's assault. He croaked, 'Please, sir, give him a chance to improve. I…I will punish him severely, he won't do anything like this ever again! Please forgive Gajanan…Don't rusticate him.'

Then suddenly he lunged at me and in quick succession rained blows on me. 'You wretch! Look what you have done… Go fall at your headmaster's feet and beg for forgiveness.'

Again, much to my surprise, it was my class teacher, Sarode Sir who sprung to my defence. 'Godbole Saheb, enough, enough! He's a kid…'

He pulled me away from my father's grip, then with a look and gesture, nudged me to fling myself at Chaphekar Sir's feet. As I did so, Sarode Sir addressed the headmaster himself.

'Sir, what Gajanan has done is very bad, but he's not a bad boy. He's generally quiet and not too bad at studies too,' my class teacher pleaded. 'That…that Nandu is pretty much… er…a headache, sir. Don't go by just what he's claimed. He may be trying to cover up his own role, sir. Let's not punish Gajanan so harshly without giving him a chance to improve.'

Chaphekar Sir scowled at Sarode Sir as if irked by my class teacher's stand. 'It's boys like him who lend others astray,' he said severely. 'It's not just about Nandu. What about the boys he led into the bad habit of buying movie tickets in black? These children spent their parents' hard-earned money on watching trashy movies on the sly; some might even have stolen it from their homes.'

He stopped and glowered all around, as if he wanted the horror of my deeds to sink in. He looked like one of those angry, sanctimonious judges who are revolted by a criminal in movies.

'If Gajanan goes unpunished, he will never learn the difference between right and wrong. He might become a menace to society.'

And that's how my trial went on and on – me crying and grovelling; my father pleading with the headmaster and denouncing me; Sarode Sir trying to get a lighter sentence for me; and Headmaster Chaphekar getting sterner by the minute.

And all because of Nandu Khandagale who had lied through his teeth and got away scot-free.

11

APOLOGY APPOINTMENT

I knew Nandu Khandagale was alive and kicking. Our paths had never crossed again after I was evicted from that school. Mercifully, after much pleading by my father and Sarode Sir, I had not been rusticated though. Fifty-seven years had elapsed since.

But I didn't remember setting eyes on Nandu again, even though we had spent all our lives in the same city. Of course, I had heard about how he and his older siblings had added to the family fortunes, in the usual way that other such families did – getting into real estate, restaurants, marriage halls, petrol pumps, car showrooms and stuff.

Nandu himself had been elected local corporator for one or two terms about 15–20 years ago, faced corruption charges like every corporator, and got into trouble with the police and income tax authorities on a few occasions. There had also, inevitably, been family disputes over property and other legal wrangles.

All in all, he hadn't really made much of his life despite the silver spoon he had been born with. I googled him and got some more details – the firms and businesses that he owned, the affiliations he had with a political party, with Rotary Club and some dubious NGOs. I found some photos and old news items in which his name had featured and, of course, his social media profile links, which were not much though. I also gleaned that he had a bungalow in one of the posher localities in the city.

Well, it was time to take the next step. I called up the car dealership he owned. 'Hello, I am an old school friend of Mr Nandu Khandagale. I'd like to contact him. Can I please have his personal mobile number?'

After a bit of humming and hawing, they gave me another number – a landline where I could call for further enquiries. The old school friend trope eventually worked, and I soon had Nandu's mobile number, on which I called one fine morning from my landline.

He didn't pick up at once, so I called again and again, till he did.

'Hullo, who's this?' were the first irritable words I heard from Nandu Khandagale, more than half a century after he'd ruined my life.

'Is that Nandu Khandagale speaking?' I asked.

'Yes…' he rasped.

'Nandu…can you recognize who I am?' I asked, sounding every bit an old, wizened schoolmate calling another.

'No…' Nandu replied tentatively. 'Who is it?' There was an impatient wariness in his voice.

'Ah well, I am your old schoolmate Vinayak Jabre,' I said, assuming the identity of one of the boys in our class back then, who I happened to know had died recently, courtesy COVID.

I waited for Nandu to call my bluff in case he knew about Jabre's death.

Instead, he said slowly, 'Vinayak Jabre…?'

'Yes. Don't you remember me? We were in New Poona Vidyalaya together…'

Probably the name rang a bell, but he couldn't put a face to it. 'Ah…right, right. Vinayak Jabre. I remember.' The tone was still tentative, but a bit of recognition had crept in.

'I don't blame you for not remembering me instantly,' I said heartily. 'It's over fifty years since we met.'

'Yes…yes. How are you, Vinayak, and how come you thought of contacting me after all these years?' Nandu asked. He had at last started sounding like the Nandu I had known. There was still a bit of nasal twang in his voice as well as the distinctive diction I remembered.

'Ah, I need to meet you, Nandu. I've been tasked with organizing a get-together of our batch.' I had no idea how fond Nandu had been of school, in later years after I'd been evicted. But it was my best bet as a pretext to seek a meeting.

There was a slight pause and hesitation that I immediately sensed. 'Get-together?' is all he managed to say, and I could detect no enthusiasm.

'Nothing big,' I added quickly. 'Nothing elaborate. No fancy programmes. Just an evening dinner at some nice place.'

'I see,' he said. 'Where? When?'

I realized I needed a better bait, to get him interested. 'Look, Nandu, with some COVID norms for functions still in place, it is not going to be easy…So, I was wondering if we can do the get-together at the marriage hall you own or your hotel property,' I said, thinking on my feet. 'Everything will be paid for, of course, and since you are an ex-corporator, you could pull a few strings in case there are any COVID restrictions…'

The commercial angle got his attention instantly. 'How many people are we talking about?'

'Oh, I don't know, but about 50 people would be a good guess,' I replied. 'It can go up to a 100, if we decide to invite wives too. Tell me, when can I come over and meet you?'

He hesitated again. 'I'm actually quite busy.'

'Oh, come on, Nandu. All I need is half an hour. Surely you can spare thirty minutes for an old schoolmate?'

After a little more show of reluctance, he finally agreed, and we fixed a date and time to meet at his house.

Three days later, I alighted from an autorickshaw, outside his bungalow. It was a three-storey structure built several years ago. Neither too posh, nor ostentatious but the design displayed a tasteless ornateness that had been in vogue about 20–25 years ago.

A morose watchman opened the gate. 'You are?' I clearly wasn't the class of visitors who generally came calling on his boss.

'I am Nandu Saheb's school friend. He's expecting me,' I replied haughtily, because underlings respected curtness not politeness.

My brusque manner ensured that he let me in. I walked past the little patch of lawn and up the verandah, accompanied by the watchman a step behind me, still unsure whether I really was what I claimed to be.

I rang the doorbell, expecting the door to be opened by a servant, but it was opened by a lady, who looked the right type and age to have been Nandu's wife. She was no Mumtaz, of course, I noted wryly, the heroine Nandu had vowed to marry. An ill-tempered Pomeranian stood with her, letting loose howls of protest as soon as he saw me. It gave me pause for I hated and feared dogs. The lady brushed the dog aside and looked me up and down curiously.

The watchman spoke before I did. 'This gentleman says he is saheb's school friend, and saheb is expecting him.'

'Namaskar,' I said joining my palms in salutation, keeping a wary eye on the dog slipping past the lady.

'Let me restrain the dog,' is all she said, caught hold of the canine by its collar and let me in. 'He's upstairs on the first floor.'

'Are you Nandu's better half?' I asked, making conversation as I stepped into the hall, casting a glance around. It was a bleak room, despite all the over-decorated ambience with chandeliers, a profusion of wooden furniture and an expensive carpet. 'Gaudy' was the word to describe it.

'Yes,' she said briefly. Like the hall, she too seemed to have a faded look about her, although bedecked with ornaments.

'Your husband and I were desk partners,' I said. It seemed to incense the dog as he barked and tried to free himself from his mistress's grip.

'Please go up,' she said, showing no further interest in me. 'He bites strangers.' By 'he', she, of course, meant the dog, not her husband.

I gave her a courteous nod and walked towards the stairs, which had a wooden wicket gate with a latch to stop the dog from bounding up. Only a short flight of stairs separated me from Nandu and I felt goosebumps.

Halfway up, I heard his voice, talking to someone, as one does when on call. There were four rooms on the first floor, two on each side of a central passage which opened up to a balcony at the far end. There, framed in the balcony doorway, his back to me, stood the burly figure of Nandu Khandagale, dressed in a pink half-shirt and navy blue trousers. He was almost bald, except for a ring of hair running across the back of his head, bridging the area between his ears.

I stood watching him talk on the phone, as yet oblivious to my presence. About a minute or two later, he ended the call and slowly began turning around, still looking into his cell phone. As he stood in profile, half turned, I saw his face had puffed up. It was adorned by a thick moustache matched by equally thick eyebrows; both were dyed. Hair also seemed to be sprouting from his ears.

He probably noticed me from the corner of his eye, so he turned and faced me for the first time, his bespectacled eyes unblinking. I could never have recognized him, if he'd passed me on the street – this man who had harmed me. Was he really Nandu Khandagale? I asked myself, as I stood searching for the boy I had known in the face that regarded me now.

'Who…' he began, then stopped, as if he'd realized who I was. 'Vinayak Jabre?'

I was still wearing a mask, so I wondered whether this was the time to reveal myself or wait. 'Nandu Khandagale…' I said in the exaggerated way people usually called out to acquaintances one were meeting, after a long time, to express bonhomie.

He moved towards me, still trying to place a face on me. 'Welcome…' he said, as he shook my hand and led me into a largish room, which was furnished as gaudily as the hall below.

'How are you, Nandu?' I asked.

'I'm good. How about you…er…Vinayak?'

'I'll tell you in a minute, Nandu, once I remove my mask. I hope you don't mind. I am fully vaccinated.'

'Of course, of course,' he said, still a little uncomfortable.

I undid my mask in slow motion, watching his expressions. 'Natural vaccination,' I chuckled, as I revealed my face. 'I just recovered from COVID.'

A wary frown appeared on Nandu's face. 'I hope you've completed your quarantine,' he said uneasily.

'Yes yes, not to worry at all. It's been several weeks now,' I replied, loving his discomfiture. 'So, now do you recognize me, Nandu?'

He was peering at me, as if still unable to connect the face to the name. 'You have changed quite a bit, Vinayak…' he finally managed to say, unable to hide his perplexity.

'So have you, Nandu,' I replied, 'and by the way, due to some last-minute hitch, Vinayak couldn't make it, so he asked me to meet you instead.'

His expression changed instantly. 'You are not Vinayak Jabre?'

'No, no. I had to take his place. Hope you don't mind?'

'Who are you then? Your voice sounds just the same as it did on phone,' he asked, scowling at me. He was clearly annoyed.

I raised my hands up as if he was pointing a gun at me, and laughed aloud. 'Ah! You got me, Nandu. Very sharp of you! Yes, it was me who called you as Vinayak Jabre, because you would never have met me if I told you who I really was. I counted on you not knowing that Vinayak is dead.'

The annoyance gave way to anger now. 'What's the meaning of this? Who the hell are you?' He leaned forward on his sofa opposite me, as if about to get up and bung me down the stairs.

'Relax, Nandu. Sorry about this, but I'm not an imposter. I am still a classmate, you just haven't recognized me yet,' I said, feeling not the slightest unease. I was floored by the cool dude I had become. 'Just look at me carefully, and you will recognize me.'

He glared at me impatiently. 'Look, enough fooling around. Just tell me who you are.'

'Okay, okay, I'll give just one more clue,' I said, refusing to be alarmed in any way. 'Brahmin!'

Almost instantly there was a spark of recognition in his eyes. My guess is subconsciously he'd probably picked on my identity and all it required was one hint to nail it, which I had just provided.

His body stiffened, then relaxed, even as his expressions shed a little bit of hostility. For a split second, I thought I saw guilt peep out of his eyes instead. 'You…you are Gajanan Godbole?' he asked, his tone incredulous.

'Bull's eye, Nandu,' I said, suddenly feeling delighted to have engineered this confrontation.

He looked at me a little chastened, a little surprised, a little uneasy! Silence prevailed for a few seconds, as I watched his disconcertment play out. He finally cleared his throat. 'So, I am guessing all that get-together talk was cock and bull?'

I smirked. 'Yes. I am afraid it was.'

'I see,' he said, still trying to decide how he should treat me. 'So why are you here exactly?'

'Just wanted to meet you, Nandu…' I said in a voice dripping with insouciant innocence. 'Am I right you would have refused to meet me, if I'd told you who I was on phone?'

Nandu gave me a long, reflective look. 'Why would I do that?' he said.

I grinned. 'Guilty conscience for what you did to me perhaps?'

The scowl reappeared on his face, doubly quick this time. 'What the hell are you talking about?'

'They say the axe forgets, but the tree remembers,' I said, enjoying the scene a great deal. 'But I don't think the axe really forgets either, it just needs a hint to be reminded…'

'Look, I don't have time to waste, Gajanan.' He cut me short. 'Tell me the purpose of your visit.'

I sighed. 'I thought you would be happy to see me Nandu. It gives you a chance to make amends.'

'Make amends! For what?'

'For having wronged me. You can't deny that it's because of you I got thrown out of school…'

He shuffled uneasily in his seat. For a minute I thought he was going to fart, like he used to back when we were bench partners, but it was his mouth which opened. 'I didn't throw you out of school. It's the headmaster who did…'

I was appalled at his ability to shirk responsibility. 'But why did it happen? Because you told them lies to save your skin and implicated me for the crimes you had committed.' I lashed out.

'Lies? Crimes? What nonsense, Gaja! You better watch your mouth,' he said, flashing his eyes at me.

'What words should I use then, Nandu? Wasn't it a lie that you told them? That you got tickets for me to sell so that I could earn money for school fees?' I said. 'Selling tickets in black was a crime, and it still is, isn't it?'

His mouth tightened and eyes turned cold. He looked as if he was going to lose his composure and let fly at me. Instead, he pinched his nose, closed his eyes for a few seconds and reopened them. 'Look, Gaja, I am not proud of what I did but I was a kid. I just said the first thing that came to my mind to save my skin, that's all. How was I to know they would throw you out of the school, damn it! I thought they'd just punish us both a bit – some slaps or call our parents…So, I just got an alibi ready for…'

'Alibi?' I burst out, 'In which I got conveniently framed as the initiator, the mastermind and you played the gullible rich brat whose actions were motivated by nobility to help me?'

Nandu shrugged awkwardly. 'You'd have done the same in my place, Gaja!'

'No, I wouldn't have,' I asserted.

He made an aggressive gesture with a downward wave of his hand and scoffed, 'You wouldn't have spilled the beans on me, if you'd been caught?'

'Let's not talk about what never happened, Nandu,' I shot back angrily. 'Let's talk about what actually did. The fact is you lied and that lie did a lot of harm to me.'

'Oh, come on! You didn't die, did you? You just had to change your school, that's all,' Nandu said, turning defiant. 'It all happened such a long time ago, Gaja, why make such a fuss after all these years.'

I didn't think I had hated him till this moment, but the insensitive way in which he reduced the gravity of the consequences I had faced – the humiliation, the banishment to a municipal school, which I thoroughly detested and all the suffering – simply blew my fuse now.

'Your lies condemned me to five years in that horrible municipal school, where I was bullied mercilessly and from where I emerged a complete loser for life! Do you understand?' I told him with a rather quiet, cold-blooded fury, 'You need to apologize to me, Nandu!'

He stared at me with a fretful, bewildered look, as if he didn't know whether to laugh or cry. His mouth was half open, with his yellowing, stained, uneven teeth peeping out. He probably was a pan-masala user. I suppose he could've simply got up, clasped my hand, put his arm around my shoulder and said 'sorry'. It might've drained all the anger out of me – the sense of being wronged.

Instead, Nandu continued being defensive by downplaying the impact of the incident. 'What are you talking about, Gaja?' he remarked with gruff amusement, masking his ego.

'I am asking you to apologize to me, Nandu…to ask for my forgiveness.'

The amusement disappeared from his face. 'Oh, come off it, Gaja,' he said dismissively.

'Why is it difficult for you to apologize, Nandu? Is it your ego?' I skewered him further.

'You are being totally childish. It's that worm Chavhanke who slyly used that clerk Rasne to entrap you and me, while he was on leave. He did that so he would remain unhindered to continue running his black tickets racket, while I'd be neutralized! I was as much a victim as you were,' Nandu put forth his stupid justification.

So, I had been right. 'I'd warned you that I'd seen Chavhanke with the clerk that day when I'd been given the punishment of standing on one leg outside the classroom,' I remarked. 'But Chavhanke wanted to settle scores with you, not me. It wasn't he who dragged my name into it, in front of the principal; it was you, Nandu!'

Nandu's mouth opened to retaliate angrily, but he suddenly stopped short, closed his eyes, as if trying to calm down. Then he opened them again and looked at me. 'All right, Gaja, I am sorry. I am sorry that I did what I did. Okay? Happy now?'

I felt a surge of triumph. My new self was rocking. I was actually getting close to what I had set out to do. But it was not done yet. There still was some way to go. 'Not like this, Nandu. I want a proper apology, a written apology, requesting me to accept it and forgive you,' I replied, pressing home my advantage.

'What? Don't be ridiculous, Gaja!' Nandu's eyebrows had collided together, and his face had morphed into nastiness. His tone was unfriendly too. All of a sudden, he got up from the sofa, pulling himself up to his full height. 'Get up and fuck off from here. I have taken enough of this crap. I apologized to you, just for old time's sake, and you dare ask me for a written apology, you bastard Brahmin! I should've kicked you out the minute I knew who you were.' And then, the stream of obscenities became a flood, as he reverted to his true self.

When I left his house a few minutes later, Nandu didn't know it then, but he had sealed his own fate!

SUNDAR NAMBIAR

12

DOGS AND PORN

Circa 2018. Sundar Nambiar would never have entered my life, were it not for a dog named Borg.

Borg was not one of those foreign pet breeds. It was an ordinary Indian mongrel, with a black coat and patches of white around its eyes and mouth. It wasn't even Sundar's own dog. Borg was one of the strays in our locality, whom Sundar Nambiar fed a packet of Marie biscuits to every day or every alternate day. You see, Sundar was one of those self-appointed canine lovers who felt stray dogs had a divine right to bark, bite and breed on city streets, and feeding a few biscuits to them made him some kind of animal rights Samaritan.

Whether he adopted the black dog or the dog adopted him, I am not sure, but Sundar Nambiar had christened it Borg. In return for the daily biscuits, Borg had taken it upon itself to escort Sundar whenever he stepped out of his house in the nearby building, for a stroll or to shop or whatever.

Borg also seemed to be the de facto leader of the pack of strays, for it was generally the one who chose the vehicles to be chased or the stranger to be barked at and the rest of the gang followed its lead. Together, these four or five hounds stalked our quiet locality, lying around on the road and starting a cacophony in the nights when they got into howling gang wars with the other dogs in the nearby streets.

Sometimes I would hear Sundar Nambiar, who stayed two buildings away, calling out to Borg to pipe down, and then the pack would go silent for a while. I had just a nodding acquaintance with Sundar, a dark man of about fifty, his eyes bulging and red, his face puffed up unhealthily, carrying a slimy, insouciant expression that hinted at pathological malice.

He was pot-bellied and his walking motion was a combination of waddling and dragging. He tended to stare at everyone who passed him, and his eyes dripped lasciviousness when he looked at any and every woman between the ages of 16 to 60. His loud, husky voice had a grating quality to it and although a Malayali, he had probably been born and brought up in Pune, for he spoke excellent Marathi with shopkeepers and acquaintances.

'Patole Saheb' or 'Ranade Saheb' or 'Khot Saheb' – Sundar would gurgle aloud from afar to the person he had just spotted and wanted to greet, then give a half salute with two fingers of his left hand. Moreover, whether he received an equally warm greeting or not, he would buttonhole the person and start chatting in his gravelly tone, as if his vocal cords were lubricated with tons of spit.

Apparently, he had been with the Excise and Customs Department and had been suspended, pending some corruption inquiry. I could well imagine, for his whole personality reeked of corruption, compounded by rumours that he was a drunkard.

My first conversation with him took place one early morning, a few years ago, when I started out for a walk and had to take shelter under a bus stop, as it had suddenly started pouring. A few minutes later, I was joined by the portly figure of Sundar Nambiar, accompanied by Borg.

He gave me a bleary-eyed grin, then ordered the dog to sit down, which it did. We sat silently for a few minutes as the rain showed no signs of relenting. Then Sundar Nambiar put a hand into his pocket, brought out his mobile, wore his earplugs and began surfing. We were about four to five feet apart and I thought he was probably listening to some music as walkers usually did.

But suddenly, he let out a loud guffaw and looked at me. I, of course, momentarily looked in his direction as a reflex reaction to his sudden laughter.

'How old are you, saheb?' he asked, amid his chuckles.

'Sixty-five,' I replied.

'Ah! Then you should watch these clips too. Very funny,' Sundar replied.

'What's that?' I enquired politely.

Before I knew it, he had thrust the phone in my direction. What I saw next, almost gave me a heart attack. Two women, with nothing on, had sandwiched a man between them and were making all sorts of exaggerated sexual movements, topped with the most obscene facial expressions.

It was a nasty shock and for a few seconds I was struck speechless as my eyes alternated between the phone screen and Sundar Nambiar's leery grin.

'Isn't it hilarious?' Sundar remarked. 'If you watch it with sound, it's even funnier and very titillating at the same time. Here.' He unplugged his earpieces and offered them to me.

'What…the…what's the meaning of this?' I said, finally finding my voice, appalled at this vulgar man having the cheek to show me something so indecent. 'This is preposterous, Mr…'

'Oh, come now…I thought you would enjoy it, Godbole Saheb.'

'Enjoy it? Enjoy it?' I spluttered with embarrassment and anger. 'We…we hardly know each other. What…what kind of a person do you take me for?'

Sundar Nambiar's eyes twinkled and mocked. 'A normal man with healthy appetites, Godbole Saheb! What's the harm? A man ought to have whatever fun he gets, especially at your age, when the action's probably all over…'

This man was not only shameless but also outrageous. If only it hadn't been pouring, I would just have walked away. But alas!

Sundar Nambiar was still looking at me with malicious amusement. Another grunt of mirth escaped his mouth. It sounded just like the snigger people give, when a prank has worked. I turned towards him again with some heat. 'Is…is this how a decent gentleman behaves with another, by showing such indecency?'

'Oh, I just thought it'll help break the ice. Most people don't mind it, Godbole,' Sundar Nambiar said.

'People don't mind?'

'Yes, I mean what's there to get offended? Watching porn is perfectly all right, Godbole Saheb, even healthy,' the filthy man continued. 'You should try it. I can send you some really hot links.'

'I am not interested in this dirty subject,' I said in the most dignified manner I could muster. 'Will you please stop talking about it?'

'Well, you can stop listening, Godbole, because I am going to continue talking with my dog, Borg, who doesn't mind at all,' the incredibly crude man said, patting his dog and openly mocking me.

For the next five minutes, he gave a running commentary on some porn clip he was watching, using graphic language to describe what was happening therein. All perhaps to spite me. How I wished that I had brought my umbrella with me, so I could escape the company of Sundar Nambiar. Was he drunk, I wondered?

His vulgar banter with Borg continued for some more time, then stopped. Silence prevailed for some time but the rain continued relentlessly so I was thankful that Sundar Nambiar had stopped his infernal bawdy talk. No sooner than I had thought that he spoke again.

'What do you think of the *Kamasutra*, Godbole Saheb? Isn't it like a manual of porn?' I ignored him haughtily. What had I done to deserve an encounter with this awful man? He broke into a giggle that made him sound like a hyena I had heard on National Geographic. 'You are such a typical prude, Godbole. It's my experience that prudes watch the most porn.'

This really stung deep for some reason, and I swung around to face him. 'Look here, Mr Sundar…'

Borg the dog didn't let me complete my sentence. It suddenly sprung up and barked at me, assuming a hostile position. That stopped me in my tracks. I'd always had a terror of dogs, ever since I had been chased and bitten by one, many years ago.

Sundar Nambiar looked at me with malice. 'Borg does not like your tone, Godbole Saheb. It's very protective about me. I can assure you its bite is worse than its bark.' He patted the dog's head gently. It quietened down and slumped on the floor again, refusing to take its eyes off me. Sundar gave a chuckle. He could probably see the fear in my eyes. 'So what were you about to say to me, Godbole? Tell me, tell me?'

'Never mind,' I replied, downcast, almost like a hostage to this sleazy man and his mongrel.

Mercifully, before he could start his dirty talk again, an auto slowed down by the bus stop. The auto driver glanced at us expectantly. I quickly hailed him, scrambled to my feet, and got in. The driver seemed disappointed that I wanted to go just a short distance – a minimum-fare passenger – but he didn't refuse me. Otherwise, that would certainly have given fresh ammunition to Sundar Nambiar, who was any way watching my hurry with bemusement.

'Nice talking to you, Godbole,' he hollered as the auto left, and I heaved a sigh of relief. 'Meet you soon…'

13

UMBRELLA vs WALKING STICK

For the next few days – I think a fortnight – I tried my best to avoid bumping into Sundar Nambiar again. I changed my walk timings and tried to keep my ears pricked for the sound of his overbearing, dreary voice, so that I could spot him before he spotted me.

When I got sent out for errands, to shop or for other stuff, I found myself anxiously hoping he wouldn't be lurking around at the same time. I had a close shave once or twice, but generally my luck held. However, not so with the dog Borg, of course, for it was a permanent feature of the lanes of our locality, and I passed it nearly every day.

While Borg didn't actually snarl or bark at me when I passed, I got the uncanny feeling that it recognized me, for it would lift its snout, sniff a bit and stare at me with what I thought was plain hostility. A few times, the dog even got up as it watched me approach, like it was ready to chase me. That's when I decided I needed to carry a walking stick or something, just in case.

Of course, walking sticks were out of fashion, and I didn't recollect any senior citizen in my locality using them. But then, they had probably never felt threatened by Borg. Where was I to get a walking stick then? Soon I remembered, we had one, tucked away somewhere – bought from Mahabaleshwar many, many years ago.

'Do you know where you kept the walking stick we purchased on that trip to Mahabaleshwar?' I asked Sumitra, one evening, when she seemed less cranky than usual.

She knitted her eyebrows then replied with a question, which was her usual style. 'Why did you suddenly think of it?'

I cleared my throat and braced myself for the interrogation. 'I…I thought I might use it…for my walk.'

Her furrow deepened. 'Why is that? You are not eighty!'

'Well…it's just lying around unused,' I replied spiritedly.

She gave me a shrewd look. 'No, you are hiding something. What's the real reason?'

'Nothing,' I said defensively. 'Just tell me where you've kept it. Is it on the loft?'

'Not until you tell me why,' Sumitra said obstinately, which was her wont.

I threw in the towel as I usually did. 'Well…those stray dogs act frisky and aggressive sometimes, so I thought…'

'Ah I see!' Sumitra said and then seemed to lose interest in me.

'Well, where is it?' I asked again, seeing her eyes glaze over and turn to her phone.

She again used her favourite ploy – counter-question. 'Don't you carry your umbrella with you?'

'Only when it's raining.'

'Start taking it daily, and you can give the dogs a whack with it if they get anywhere near you,' she said casually.

I felt exasperated. 'But where have you kept the stick?'

She frowned silently for a few seconds as she began checking some WhatsApp messages on her phone, then spoke, 'I think I gave it as a present to someone. I am not sure…'

'What?' I screeched, my voice rising a little above my normal level.

She immediately gave me a nasty look. 'What do you mean "what"? How was I to know you'll need it, after so many years, to clobber some dogs, of all things.'

My withdrawal from battle was swift for I knew I was neither built nor equipped for conflict. 'I guess an umbrella might do for now,' I mumbled lamely. There was no point in arguing with Sumitra, because she was always itching for a fight.

She cast a disappointed glance in my direction, as if sour that I hadn't provided her with any cue to make some devastating final retort.

'I don't want you breaking the umbrella while trying to fend off dogs, okay?' she said finally.

I gave no rejoinder as we settled in to sleep. Then something really scary happened. As Sumitra shut off the lights, heaved into position, turning and twisting, Sundar Nambiar's words about porn and the *Kamasutra* mischievously erupted in my mind. All of a sudden, my brain and consciousness were flooded with vivid images of naked women and hot bodies, from God knows where. Within moments, my mind had turned into a sex riot, as if someone had just turned on a libido switch, which I had no idea how to turn off.

I panicked, sat up in bed and quickly rushed towards the bathroom to get a grip on myself. I heard Sumitra grumble something but was too disturbed to listen. No sooner had I entered the bathroom than the images of nude women vanished and instead Sundar Nambiar's lecherous, lewd face filled my mind.

It took a few more minutes for my brain to go blank and normal again. I flushed and stepped out to avoid any questions from Sumitra about my uncharacteristic dash to the bathroom. Mercifully, she was snoring away. Perhaps I had been inside longer than I thought. Fifteen more minutes elapsed before I began to drift off to sleep, scared to death that I would dream of naked women.

Now I would have welcomed it, but back then I was still the old Gajanan Godbole.

14

BARKS AND BITES

Another week passed and I'd still managed to avoid another encounter with Sundar Nambiar. Borg too had not engaged in any overt show of aggression with me, although I thought I always heard a low growl every time I passed the canine. The umbrella didn't make me feel any safer. How I wished I could get a sturdy walking stick. But for that I would have to go somewhere in the city, where they sold it.

'Here's the walking stick you were clamouring for,' Sumitra announced one day. I looked up, surprised, from the newspaper, to see her holding a wood-coloured stick with a curved handle in her hand.

'I thought you said you had gifted it to someone.'

'You want it or not?' Sumitra asked curtly. Admitting mistakes was not in her nature.

'Yes,' I replied, feeling gratified that, for once, my wife had thoughtfully arranged for something that I needed.

She handed it over to me haughtily as if bestowing a knighthood. 'Don't lose it, don't break it,' she said cryptically.

I nodded and suddenly felt a little self-conscious. How would I look carrying it around? Some kind of dandy old codger, inviting sniggers and ridicule? Besides it was the rainy season, and an umbrella would be more handy in case of a sudden shower. The chances of being caught in a drizzle were far higher than a dog attack. But then being drenched in the rain would probably mean nothing more than a change of clothes, while a bite from Borg would result in anti-rabies injections. Also if I didn't use the walking stick now, after Sumitra had searched for and found it, I would never hear the end of it.

So, the next day when I stepped out for my walk, I had the stick in my hand. It felt incredibly silly and was quite a task getting used to it. I couldn't decide whether to actually use it as a walking accessory or to just hold it in my hand, swinging and twirling it, as a kind of style statement. I didn't really need it for walking, and it interfered with my rhythm. But just holding it in my hand was mighty inconvenient.

Other everyday walkers gave me a glance or a stare, probably noticing the addition to my walking gear, which only made me feel even more like a septuagenarian or a show-off. But all that discomfort was worth it when I spotted Borg and its gang of mongrels, for the stick did make me feel remarkably safe. I had the means to protect myself, if Borg tried to act smart. I am not sure whether Borg noticed the stick in my hand or not, but I don't think I heard its usual low growl that day. I was elated when I reached home.

Little did I know that my relief was to be short-lived.

Three days later, I was up much earlier than usual and couldn't go back to sleep, even after much tossing and turning. So I decided to set out for my walk early. There was little chance of bumping into Sundar Nambiar at that hour, so I wasn't particularly concerned. To add to it, the dogs were not in their usual place too. I therefore had an excellent walk, followed by some stretching that I did every day in a small park nearby.

In a good mood, I started on my way back home. I had walked about a hundred metres, when I spotted Borg and its pack. Instead of lounging around in their usual prone positions on the ground, they all seemed to be agitated about something, barking loudly, and trotting around in little circles.

I guess I should have just retreated to the garden or sat down on a bench for a few minutes till they calmed down. But I simply needed to get back home to use the toilet. I could hardly relieve myself by the roadside as we lived in a locality which had no such nooks and crannies to do so, without being observed.

I was apprehensive as I approached the dogs, gripping my stick tightly, hoping they wouldn't direct any aggressive attention towards me. I was a little heartened by the fact that two other walkers were also approaching from the opposite side, so I wouldn't be the lone centre of the pack's attention.

I tried not to look at the dogs directly, shooting only brief glances at them from the corner of my eye, while looking as unflappable as possible. Display no fear, as they say. When I was about twenty metres away from them, Borg issued a tentative bark in my direction and fixed its glare on me.

Once again I wondered if I should wait by the roadside bench to let the dogs settle down and their excitability to abate. But nature's call was getting rather urgent, and I decided to push on. There was no earthly reason for Borg and its gang to attack me. They were familiar with my scent and presence on the road; neither was I riding a scooter or bike for them to give chase, nor was I doing anything to provoke them by just walking by.

Still, my heart was in my mouth. Dogs were unpredictable creatures, and I did not like the way Borg was watching me right now, as if itching for a confrontation. It produced another guttural sound but no bark. A few tense moments later, it seemed to lose interest in me and looked away.

I was just a few paces away from the pack now and despite my full bladder I quickened my strides as I braced to pass them. But, as my god-damned luck would have it, I failed to notice a small juice carton, littering my path, which I fatefully stepped on. It produced a 'pop', which startled both me and Borg. My right hand, which held the stick, shot up in reflex to balance myself and the next instant Borg let out an offended, full-throated bark, leaping forward.

Blind panic engulfed me and, convinced that it was about to attack, I gave a little shout of fear and struck out at Borg with my stick, to pre-empt its charge. I hadn't even aimed the stick at the dog or swung it with any conviction, but it hit the mongrel on the rump like a bat sweetly thwacking a ball, although totally unintended.

Borg produced a howl of pain and with lightning swiftness leapt towards my calf, nipped my flesh and backed away. It was my turn to yelp, and I began to wield the stick like some lathi-charging cop. Borg received another whack and another dog, which had bared its teeth, got one on the snout from me, following which both took to their heels.

The two walkers, coming from the opposite side, had witnessed the entire fracas. They first leapt out of the way of the scurrying canines, then looked at me, dumbstruck. I stood trembling and panicking, convinced I had wetted myself, my bladder having burst.

'Are you okay?' one of the men asked me.

'It…it bit me…' I managed to say hysterically.

'Oh! Okay,' said the first man.

'But you hit the dog first, so it bit you,' the other man said in a tone where the reproach outweighed sympathy.

I was so aghast, so as to be rendered speechless, in addition to the panic that was still sloshing about, not to speak of the urine in my bladder. 'No, no…that's not what happened…'

I said, shaking like a leaf and trying to pull up my trousers to check the extent of the bite.

The men didn't look particularly concerned. 'You live somewhere nearby, right?' the first man asked. I nodded.

'You want us to call any family member?'

'No, no…' I said, aware that nature's call was getting urgent. 'It's okay, I'll go home now.'

They watched me walk away, looking bemused and I heard the first man comment, 'He's going to need anti-rabies shots.'

'Silly fellow,' the other man responded under his breath. 'Wagging a stick at a dog…'

I had no energy to refute the ridiculous remark since all my concentration was now focused on not wetting myself in public. I reached home, after what seemed an eon, praying that Sumitra wasn't occupying the toilet. Otherwise, I would've had no choice but to relieve myself in the washbasin outside, or in one of the flower pots in our balcony.

Luckily, the toilet was unoccupied, so I bolted in and locked myself inside, ignoring Sumitra's comment about how I had disturbed her sleep. Off came the belt buckle, down came the trouser zipper and then I think I took the longest pee of my entire life.

It took me the rest of the morning to calm down. Apart from my wildly pumping heart, I had to also contend with Sumitra's rebukes and hysterics, after hearing about the incident. Then, of course, around noon I visited the doctor, who grimly advised that both rabies and tetanus shots were unavoidable. That painful ordeal done, I got back home, had lunch with Sumitra's reprimand as a side-dish, after which I slipped into a deep slumber.

15

THE ABUSE SQUAD

When I woke up it was probably past 5 p.m., and although groggy, I had stopped feeling I'd die any minute. Sumitra appeared decked up, getting ready to go somewhere. Her hawk eye noticed I was awake.

'Ah, good, you are up and about,' she observed. 'I was just leaving.'

'Where to?'

'I have a haldi-kumkum ceremony to attend nearby. I'll be back by 7.30 p.m.,' she replied. 'Don't go frolicking around anywhere.'

I said nothing, not even my usual 'okay'.

She began leaving and then suddenly said, 'Oh and someone's been calling on your mobile. Some idiot, who cut the call when he heard my voice.'

I couldn't make any head or tail of it. 'Can you make some tea for me?' I asked hesitantly.

Sumitra gave me her special vexed look, but then grunted and went to the kitchen. I could hear her make tea. Meanwhile, I checked my phone. There were calls from two unknown numbers, and I wondered who had been trying to call me.

'Here,' Sumitra said, handing me a tea mug and throwing a scowl at me. 'I'm late…'

Soon I heard the door close and I was left alone with my tea. I found a few biscuits and had just dipped the first one into my mug when the doorbell rang. With mug in hand and biscuit in my mouth, I hobbled to the door and opened it. The mug almost slipped from my grip when I saw who stood outside.

It was Sundar Nambiar, with malevolence in his gleaming eyes and hands on his hips. 'Thought you would get away with it, Godbole?' His unpleasant saliva-flaked voice fell on my ears.

I blinked, beating back the urge to slam the door in his face and hide under the sofa. I swallowed meekly. 'Get away with what?' I asked.

'Animal cruelty!' Nambiar said coldly, liberally sprinkling me with saliva. 'Assaulting harmless stray dogs with a stick, you nasty old man.'

'What?' I croaked.

'Yes, I have witnesses! Do you know it's a punishable offence? You are going to jail.'

'Jail?' I stuttered. 'That's absurd, the dog attacked me.'

'Don't lie, Godbole, don't lie.' Sundar smirked vehemently. 'They didn't come chasing you. They were minding their own business. You thwacked Borg for perverse pleasure. People saw it.'

I looked at him, aghast, my head swimming. 'No, no, that's false,' I said. 'That dog bit me, and I had to get a rabies shot.'

'Serves you right, Godbole,' he said, almost frothing at the mouth. 'Hope you get rabies despite the shot.'

I was shocked and shaken to the core. All I needed was the nerve to say 'Get lost' to Sundar, but instead I whimpered, 'You…you…what right do you have to speak to me like that? It's not even your dog.'

'All the dogs in this locality are my dogs, and Borg is special,' Sundar Nambiar declared. 'I'm an animal lover, that gives me the right, okay, Godbole? You just wait and see what happens to you now. Prepare to go to jail. I've already spoken to the local animal welfare officer and tomorrow morning the cops will drag your arse to jail, and I'll be there watching them do it.'

I could have collapsed with anxiety. Why was this man doing this to me? How was I to deal with it? Could the police really arrest me? Had Sundar really set a police case in motion? I had heard of animal rights laws being very strict and stringent, but for heaven's sake, what had I done to deserve this?

I almost felt like begging him not to do it, to apologize to him abjectly, but I could not get myself to. 'Please go…' I said, and began shutting the door.

'Godbole,' Sundar hissed, 'you are going to regret that you ever touched Borg, that you ever offended me.'

I gulped uneasily and shut the door, then sat on the sofa, cursing my luck for ever having bumped into this obnoxious man.

~

Sundar hadn't been talking in the air. The police did turn up next morning and when I saw the two constables at the door, my heart missed several beats. I had already spent a sleepless night worrying myself sick over Sundar's threat, trying to wrap my head around the fact that one could actually go to jail for hitting a stray dog that attacked you. It had been unthinkable in my time. When had the world become so sensitive to dogs, yet remained completely callous to human beings?

But the constables didn't make any move to take me into custody. They just asked me what happened, and I narrated the incident. Then they left.

Still jittery, I called up Ravi and requested him to drop by at the police station, meet the constables or the station officer and check how serious the matter was and whether I really was in danger of imprisonment. I sat through the day, half expecting to be arrested every time the doorbell rang. Sumitra scoffed at the possibility, but she had never been much of a comforter.

Ravi called up late in the evening and told me that there was nothing to worry. The constables had told him that although Sundar and the animal welfare officer had called and tried to raise hell, they found no substance in the complaint. The two men who had witnessed the incident had refused to get involved or testify that I had deliberately been cruel to the dog. There was no CCTV footage whatsoever, and the dog itself had not been badly injured or anything of that sort. So, they were not going to drag me to the gaol and pursue the matter.

It was only then that I felt reassured enough to relax. Moreover, I was showing no signs of hydrophobia, so rabies too was out of question. Although Sumitra, as always, came up with the perfect remark to throw me into turmoil again. 'You ought to keep an eye out for the dog. They say if it dies within forty-eight hours of biting someone, it's a sign of rabies and you might be in danger.'

It was enough to give me another sleepless night, wondering if this was true or one of those myths. I finally fell asleep, only to wake up feeling no inclination to bite anyone, but my troubles were still not over.

Sumitra had a dental appointment that morning, so she left and I was looking forward to a few peaceful hours. But that wasn't to be. The doorbell rang a little while after she left and once again, I found myself face to face with the ugly visage of Sundar Nambiar, this time accompanied by a rather intense and attractive young lady of around thirty years of age.

'That's him!' Sundar began, his evil eyes on me. 'You think just because the cops didn't take action, you will escape the consequences of animal cruelty, Godbole?'

Again, I now wonder why I was such a wimp back then that I couldn't just slam the door in their faces. Instead, like a deer caught in the headlights, I looked from Sundar to the young lady and asked meekly, 'Who are you?'

'She's the local animal welfare officer,' Sundar replied. 'I won't let you get away. You are in serious trouble.'

The woman nodded. 'What you did is reprehensible, Mr Godbole. You may have escaped police action, but my higher up at the Animal Welfare Board wants to speak to you personally about the incident and warn you against repeating such a heinous act!'

'What? Who?'

Before she could reply, Sundar blurted out the name of a famous union minister in the present government, who had been single-handedly responsible for banning the culling of stray dogs in India. It was because of her that Indian streets were full of menacing mongrels.

'We better go inside so that I can connect her to you,' the young lady said. Completely befuddled, I yielded and allowed them to ambush me in my own house.

Sundar looked at me triumphantly. 'Just you wait, Godbole. After this call you'll wish you were never born. You won't know what hit you.'

The animal welfare officer had already started dialling a number. 'Yes, madam, Madhuri here. We are with Mr Godbole in Pune. It's about the incident the other day. He's the man who hit the dog with a stick.'

Madhuri listened, then said, 'Yes, I'll put the phone on speaker.' She held the phone close to me, and I heard the surly, heavy voice of a woman. 'Listen old man, do you know who I am?'

My throat locked and I was speechless.

'He's listening, madam,' Sundar piped in. 'Sundar Nambiar here. This guy, Godbole, needs to be taught a lesson.'

'It's good that you have been vigilant, Nambiar…' the voice over the speaker replied. 'Look, Godbole, I am the lifetime chairperson of the Animal Welfare Board, okay! How dare you hit dogs, you piece of shit?'

I felt as if I had just been socked in the jaw. I couldn't believe my ears, that I had just been called a piece of shit by a dignitary!

The woman continued in the same vein. 'How would you like to have a few of your bones broken with that same stick, you senile old prick? Answer me. Are you listening?'

Even in a lifetime of insults, I had never been subject to such brazen use of cuss words by a woman.

'How…how can you use such language…' I found myself protesting uncharacteristically, so appalled was I.

'I can do much worse, okay, arsehole! I have no mercy for bastards like you who mistreat animals,' the minister snapped back, as if she was some roaring drunkard who had lost control of her tongue. 'I am warning you. Dogs are divine and noble creatures. I love them, even more than the holy cow! If you dare touch the poor dog again, or any other dog, I'll make sure that your shrivelled scrotum is fed to them.'

I felt a burst of shame overcome me, as if I had just been stripped naked in public. This was a woman speaking to me, a minister of the government. To me, it felt like some mafiosi making threats. I caught the eye of Sundar who was watching gleefully. A ribald grin had settled on his face, growing wider.

'I…I didn't do anything…the dog bit me,' I whimpered brokenly.

'Just shut the fuck up and listen…Don't interrupt! As a penalty for your offence, you have to feed all the dogs in the locality for a month – twice a day. Understood?'

I was trembling like a leaf by now. 'But…but…I am telling you, madam.'

'Don't lie and waste my time…Just do what I say, you motherfucker,' the minister snarled, intoxicated perhaps by her power. 'Sundar will keep watch and if you fail to feed the dogs, remember we'll get all sorts of cases filed against you – molestation, passing lewd comments on women, eating beef, hurting public sentiment. I'll make sure you wet your pants with fear. Understand?'

I was so numb and dizzy with fear that I thought I was about to have a stroke. My mouth refused to open – as if I had lockjaw, although that wasn't a symptom of rabies. Maybe I had contracted tetanus instead.

'I need to hear your reply,' the minister snapped over the phone.

'Answer her, sir,' Madhuri, the animal welfare officer prompted. 'Tell madam that you agree.'

Sundar only gave an evil chuckle.

'Yes…' I said finally.

'Say it clearly.'

'Yes, I'll do it,' I replied.

'Good! Bye, Sundar. Bye, Madhuri,' the minister said and cut the phone as the two people opposite me chorused 'Bye, madam.'

I wanted to burst out crying. Never had I ever felt so humiliated and violated in my entire life. With great effort I held back the tears that were threatening to roll down my face, as I caught Sundar's gaze, in which malice danced.

'I told you, you'll regret it,' he said in that hateful, mocking drawl of his.

'We'll take your leave now,' Madhuri said, moving towards the door. 'Please feed the dogs daily, as madam said.'

I could barely nod.

'At 7 a.m. in the morning and 7 p.m. in the evening,' Sundar said. 'Remember, I'll be watching you.'

He winked at me with a malevolent grin. Then both were gone. The dam burst and I think for the second time ever in my adult life, I sobbed.

~

The next month was pure torture – Sundar Nambiar behaving like some jail warden and I like a convict under his watch. I hadn't dared tell Sumitra about what had transpired. I didn't need more taunts and ridicule. I had faced all the vituperation I could bear in life.

Every day I would buy bread and biscuits from a nearby shop and then feed the dogs, like I had seen Sundar do. Sundar himself would be there, overseeing my wretchedness, mocking me, gloating, instructing me to do this and that, pet Borg and the other dogs, talk about sex and pornography so as to embarrass me, in his grating husky voice that was terrible to hear.

I hated every minute of it, burning with shame and humiliation that I had to undergo this. I hated myself more than ever, more than I had in any other situation in life. How could I let someone subject me to this kind of perverse, private punishment?

Several times I thought of discontinuing feeding the dogs, or going to the police and lodging a complaint for harassment and threats. But which police officer would accept a complaint against a powerful government minister? And even if they did, what if the minister retaliated exactly as warned and filed all sorts of complaints against me?

I shuddered at the thought. No, it was better to get it done with. Only a few days were left for the month to end, then it would all be behind me. At least I hoped so!

'Godbole,' Sundar said one day. 'These normal biscuits are no good. I want you to get some dog biscuits for Borg this last week.'

'Dog biscuits? But I've never seen you feed Borg dog biscuits, so…'

Sundar gave me a cold glance. 'Just get dog biscuits tomorrow. Don't argue.'

I wanted to tell him to go to hell but I simply couldn't get myself to defy him. I managed to get hold of a packet of dog biscuits. The price scandalized me – five times the cost of human biscuits.

'Good boy, Godbole,' Sundar mocked as soon as he saw me with the dog biscuits. 'You are such a pet.'

I looked away, not wishing to engage in any further conversation with him. He watched me with malice as always, whistling and making all kinds of grating noises with his mouth, probably wondering how to needle me some more.

As I finished feeding the dogs, he spoke again, 'There's one last thing you need to do, Godbole.'

'What?' I asked, my heart in my mouth.

He gave a sly chuckle. 'Well, you have to watch a video clip with me.'

'What video?' I said, alarmed. His face broke into an evil smile again. 'Well, since you don't like to watch humans engaging in sex, I have a special treat for you – a video showing dogs in heat, mating.'

I grimaced. 'I can't. No…Why are you doing this? Please…'

He let out a rumble of laughter and his potbelly shook. 'Okay, if you can't even do that, then there is another alternative.'

'What?' I said, flustered and weary.

He let a few beats pass. 'Eat a dog biscuit then,' he said in his gravelly voice, his bulging eyes dancing with sadism.

And, he made me do it!

16

SNOOPING TIME

Sundar Nambiar had continued his sick existence. He had even survived a bout of COVID, proof enough to me that the scourge was not godsent to rid Earth of its vilest denizens. He was puffier and nastier. Although he had more or less lost interest in me, he had not entirely stopped picking on me.

I was looking forward to getting even with him. Borg had died but new stray dogs had appeared in its place. Sundar had, of course, started patronizing the new lot too – feeding them and generally ensuring that they became as much a nuisance in the locality as the previous band was.

Why other people never complained about these strays mystified me. We could hear them barking at all hours, chasing cars and scooters, indulging in never-ending howling matches in the night, while looking ferocious enough to worry most passers-by and other people. But India is a land of wonders, where people live with all kinds of crap. So, the canines and Sundar continued to dog the locality.

I would need to plan my opening gambit, of course. Unlike Nandu Khandagale, there was no point in just going to Sundar and demanding an apology. It would be a damp squib. My approach needed to be more dramatic than that. What did I know about him, except for the fact that he was a loudmouth, a drunkard, a pest who fed stray dogs and was probably a suspended excise and customs officer with a sadistic streak for watching pornography and thrusting it on others?

I needed to glean more information if I was to find his weak spot. I decided I would watch him for a couple of days, perhaps even follow him around a bit. But would I be able to do that – stake him out at my age? And even if I somehow did manage to do it, there was always the possibility of being spotted.

Then an idea came to me. How about hiring one of those private detective agencies that dig out dirt on adulterous husbands and wives or prospective grooms and brides or any individual, no questions asked? The more I mulled over it, the more I felt it would work. But it would also leave a trace that could be linked back to me if things took a serious turn. Well, that risk had to be taken, I concluded. So off I went to the office of a small private detective agency.

'Yes, sir.' A rotund, jolly man beamed at me. 'We do background checks and surveillance. Is it for matrimonial investigations, sir?'

'No,' I replied. 'It's a man who has been blackmailing me.'

The rotund man's face remained genial, as if blackmailers were a common species he dealt with. 'What exactly is the nature of the blackmail, sir?'

'I'd rather not say. Can you just have the man followed and get me some information that I can use to neutralize him?' I asked.

The smile became a little wider and the rotund cheeks now bulged on both sides of his face. 'Ah, you want to blackmail the blackmailer, sir? Very spunky, but what if he hasn't got a dirty enough secret?'

'He's a sleazy man. He's bound to have something I can squeeze his nuts with,' I asserted. 'I would've followed him myself and dug it out, if I were younger.'

Rotund Face beamed some more. 'I really like your spirit, sir. Please tell me more about the man you want followed.'

'First tell me how much you charge.'

'Here are the various packages, sir,' he said, quickly showing me a sheet of paper, 'from basic to premium to high-tech surveillance.'

I glanced through the descriptions and figures, and marvelled at the types of investigations they undertook. 'A week,' I said finally, tapping on a package. 'This level of activity should suffice.'

He looked at it and beamed at me yet again. 'You've chosen wisely, sir. I was going to suggest that myself.'

'Surely you'll give me a discount, won't you?' I said.

'These are already discounted packages, sir.'

'How about an additional senior citizen discount then?'

Rotund Face's smile suddenly turned to matter-of-factness. 'Sir, this amount must be a fraction of what the blackmailer must be demanding.'

I looked at him witheringly, then with some hurt, and finally began hauling myself out of the chair. 'Perhaps I'll try following him myself after all,' I said, and turned to walk out of the office.

Rotund Face showed surprising agility for a man of his girth and was beside me in a flash. 'Arre sir, don't say that…Let's work something out.'

He led me by my elbow and seated me back in the chair. 'Chalo, I'll give you another 10 per cent senior citizen discount.'

'20,' I said.

He sighed. 'Okay, sir. You win. 20 per cent.'

'And what if you don't get results?'

'Sir, I can assure you that we'll get you everything there is to find out about him – every place he goes, everyone he meets, everything he does – for the next seven days.'

'Fair enough,' I said finally and pulled out some cash for an advance payment. Then I told him what I knew of Sundar Nambiar – who he was, what he did, his proclivity for porn and his perverse pretensions of being a dog lover.

~

Rotund Face was as good as his word. He called me, one day before his week ended. 'Sir, please come over tomorrow, I think you might be happy with the result.'

All the way to his office, I wondered what he must've got on Sundar Nambiar, for me to make him squirm. Could it be information of Sundar's involvement in pornography, prostitution, maybe even drugs or an affair, that I could dangle over him and make him beg?

'Well?' I said eagerly, slipping into the chair across Rotund Face's table, all sorts of possibilities exciting my nervous system. Rotund Face beamed at me, then laid the results of his surveillance on the table in front of me.

It would be the understatement of the year to say I was disappointed. No, I was abjectly dismayed. The old saying came to my mind – 'shovel up a hill to find a mouse'.

Shadowing Sundar Nambiar was supposed to yield a minefield of his vices, which I could milk to bring him to his knees. But all that Rotund Face had got me was the underwhelming secret with evidence that Sundar was a vehicle slasher and a petrol thief.

Now, how the hell was I to convincingly threaten him with this damp squib of a revelation and hope to get him to grovel?

'It's laughable,' I snapped. 'I'll just make a bloody fool of myself. You think he's going to quake in his boots with this?'

Rotund Face's smile was intact, although tinged with some concern. 'You are underestimating the power of this information, sir. Would any educated, middle-class person like to be exposed as a petrol thief and slasher of cars? And these crimes are punishable with three months' imprisonment or a fine or both and petrol thieving is…'

'These are petty misdemeanours,' I grumbled.

'Precisely, sir,' Rotund Face said. 'It's the petty nature of these crimes that makes it so acutely embarrassing for middle-class people, sir! People are pretty brazen about big crimes – land grabbing, black money, bribe-taking, all white-collar crimes, sir…But to be exposed as a petty petrol thief or car slasher is more shameful than you can imagine.'

He had a point there and I reflected over it but still felt crestfallen. 'You had promised results,' I said. 'I didn't know I was paying so much for this.'

The smile on his face had gone. He looked concerned and anxious. 'But, sir, I can only dig out the dirt that's there. I…I can't invent it.'

'You've seen the man, Sundar Nambiar, right? You think that guy only has these minor bones in his cupboard, not a whole, juicy skeleton?' I said heatedly.

Rotund Face looked at me apologetically. 'Sir, it takes more time to dig deeper. That costs time and money. It goes beyond budget. And let me tell you, sir, you'll be surprised how effectively the things I have discovered might work.'

I sighed. To be fair to Rotund Face, he'd certainly stalked Sundar enough to find this stuff. The photos and videos he'd got were pretty clinching evidence of his car-slashing and petrol-thieving. The ghastly man apparently went out on car-slashing expeditions armed with a rather ugly, sharp metal nail. Every time he saw a parked car with no scratches, he brushed past it, slashing at it, peeling away paint, leaving scratches, which would be enough to dismay a car owner.

It was quite a perverse, though essentially low-risk pastime. And with his mobile camera, Sundar's shadow had picked up clear images and clips of him in action, on at least three to four different days and in different areas, and made a note of the car numbers. Ditto petrol-thieving! Just how Rotund Face's operatives had managed it, God alone knows, as they followed Sundar, clicking him red-handed.

I got up. It might just work. I decided to mull over it, paid the balance money to Rotund Face and left. I had only one shot at this and if I failed then my avenge-grudge operation against Sundar could boomerang on me.

~

I was still undecided whether to proceed and if so, how to best use my material effectively against Sundar Nambiar, when my cell phone rang a few days later. It was Rotund Face.

'Sirji,' he said, 'I've got something more for you.'

'But I hadn't asked you to continue surveillance,' I said, chagrined.

'I know, I know, but you looked so disappointed that day that I felt like I needed to make it up to you…' Rotund Face replied. 'I did it on my own and you'll be thrilled to see what I have dug up. You'll reward me, sir.'

I felt curious and also gratified by his eagerness to help. 'Okay, I'll come over a little later.'

And what's more, Rotund Face proved his worth. He gave me just the kind of stuff I was looking for to catch Sundar Nambiar by his balls.

17

COMEUPPANCE

Sundar had certainly never expected me of all people to turn up at his doorstep. His bulbous eyes didn't exactly pop out of their sockets, but they did widen. His eyebrows shot up and the expression on his lecherous face seemed momentarily wary.

It reminded me of a scene in the Amitabh Bachchan film *Deewar*, when a bunch of goons after failing to hunt down the hero return to their den to find him waiting for them.

'Godbole? Why are you here? You got the wrong flat or something?' Sundar asked me in that irritating drawl of his.

'I've always wanted to pay you a return visit, Sundar, after you came to my house uninvited back then,' I said.

He looked at me oddly, as if trying to figure out the change in me, from the crushed old man he'd bullied almost three years ago. 'What's this about?'

'You want your neighbours to hear?'

'Hear what?' he asked with a scowl.

I smiled. 'I promise you'd prefer to hear what I have to say in private. I know your family is not at home just now so let's sit in the drawing room and talk.'

His face grew nasty, as if trying to grapple with the new Godbole, who appeared quite different from my old self.

'How do you know my family is not home?' he asked angrily.

'I watched them leave,' I replied. 'It would be very awkward for you otherwise.' Anger and unease wrestled with each other in his eyes. I had certainly pushed a button.

Suddenly the door of the flat opposite his opened and someone stepped out. 'Come in,' Sundar said gruffly and shut the door behind me as I stepped inside. Before he could say anything further, I sat down on his sofa.

'What is the meaning of this? What are you doing?' he asked, frowning.

'Sitting down. I'm an old man, I can't do this standing up,' I responded with a grin.

'Look, Godbole, I don't know what the hell you are playing at.'

'Shut up, Sundar, and make me some tea,' I snapped at him.

He goggled at me, speechless, with such fury, as if I had landed a sock right on his nose. 'How dare…' he fumed apoplectically. 'Get out of my house.'

'Of course, I will. As soon as you've fallen at my feet and begged forgiveness for what you did to me three years ago,' I shot back.

'What?'

'You heard me, if you know what's good for you, do as I say Sundar,' I said calmly, watching him get flustered, 'But first, get me some tea.'

'Tea?'

'Yes! Quick! And don't try to poison it.'

'Fuck off,' he exploded. 'Make tea, beg for forgiveness. Who the fuck do you think you are? Wait till I kick your arse…' The next moment he had his hands on my collar and began heaving me up. I had prepared for this, for two seconds later

Sundar gave a yelp and fell down writhing on the floor. With exquisite timing I had rammed my knee into his groin and his testicles were right now clanging around in his brain like church bells.

Of course, my knee hurt a bit, but it was well worth it. I wasn't done yet. I stood up and gave him another well-aimed kick in the same area. This time he howled.

'Now listen, while you gather your breath,' I said. 'I know you've been a very naughty boy, Sundar, so unless you do as I say, there is much pain ahead for you.'

He answered with a stream of curses, still writhing on the floor.

I cast a stern look at him. 'Every abuse you throw at me is going to cost you, you gutter-mouth,' I said. 'Now, don't waste time. I've come to make you repent and atone for your sins against me.'

Sundar had dragged himself into a sitting position on the floor and was glaring at me as if he'd like to murder me. 'I'm going to give you the thrashing of your life, Godbole, and then...'

'Empty threats,' I said dismissively with a giggle. 'Right now, you can't even stand on your hind legs. Anyway, here is what I want you to do first – fold your hands, apologize, and beg for my forgiveness.'

'Go to hell.'

'Let me complete. Don't interrupt. After you are done apologizing, the second thing you'll have to do is to call up the bloody chairperson of the Animal Welfare Board, the honourable minister herself and scream obscenities at her loudly – all the foulest things you can think of.'

'What? Are you crazy, Godbole?'

'Wait till you hear the third thing you have to do for me,' I said with a chuckle, loving this moment. 'Knowing your fondness for pornography, I want you to take nude selfies of yourself, performing various sexual acts with a hole in the wall or something and post it on your favourite porn site.'

Sundar gawped at me, looking like one of those Hindi film villains who don't know whether to laugh mockingly or strike a menacing pose. He began raising himself to his feet, still unsure of the state of his testicles. 'Have you lost your marbles, old man?'

I burst into laughter. What was it? A Freudian slip that Sundar should mouth these words at this moment.

'No, but you probably might have,' I guffawed. Oh, wasn't I enjoying this!

Sundar eyed me with fierceness, although tempered with the ginger-ness that made him incapable of trying any physical manoeuvre on me. 'Get out,' he snarled, his bulbous eyes trying to look smouldering.

'I have no intention of staying overnight, Sundar,' I said reasonably. 'Of course I'm going to leave. Relax! Let's do one thing – you grovel in front of me, right now, then you make a quick, nasty call to the minister, and I'll come back later for the nude video. You can do it any time, at your convenience, in the next forty-eight hours. Fair enough?'

'I'm not going to do any of it.'

'You are! You are!' I assured him. 'Else you are going to get into a lot of trouble.'

He glowered and tried to move forward aggressively, then realized it would be physically unwise given the state of his nuts. 'Fuck off. Go to hell.'

I sighed. 'You do have a very limited vocabulary you know… Now be a good boy, Sundar, and avoid trouble.'

'What "trouble"? What the hell are you going to do if I just kick you out of the house?'

'Ah, at last you are asking the right questions,' I said with contentment. 'The answer is that I have evidence of your car-slashing and petrol-stealing.'

His belligerent face fell with the speed of light. He was rendered mute, as he stared at me with baffled hatred.

'Bullshit,' he finally spluttered.

'Oh, no…no! It's all on camera…Lovely visuals as you do your handiwork on different cars, different locations, different days…Everything is neatly recorded. Including car numbers – all the scratches made, the cracking of car mirrors! Ditto, your petrol-thieving activities from two-wheelers. Open and shut cases of vandalism and petrol theft, which are punishable with imprisonment and fines. It'll also be posted on the net, making you immortal.'

Loathing and rage were oozing out of his eyes.

'Show me…'

I giggled. 'No need to. I'll just remind you; a red Tavera on FC Road, last week on Tuesday, near Vaishali Restaurant. Neat scratches on the front door, left side. You checked for a car alarm first, then slashed merrily…'

Sundar's face darkened further, probably at the vivid recollection. He was quiet for a few moments, then finally glanced at me. 'Look, I am ready to apologize for…for…that incident three years ago.'

'Good! Good! Go ahead,' I said encouragingly.

'But…but you can't seriously expect me to do the other two things,' he said stiffly.

'Why not?' I said. 'But first things first. Bring on the apology. I am going to record it. Remember, it's got to be grovelling and detailed, okay? Not just, "I am sorry". You have to admit how you acted like a total jerk.' I gave him directorial guidelines as I got ready with my mobile phone camera and began shot framing.

'Why are you recording it?' Sundar asked me hoarsely.

'Not to worry. It'll be for my personal viewing only, for whenever I wish to relish this moment again and again,' I replied. 'Come on now, quickly! Do you want to rehearse it a bit? Look, I've written down exactly what I want you to say...'

He took the paper I held out and began reading my scribbles. 'You...you want me to say all this?'

'Yes. And, you should clasp your hands together as you say it. At the end you can touch my feet,' I said. 'Tell me whenever you're ready. Let's do it in one take.'

He rolled his eyes then read through once more. 'Okay, but I...I'm not going to fall at your feet.'

'I am not really giving you a choice, Sundar,' I replied. 'You made me eat a dog biscuit, you bastard. Remember?' His Adam's apple bobbed up and down as he looked away.

I aimed my camera at him and shouted 'action' like a film director.

Sundar paused a few seconds, and then clasped his palms together. He began speaking in a morose voice.

It took him four takes to get it right, just the way I wanted it. Sometimes he mumbled, or forgot the words, or skipped the part where he had to fall at my feet. Every time I hollered 'cut' and made him repeat the whole thing.

I was beaming at the end of it and praised him lavishly. 'Good! That was satisfactory,' I said as I played it back for him. He cringed and looked distinctly unhappy.

'Well, now to the next task,' I said.

'Godbole, I told you I am not going to do anything else...' Sundar began arguing. 'I've given you an apology...That's it...'

'But an apology is not enough punishment, Sundar, for what you did to me,' I reasoned. 'I'll have no choice but to bring your criminal vandalism to the notice of the police as a good citizen and inform the owners of the various cars you damaged. And post the clips online too...'

'Come on, Godbole. You can't expect me to call up the lady, the minister, and abuse her like that…' Sundar said, exasperated and desperate.

'Why can't I? You called and made her abuse me. The honourable chairperson of the Animal Welfare Board.'

'Hell, she'll screw up my life, Godbole. I'll be arrested before I know it and get thrown into jail,' Sundar shrieked.

'Oh, come on, Sundar. You can disappear for a few hours and then send her an abject apology the next day, saying you were drunk or suddenly had a bout of schizophrenia or something,' I said reasonably.

He stared at me wild-eyed. 'Are you crazy? Do you realize just how powerful she is? She'll have me disembowelled. I'd rather go to jail for slashing cars and stealing petrol. No, no, no! I won't do this.'

I looked at him and shook my head in disappointment. 'You are not cooperating, Sundar. That woman abused me disgracefully, used such vile language, and you are not helping me get my own back on her!'

'Why don't you abuse her yourself, Godbole,' the little weasel said. 'Tit for tat. I'll get you her direct private number.'

I tut-tutted knowingly. 'That wouldn't be half as much fun as you doing it, Sundar. Okay, here's another idea. Why don't you abuse her like I tell you to and then later claim that you did it under duress, that somebody had a knife against your throat and forced you to call her?'

He groaned, then covered his face with his palms. I let him think it out. Finally, a few minutes later, he pleaded, 'Then let's just do it some other time of the day. Maybe tomorrow so that at least it'll seem plausible, from some other place, so I can say some animal abuser attacked me.'

I shook my head sagely at his pathetic attempt to wiggle out of the situation. 'That won't do, Sundar. I don't like the idea of delaying my gratification any longer. I have already waited too long to punish you and that foul-mouthed bitch.'

'You are mad! Bonkers! She'll come after you too,' Sundar lashed out.

'Not unless you squeal on me, but that will put you behind bars too…which you wouldn't want to be,' I reasoned lucidly. 'So your best bet is to call her now, get it over with, and then claim some unknown people made you do it – that will save you from her wrath and mine.'

Sundar sat for a few minutes and then glared at me. It was good to watch him crumble bit by bit, then fold altogether.

'Okay,' he cracked, then took his mobile, as if ready to dial.

'You are sure you want to do this extempore?' I asked.

'What's extempore?'

'Launching into abuse without rehearsing what you are going to say?' I said. 'I guess you are naturally good at talking trash.'

Sundar gave me a sour look. 'You just want me to call up and start abusing her, right? Bitch, whore…slut…That kind of stuff?'

I smiled. 'Ah! But abuse requires context to really sting, Sundar. So, here are a few lines you could mouth. Of course, mix it up with your colourful language.'

I passed on a written note to him, which he quickly read and looked aghast. 'Your mind is filthier than mine, Godbole. I can't say things like that.'

'Oh, yes, you can and you will,' I assured him. 'Just show me your dialogue delivery.'

I grinned encouragingly and for the next few minutes he muttered under his breath, as he practised the lines I had jotted down.

'Ready?'

He didn't reply.

'You want to practise it aloud once?'

Sundar shook his head, as if sure of his abilities.

'Well, your choice, but if I sense a below par performance, I am not going to be happy about it, Sundar!'

He made a face. 'You don't have to keep telling me that.'

'Go on then…Dial her number,' I replied brightly. 'And put it on speaker…'

Sundar's facial muscles did a little jig, then he licked his lips. I guess even abuse artistes get nervous sometimes. His hands were shaking as he held the phone and began searching for the minister's number to dial.

'Show me it's her number that you are dialling, before you actually do,' I remarked, quite aware that the sly bastard could try some last-minute trick.

He showed me the display, then jabbed the dial button and put the phone on speaker. He was still aquiver, and his panic was a treat to watch as the rings began passing. His tongue moved in and out, as if he were a lizard in human form, which of course he was.

A minute passed – the call went unanswered. A hint of gleeful relief appeared on Sundar's reptilian face.

'Try again,' I said curtly.

'But she must be busy.'

'Who cares! Dial, continue dialling until she picks up.'

'What? This isn't an ordinary person I can keep calling, Godbole. It's the minister's direct personal number.'

'Get on with it, Sundar.'

His face tensed up again as he dialled. Yet again the call wasn't picked up. Reluctantly, he attempted a few more times with rising panic. I must confess I hadn't considered the possibility of the calls going unanswered.

'Hmmm…Keep trying, Sundar.'

He grunted with exasperation. 'I…I need to pee first.'

'Not before you've made the call, Sundar.'

'Oh, come on, Godbole...I've got to go...my bladder's full!'

'I don't care if you wet your pants or your bladder bursts, Sundar.' I chuckled.

We eyeballed each other back and forth – a kind of battle of wills. Of course, I had no clue what I'd do if he insisted upon going to the toilet in his own house. It wasn't as if I had a gun to prevent him. But I knew a man with a full bladder was pretty vulnerable and helpless till he'd emptied himself. And then, just as I was wondering whether to relent, Sundar's phone gave tongue. We both reacted differently to the incoming call.

He was startled and morose, whereas I was elated and excited.

'It's her, Sundar! Your big moment is here. Go for it. Don't let me down,' I said.

He remained inert, making no move to take the call, glancing at me as if thinking of bolting. I sighed. I guess I had to get violent again. The next moment, my cane thwacked him on the fleshy part of his hips. Did I tell you, he had protruding buttocks like a Neanderthal? Well, he definitely did.

'Ow...' he squealed and almost immediately took the call.

I raised my cane again to strike, and Sundar let loose his volley at the minister, delivering a performance that warmed the cockles of my heart. Sweet revenge was mine.

~

Two days later, I rang Sundar's doorbell again. I had waited for the midnight knock from the police, expecting Sundar to have been subjected to some mild third degree, after which he would spill the beans about me. But that never happened. There had been a buzz in the neighbourhood that Sundar had indeed been taken to the police station, but no details were forthcoming. Naturally, as a good neighbour, I wanted to check on his well-being. So, here I was.

'What do you want?' Sundar asked belligerently as soon as he saw me. I was a little disappointed not to see him covered with welts and bruises, inflicted by the cops, but he certainly was looking a mental wreck. That cheered me up infinitely.

'Tell me everything about your ordeal, Sundar. Tell me, buddy.' I said heartily.

He looked daggers at me, seeming to wrestle with the urge to tell me to go to the blazes on one hand, and on the other, the need to blithely vent an impotent rant at me for what I'd put him through. 'I hope one day I can throw you into a pool full of piranha, Godbole,' he hissed as he let me in.

'Ha ha! I'll pull you in, Sundar, and they'll probably devour you first because you are such an animal lover,' I shot back. 'Are fish animals too, Sundar? I mean, why isn't there a Society for the Prevention of Cruelty to Fish? I have always wondered.'

He ignored me, then struck an accusing pose, his hands on his hips. 'Do you know what they did to me?' he cried hysterically.

'What?' I asked earnestly. 'That's exactly what I've come to hear.'

Sundar stared at me with his bloodshot eyes popping out of their sockets, as if hoping the hate he felt would produce rays that could reduce me to ashes, there and then. It was greatly titillating to see him suffer like that.

'Well…' I prompted.

In response, Sundar literally burst into tears. 'You bastard, Godbole. You motherfucker, I'll kill you. I should've told the cops it was you who forced me.'

A roar of laughter from my innermost depths surprised me as much as it did him. It was so funny to hear the pathetic twerp. I rumbled heartily, watching his miserable self-pitying rage.

'Go on…Do it…I dare you.'

He watched me, turning red with shame and humiliation, helpless to turn the tables on me. Yet his need to lick his wounds was so powerful that he narrated all that had transpired after his call to the minister.

The police had descended, like a ton of bricks, within half an hour of the call and picked Sundar up. He'd been taken to the police station like some dangerous criminal, subject to multiple rounds of questioning, free-flowing abuse and later a few slaps too. He had pleaded pathetically that he had been under duress and had made the call while being held hostage by unknown people – dog-haters probably – who'd wanted him to get into big trouble. He claimed that was the reason why they made him call the minister and shower the choiciest abuse. The cops had taken a long time to swallow the story.

But Sundar had whimpered and grovelled through the grilling and stuck to his tale till the cops grudgingly accepted his imploring. After all, if it hadn't been a minister at the receiving end, abusive rants could at best be a non-cognizable offence since no threats had been made. Of course, a case for obscenity and sexual harassment of a lady had been registered, but Sundar had been abject in his apologies; he hadn't been found drunk nor seemed to have any earthly reason to abuse the minister the way he had.

Sundar had also begged them to call the animal welfare officer of the area, who then reluctantly spoke to the minister, clarified what had happened, and sought forgiveness on Sundar's behalf. Finally he was let go after being issued a stern warning. Of course, the police case would remain, and the legal process would have to be dealt with, but for the moment Sundar was off the hook.

'So, it wasn't so bad after all, was it, Sundar?' I remarked after he had stopped yapping. 'What's a day of humiliation compared to the month-long dog feeding you made me endure?'

He scowled at me, looking uneasy. 'You've had your fun and revenge, so leave me alone now.'

I giggled and cackled and wagged a finger at him. 'No…no, Sundar, not yet. You are still a long way from making amends.'

His face turned defiant. 'No, I am done dancing to your whims. I am not doing the nude thing. You can't make me.'

'No?' I teased. 'You are missing the chance of a lifetime to trend on the internet. I've even thought of a hashtag – #sexysundarstrips. Believe me, you can become an overnight sensation.'

'Oh, shut up,' Sundar snapped. 'I am not doing anything of that kind, just get out, Godbole. Beat it…'

'Tut, tut, wrong tone to take with me, Sundar,' I rebuked him. 'You aren't getting rid of me just yet.'

'Fuck off, you can't blackmail me any longer after what I've gone through.'

'You are mistaken. I can…I can…because I know something worse about you than I have let on,' I said gleefully.

I heard a sharp intake of breath. Sundar froze, his eyes slowly bulging as if he were suddenly turning into a toad, starting with his face. 'Bullshit!' he said with hollowed out aggression.

'Add some variety to your cuss words, Sundar,' I chided him. 'Any way, I know a really shocking secret of yours, my boy, that could put you inside for seven long years of hard labour, promise!'

Sundar went on turning into a toad, his features puffing up, as he palpitated and groaned. 'What are you talking about?' he asked querulously.

I gave him the widest grin possible, because even blackmail can be done pleasantly, can't it?

'Turtles,' I exclaimed. 'Olive Ridley turtles.'

Have you ever heard the term 'poleaxed'? Well, I got close to seeing what it meant as Sundar went down. He didn't exactly fall flat on his back with a thud, rather tripped on something as he backed away, and fell on his rump, as if I'd delivered a knockout punch.

He didn't even try to deny it – this bogus, slimy animal lover. 'What proof...?' he managed to stutter as he crawled back to his feet.

I smirked. 'Let's just say, last Wednesday at 4.30 p.m., you and that lady, the animal welfare officer, got into a car and exchanged a blue icebox with a man in a Mercedes, and drove away with a bag. Am I right?'

Sundar's face and body language were dead giveaways. All the cocky pretensions were gone. He knew he was done for. Game, set and match to me!

'Smuggler Sundar, no wonder you talk of feeding me to the piranhas. You are a member of the wildlife mafia, behind that phony front of being an animal lover!'

'Don't call me mafia or a smuggler,' he said in an almost inaudible voice.

'Then what? Poacher?'

He sat silently for a while, then gave a low moan. 'It's harmless, just a one-off thing. As a pet...for a child.'

'It's illegal, you bum. No one can keep Olive Ridley turtles as pets, or any other turtles, for that matter. You know that, as well as I do. And you've done it before,' I blasted him. 'There's money in it, you turtle thief! Your goose is cooked. Both you and your lady friend are going to jail.'

He suddenly began sniffling and sobbing. 'What do you want me to do? Why do you want me to do the nude thing? Please, Godbole, have some pity.'

I loved it. I loved this meltdown of his. I chuckled and revelled in it a bit, watching his wheedling and whimpering.

'Well, what the hell, Sundar. I won't hold you to the nude selfies if you do something else for me,' I finally said with a rollick.

'What?' he said warily, his heart in his mouth. 'Something illegal?'

I smiled. 'Oh, something illegal, definitely, which you've already proven that you have a talent for, Sundar – you and your lady friend,' I replied, patting him on the back.

18

TURTLES AND JACKFRUITS

'You want us to plant a dozen Olive Ridley turtles in his house and get him arrested?' Sundar asked, gawking at me, twenty minutes later.

'What I'd really like is to have him bitten by a rabid dog or venomous snake, if you can arrange that as an animal lover. But since you obviously cannot, planting turtles would do splendidly,' I replied. We were talking about my school friend, Nandu Khandagale, against whom, you'd remember, I had sworn revenge.

'But where the hell will I get a dozen Olive Ridley turtles?'

'The same place where you got the earlier one,' I said. 'Your nubile friend...'

'A dozen? Are you crazy? Do you know how much they cost?'

I nodded sagely. 'I have some idea...but that's not my lookout.'

'Means what?' he asked anxiously.

'It means how you get those turtles is your problem...It's part of the debt you owe me, Sundar.'

He freaked out. 'What do you take me for, Godbole? I'm not some animal mafia! How am I going to get twelve turtles without paying a dime?'

'You'll think of a way, Sundar. It happens when you are caught between a rock and a hard place,' I said cheerfully.

'But…'

'Talk to your friend, tell her I've caught you both red-handed, on camera. It'll act as a great motivator…and let's meet again tomorrow to plot further,' I said, just in time, since Sundar's doorbell rang at that very moment.

It was probably his wife and daughter, who were back from shopping or whatever they'd gone out for. He threw me another one of his hopeless looks.

'You wish you hadn't tangled with me now, don't you, Sundar?' I preened at him, with a kind of amused menace in my eyes. 'If only you'd known the way I nurse my grudges.'

He seemed shaken and quickly glanced in the direction of the door. I read his mind.

'I'm leaving, Sundar, don't you worry. Let your family in.'

~

Twenty-four hours later, we foregathered at a restaurant in a faraway locality of the city, where no one was likely to know us – Sundar, the animal welfare officer and me.

The lady's name was Madhuri – and my newly acquired glad-eye noticed that though she was nowhere in the league of Mrs Dixit-Nene, this Madhuri was also not bad-looking in the least. And, she was curvy as hell! I absolutely wouldn't have minded being an animal, if she was indeed willing to express her love for animals, even here and now.

She was looking tense and anxious – a damsel in distress.

'It can't be done,' Sundar huffed in an undertone. 'You can ask Madhuri yourself…'

Madhuri shook her head when I glanced at her.

'What can't be done?'

'What you asked for,' Sundar replied. I ignored him and kept looking at Madhuri.

Her slightly pouty lips parted, and she looked away first, then finally replied. 'It's impossible…A dozen…' She shook her head again for emphasis.

'How many can you arrange then?' I asked and pre-empted Sundar from answering by gesturing to him. 'I want to hear directly from her, Sundar.'

Madhuri glanced in Sundar's direction and then at me. 'Only one.'

'Don't bluff, Madhuri. How many? Eight or ten? Half a dozen?'

She flashed her eyes at Sundar again. 'It's not that easy, two or three perhaps.'

'Get me five,' I replied.

'Five!' both of them chorused. They looked at each other and then at me, as if I had asked them to fetch some temple treasure.

'How can I get five?' Madhuri said. 'Mr Godbole, please, I am telling you…you are asking for the moon.'

'It's just about money, my dear Madhuri, and contacts. I know you can do it,' I said, turning on my latent charm.

'But why do you want five, Mr Godbole? Even one will do the trick,' she said. 'He gets the same sentence whether he is found in possession of one or five.'

'Come on, don't pretend to be naïve, sweet Madhuri,' I said, taking liberties, which she didn't object to, although her expression changed slightly. 'If Nandu is found with just one, he can plead being a customer. But with five, he becomes a supplier and a smuggler. It is just like the difference between a junkie and a drug dealer.'

She and Sundar were quiet again. 'Can we just discuss this amongst ourselves?' Sundar asked me.

I shook my head. 'Nope! Five is fair. No scope for discussion.'

'But Mr Godbole, it's not just expensive, it's also very risky,' Madhuri said. 'I've never procured so many at a time before and got them here.'

'Oh, come on. All you have to do is to take Sundar's car and drive down to Velas, right? Contact your friendly turtle smuggler, pay and bring them back,' I said.

'Shhh…Shhh…Godbole, not so loud!' Sundar said, panicking and glancing all around. Madhuri, however, was eyeing me with new-found respect in her expression. 'You know about Velas?'

'Of course I do. I have done my homework, Madhuri dear,' I replied, and she still didn't object to my far-from-fatherly endearment.

'Then you would also know that it's not easy getting in and out,' she said. 'There's plenty of checking in the area around hatching season.'

I bubbled with laughter. 'Human trafficking continues unabated everywhere, despite all the checks in the world! What's with a few tiny turtles, Madhuri…You can do it.' Then I turned to glare at Sundar, 'And weren't you an excise and customs officer once, Sundar? Surely, you have served on the Konkan coast.'

He looked at me with a start. 'How do you know about my background?'

'I also know that you were suspended for disgraceful conduct, pending an inquiry into serious corruption charges against you.'

'That's false, totally untrue,' he snapped, turning pale.

'Then what?' I mocked. 'You were suspended for being too upright and honest?'

He gave me his 'throw you to piranhas' look again but said nothing. I turned to Madhuri. 'So shall we say that next week you'll be back with the turtles from Velas?'

'Next week? That's too short,' Madhuri said quickly.

'One week is more than enough,' I said, waving her protest aside. 'Okay, Sundar?'

He gave me a glazed-over look and nodded slightly.

'Good! One last thing,' I said.

Madhuri and Sundar looked at me, wondering what more I was going to say.

I smiled. 'Are you married, Madhuri? Or engaged or something?'

She was taken aback by the question and a frown appeared on her face. 'No! Why?'

'Nah! Just asking! Neither am I,' I replied. 'But do you know what I am? A widower on Viagra, ready to date and mate.'

I said it with a flourish and caught the look of astonishment on her face. Not shock, mind you! Well, what the hell was she going to do anyway? Charge me with POCSO? I didn't think so!

~

Four days later I got a call from Sundar.

'We've arranged for the jackfruits,' he whispered in his annoying, husky voice.

'Jackfruits?' I asked, before it struck me that the idiot was using it as a code word for the turtles.

'Yes, the *jackfruits* you ordered,' he said hastily, emphasizing the word as if we were actors in some amateur spy movie. I giggled. It wasn't a bad code word, because jackfruits are a speciality of the Konkan area.

'The full quantity?' I asked, to ensure he wasn't selling me short.

'Yes, yes, so…so we are starting from here tomorrow morning,' Sundar said. 'What's the plan? I mean, what next?'

'Well, day after tomorrow morning, you deliver the jackfruits where I tell you to,' I replied. I had it all worked out.

'Deliver? How?'

'I'll explain when you get here. I need to check the quality and quantity myself,' I replied.

'So, we bring it to your house tomorrow, to store it overnight and you'll deliver it the following day?' Sundar said quickly.

'No, Sundar. I'll just check the jackfruit when you get here. But they remain with you and you deliver it the following day, as I tell you to,' I said, nipping in the bud his attempt to be too clever by half.

'But, I can't keep it overnight at my home…' Sundar wailed. 'I mean, I just can't.'

'Well, then Madhuri can keep it. You decide between the two of you,' I replied, relishing the whole set-up, since I held all the cards. 'See you and the jackfruits tomorrow,' I said and hung up.

I had heard his yelp in protest, yet I hung up nevertheless. My phone rang again a couple of times, but I just didn't bother.

19

BRINGING DOWN NANDU

'Are they alive?' I asked a terrified Sundar as I looked down at the five tiny creatures, each no bigger than the size of one's palm.

'Of course they are,' he snapped hysterically, looking at Madhuri and then all around to see if anyone was watching.

We were seated in his car – him in the driver's seat, half turned, and Madhuri and I in the back seat, with the icebox containing the turtles, between us.

'Why aren't they moving then?' I persisted.

'How should I know, Godbole?' Sundar remarked, looking quite near the edge. 'What difference does it make whether the turtles are dead or alive?'

I looked at him reproachfully. 'Aren't you supposed to be an animal lover? I don't want anything to happen to the turtles, just to my enemies.'

Sundar seemed to be in a belligerent mood. 'They are reptiles. I am not a reptile lover.'

'Despite being a reptile yourself?' I couldn't help quipping and then winked at Madhuri, who looked rather fetching despite the long drive from Velas that they were just back from.

Sundar bristled. 'Look, Godbole,' he said.

'Relax, Sundar. What's a little harmless ribbing between friends and co-conspirators…' I said, tapping his hand to calm his nerves.

Madhuri, who had been quiet so far, now cleared her throat. 'Mr Godbole…'

'Yes, Madhuri dear…I wish I had a trendy first name, which I could ask you to call me by, instead of this formal "Mr Godbole",' I said. 'But unfortunately for me, it's "Gajanan" and does not lend itself to a sexy abbreviation either.'

She gave a pre-occupied smile and looked even more desirable. I wondered if I could attempt a quick kiss. But tomorrow morning was crucial and there was no point in trying anything foolhardy on the prompting of my long-dormant loins, which had started stirring recently.

'Anyway, what were you saying?' I asked. She glanced at Sundar, then spoke. 'Sundar tells me you have a plan for planting these on that man tomorrow.'

'Ah yes,' I beamed, 'very simple and easy to execute.'

'But then why don't you do that yourself, Mr Godbole,' Madhuri said earnestly. 'After all, Sundar and I have gone through a lot of trouble and risks already…'

'No…no…no, Madhuri,' I said, 'the roles are crystal clear – I'm the boss and mastermind, while Sundar and you are my henchmen…sorry…henchpersons. Besides, the plan needs some nimble footwork and faces that are unfamiliar to our quarry. So that's how it's going to be…'

For a few moments I thought a rebellion was brewing in the ranks, as I noticed mutinous expressions on Sundar's face, while Madhuri looked exasperated. But good sense prevailed in both.

'Tell us what exactly needs to be done,' Madhuri asked finally.

'That's the spirit, sweet Madhuri,' I said. 'Our target, Nandu Khandagale, goes for a morning walk daily on Vetal Tekdi. He leaves home around 5.30 a.m., parks his car around 5.45 a.m. and then begins his trundle. He returns around 6.45 a.m., stands and chats with a group, then gets into his car, drives a short distance and stops by a small line of counters – tables set up by individuals offering tea, juices, health drinks and stuff like that to daily walkers and joggers. He gets out of the car, crosses the narrow road and goes to a counter offering bottle gourd juice.'

I watched an involuntary shudder pass through Madhuri. 'I know. Yuck,' I responded.

Sundar belched. 'Oh, he's one of those freaks who has bottle gourd juice, is it?'

'You bet. Shows you the kind of man he is. Have you tried it too?' I asked.

'No way,' Sundar replied.

'Well, you always look and sound as if you consume it daily,' I said with a chuckle.

He gave me a sour look. 'Stop those wisecracks, Godbole…'

'Or what?' I dared him. He glowered at me, looked at Madhuri, then looked away.

'Continue narrating the plan, Mr Godbole,' Madhuri said.

'Ah well…Nandu takes about ten minutes there, as he downs the bottle gourd juice and pays for it, then gets back into the car and drives home,' I said. 'But the crucial thing is when he stops for the juice, he does not lock the car, because it's just across the road and within eye range. That's when one of you will have to quickly open the back door of his car and place the icebox on the back seat floor – in the leg space.'

'What?' Sundar asked.

'Yes, you heard right, Sundar. Nandu's busy chatting with the lady or other customers, then swallowing the stupid drink in small little gulps, because it's really awful and thus takes some time to finish.'

'This is your masterplan?' Sundar asked in a strangled, outraged tone.

'Yes,' I said. 'Simple, quick, uncomplicated. Over in the blink of an eye. Nandu won't notice even when he gets home and then all that needs to be done is to tip somebody off that he's in possession of Olive Ridley turtle hatchlings…' I replied with a flourish. 'And Nandu will be in big trouble.'

'Are you mad? It's the stupidest plan ever,' Sundar said, returning to hysterics. 'Someone's bound to see. Hell, even your friend, Nandu, himself might see! I am not going to have anything to do with this, Godbole. No way.'

'Calm down, you idiot. What are you getting all worked up about? All one of you has to do is to keep watch and the other has to open the rear door of Nandu's car, place the icebox inside and shut the door again…Easy-peasy! Less than a ten second job…' I said. 'It's child's play, Sundar…I don't know what you are freaking out about.'

I glanced at Madhuri, who was listening carefully, her eyebrows knit together, her lip curled up at one corner, which she was nibbling on. 'What do you think, Madhuri? Isn't it just brilliant – a plan so simple and easy to execute, low risk?' I asked her. 'It would be done in a flash.'

Madhuri chewed on her lips a bit more, and I was disappointed she wasn't appreciating the ingenuity of my diabolical scheme, yet.

'It's not a plan, Godbole, it's a sure shot way of getting us arrested,' Sundar continued his tirade. 'You are batshit crazy.'

'It's you who is a numbskull, Sundar,' I said. 'Nothing of the kind will happen. You will already be waiting around the spot where Nandu stops his car. As soon as he parks and hops across the street, you casually walk up to his car, open the rear door on the passenger side, slip in the icebox, shut the door, and stroll back to your position.'

'But, Mr Godbole,' Madhuri said hesitantly, 'what if the target just glances over his shoulder or maybe an acquaintance of his or even a bystander happens to notice?'

'It won't happen, believe me,' I said to her. 'And even if by chance someone…even Nandu notices…all that Sundar or you have to pretend is that you opened the door of the wrong car by mistake, instead of your own. That's the beauty of the plan, you see – the car door will be opened for just a few seconds and then immediately shut again. And whoever is placing the icebox has to just pretend that they were momentarily confused, just in case.'

'Oh, come on, you are just making it sound easy,' Sundar began whining again, but before I could shut him up, Madhuri spoke.

'It could work, you know, it's quite a clever tactic. And yes, it won't look suspicious at all to claim Sundar opened the car door by mistake, thinking it was his.'

Sundar turned on her. 'Why me? If you are so convinced, why don't you do it? I'll keep watch. Anyway, as a lady, it'll be more believable and no one's going to manhandle you or anything, even if you are caught, whereas…'

I was about to shoot down Sundar's attempt to evade, when I realized it wasn't such a bad idea after all. 'He has a point, Madhuri. It could go much smoother and arouse less suspicion if a lady did it…'

'You forget that I am the animal welfare officer of this district and might have to get involved in proceedings, especially since I am the one who is going to provide the tip-off,' Madhuri replied. 'If the target happens to see me tomorrow, he might recognize me later on at some stage in case we come face to face then.'

'Hmm…you are right, Madhuri. Smart girl!' I said and turned to Sundar. 'Sundar, my boy, it's got to be you, I'm afraid.'

'Shit man!' Sundar grunted. 'Curse you, Godbole, I'm going to kill you. I really am.'

'Stop being a sissy, Sundar. Someone would think you are being asked to plant a bomb,' I chided him.

He gave me a dark look, which I ignored and soon we were discussing what would happen after Nandu drove home with the turtles.

~

Sundar fidgeted in his seat as we waited for Nandu to turn up near the row of roadside tables and counters offering tea, coffee, health concoctions of all kinds, even coconut water, and some herbal stuff.

We had first watched Nandu arrive at Vetal Tekdi, park his car and then start his walk. An hour later, we were expecting him anytime now, to show up for his bottle gourd juice, on his way back.

A middle-aged woman with a ready smile was the one who sold three types of juices, including bottle gourd, which were placed in big glass jugs. All her customers seemed to be regular walkers and joggers, men and women, joking or chatting with her or among themselves, holding their paper cups and sipping the poisons of their choice.

'Is he late or what?' Sundar grumbled and tugged at his crotch yet again.

'You are soon going to break the record for maximum number of crotch adjustments in a sixty-minute period, Sundar,' I remarked. My pinprick turned Sundar's face red with embarrassment, and he cast a quick glance at Madhuri, who seemed to have heard my barb too.

'It's a stupid plan. It's not going to work, someone's going to see,' Sundar said vehemently. 'Let's call it off, damn it...'

'Will you stop being a fusspot! He'll be here any minute, and it's going to be all right,' I asserted.

'Well, I'm sick and tired of all this, Godbole. I bloody well am getting some tea,' Sundar said, opening the car door and starting to get out.

'Wait,' Madhuri said, 'I'll go and get the tea. I need some myself and it'll also give us something to do as we wait...'

I checked my watch. Nandu's usual time was about 5–7 minutes away, but he could also reach earlier. 'Okay, but make it quick...' I said.

Madhuri got out of the car and crossed the road to fetch tea. As soon as we were alone, Sundar swivelled around and glowered at me. 'Don't you dare humiliate me in front of her again, Godbole! I'm warning you...enough of your cheap shots...'

'Why, you got a thing for her, Sundar?' I chuckled slyly.

'None of your business...And stop propositioning her, you obscene old man...' he growled.

I was about to remind him that I had his balls in my hand, when from the corner of my eye I noticed Nandu's car coming into view, slowing down and preparing to ease into a parking space, just one car away from us.

'He's here,' I hissed. 'Get ready...look...'

Sundar stiffened then turned around as if he were a wound-up toy that had just been set-off. 'Where? Where?'

'Shhh…stop making such a racket,' I said. 'Look…' I pointed Nandu out to him, as he got out of his car and shut the door. But just as he was about to cross the road, he reached into his pocket and took out his phone, as if he'd just received a call.

'Get ready…' I said and quickly repeated the plan again. 'Get out of the car and wait for him to cross the road. As soon as he reaches the counter, move towards his car with the icebox. Then, when he is busy being served or paying for the juice, open the rear passenger door, place the icebox, shut the door and walk back to our car. Understood?'

Sundar nodded, still shaky, but got out of the car.

'Where's Madhuri?' I cursed. 'Signal her to come back.'

'What? Her…her back is turned toward us…' Sundar replied, clearly disoriented and nervous.

'You and your bloody tea…' I said furiously. 'You better make this work, Sundar, or you are done for…'

'Stop…stop badgering me…Let me concentrate…'

Beads of sweat had already appeared on his forehead. He was watching Nandu, who seemed to have been engaged in a conversation on his phone, leaning against his car. I could even hear his voice, a word here or there, although not exactly what he was saying.

Madhuri, meanwhile, had turned around, two cups of tea in her hands, to cross the road and return to our car. She seemed to have seen Nandu, but her face remained totally impassive. The problem, however, with even slightly pretty women is, they get noticed by men. And as Nandu stood there talking on his mobile, I saw his head tilt in her direction, as Madhuri came into his field of vision while crossing the street.

'Shit…' I cursed as I watched his eyes follow her, right towards our car. I was sure he would now notice Sundar too, standing outside. 'Don't let him see you, Sundar…'

'What the hell do you want me to do?' Sundar hissed back. 'I can't cover my face or something, can I? He'll notice that.'

Madhuri had crossed the street and handed over one cup to Sundar. Nandu was still looking but he had lost interest now and his neck swivelled back away from us. He'd probably had a glimpse of Sundar distractedly, but there was no question of him having seen me, since I was inside the car.

'Should I go back to get the third cup?' Madhuri asked.

'No, no,' I said. 'Wait. He's already had a good long look at you. Damn, Sundar, hope you scald your tongue.'

Sundar had already begun slurping his tea greedily, with no signs of scalding. 'No one taught you to sip silently?' I asked angrily.

Sundar paid no attention, his eyes fixated on Nandu. 'He's never going to stop yapping on his phone,' he remarked impatiently.

'He's looking at his watch,' Madhuri observed.

Sure enough, I could see Nandu look at the time and then towards the counters, as if in some kind of a dilemma. Finally, he hung up, but instead of crossing the road for his bottle gourd juice, he got back into his car and started it. Clearly the phone call had made him skip his routine. Something more important than bottle gourd juice had probably come up.

I turned away a little, as Nandu pulled out and drove past us.

'What the fuck? He's left…' Sundar said with disbelief and relief. 'I told you it was a stupid plan, full of holes! Bottle gourd juice, for heaven's sake, all he needed was an excuse to give the foul drink a miss. How the hell could your plan hinge on someone consuming bottle gourd juice by the roadside?'

'Shut up, Sundar. It's a perfectly workable plan. Consider this a dry run. We'll try it again tomorrow,' I replied.

'What? No way. I can't do this again tomorrow. Besides, he's seen our faces, damn it. It'll be suicidal. I'm not letting myself get dragged into this idiotic plan tomorrow...' Sundar began ranting.

'So what? He'll just think you are new walkers at Vetal Tekdi. Why would he think differently?' I reasoned. 'Nandu doesn't know you. He doesn't have any idea what's going to befall him. And even later, why will he connect anything to you, Sundar, a total stranger?'

'But he's seen me too, Mr Godbole, and if he sees me again tomorrow, he might just recognize me later on if I come face to face with him as the animal welfare officer,' Madhuri said.

'So he should definitely not see you tomorrow, Madhuri,' I said. 'No getting out of the car to fetch some blithering tea, understood? We do exactly what we did today and execute the mission successfully tomorrow.'

Sundar gave his characteristic whiny grumble. 'No, no, I'm telling you it's no use. Maybe he's just given up on bottle gourd juice or maybe he even won't stop at all tomorrow! So let's abandon the whole thing.'

'Abandon the plan and do what exactly?' It was Madhuri who spoke with slight irritation. 'We would still be stuck with the turtles. What are we going to do with them otherwise? How would we look after them? It's not as if we have an alternative, like ready buyers.'

Sundar fixed her with a searing et tu Brutus look. 'Can't we just throw them in the river or Pashan lake or something?' he said. 'Or take them back to that chap in Velas and get a refund?'

'Refund? Don't be silly...Who do you think we are dealing with? A grocer?' Madhuri snapped.

'Look,' I intervened, 'let's try this tomorrow again. I'm sure it's going to work. If it doesn't work, we can throw them into the river or something.'

'They won't survive that,' Madhuri said.

'Well, that's why, let's make sure that we damn well succeed tomorrow,' I asserted.

'Curse you, Godbole,' Sundar muttered under his breath. Madhuri nodded silently.

'Well then, that's it. Now, did you pay for the teas?'

'Yes…' Madhuri said.

'Then perhaps you can get the third cup, which you haven't gotten around to bringing yet, my dear Madhuri…'

She got out of the car without a word and got me my tea. I was the boss, after all!

~

'Ex-corporator Khandagale booked for smuggling Olive Ridley turtles' flashed the headlines of a leading news channel, with visuals of Nandu being led away by policemen, his bungalow besieged by cops and a crowd of bystanders and of course the recovery of the Olive Ridley turtles in the icebox.

I chuckled as the anchor and news reporter did a short Q&A, making it sound as if they'd dug up a couple of bodies from the house of a psychopath. I channel surfed and watched another report on another news channel, that sensationalized the facts even more.

'Is Ex-corporator Khandagale a part of the animal trafficking mafia?' Here the reporter hyperventilated, about the value of Olive Ridley turtles found and how the discovery was perhaps the tip of the iceberg of a multi-crore illegal racket. There was also a quick profile on Nandu, a lament on a possible criminal-political nexus and how Nandu was just the kind of guy who could be involved in such shady activities – all defamatory to the hilt.

I was, of course, beside myself with joy. The plan had gone like a breeze the next morning. We had lain in wait; Nandu had parked and crossed the lane to fetch his bottle gourd juice. A jumpy Sundar had managed to open the rear door of Nandu's car and place the icebox without a hitch. No one had been watching or had noticed, and nothing had gone wrong despite Sundar's clumsiness. An unsuspecting Nandu had returned to his car and without so much as a backward glance, had driven home with the turtles in the icebox.

We had followed him all the way, and I watched gleefully as he drove inside the gates of his bungalow. We had a quick celebratory breakfast at the nearby Udupi restaurant, and I magnanimously paid the bill, even for slimy Sundar's dosa and coffee.

Then an hour later Madhuri had called the cops, saying she'd received a tip-off that a gentleman named Nandu Khandagale had recently smuggled some Olive Ridley turtle hatchlings to Pune. The cops had questions and probed about her source. Madhuri had hinted it was an environmental activist from Velas, who would remain anonymous. The cops had hummed and hawed and told her they needed something more specific to even attempt a raid or search, especially because Nandu was an ex-corporator. Madhuri had said she would try to get more information, but time was of essence to catch the man red-handed. Half an hour later, she called them again, and told the officer fresh details – five Olive Ridley turtles in a blue icebox.

The officer hummed and hawed some more, saying it still wasn't enough. That's when Madhuri pulled her trump card; she said she didn't want to force their hand, but was left with no choice but to report it to the animal welfare chairperson, the union minister. She, Madhuri, couldn't with good conscience be party to dereliction of duty, and since Nandu was anyway just an ex-corporator, that too from a rival party who were not in power, she couldn't understand the cops' hesitation.

That finally did the trick and, reluctantly, the cops sprang into action. They found the icebox with the turtles exactly where Sundar had left it – in the well of the backseat.

What followed was inevitable and I felt like an Indian screen hero who'd succeeded in avenging himself and putting the villain in the dock. What would ensue was, of course, slow burn – given the Indian legal system. It would be a long, long time before Nandu was tried, proven guilty and punished. But then the process itself would result in ample punishment and harassment for him. I relished the prospect of his forthcoming sufferings and what he would be put through for several weeks and months to come, even years, till the case was decided.

Mind you, I was still not done with him. This was just my first gambit, and a few weeks after he had endured the suffering caused by the turtle fiasco, I was planning an endgame – a check and mate. You see, Nandu's fondness for bottle gourd juice had given me some rather naughty, nasty, murderous ideas. I just needed time to let things marinate in my brain and throw up a workable plan.

Meanwhile, I would be putting my mind to seducing the buxom Madhuri, while also thinking of ways to quench my thirst for revenge against Sundar, which wasn't satiated yet. He didn't like bottle gourd juice, but as they say, there are many ways to skin a cat and murder a man!

20

COURTING MADHURI

'Madhuri,' I said as she picked up the phone, 'what do you think of me?'

'I didn't quite get you, Mr Godbole,' Madhuri replied in a voice that I recognized as wary. She understood me all right.

'Oh, come on, you know what I am talking about, dear. To use that American phrase – you turn me on, Madhuri,' I said, oozing with ardour.

I heard a sharp intake of breath and a pause. 'I…Mr Godbole, I'm quite flattered but…'

'But what, Madhuri? I am too old? Is that it?'

'I mean…' She probably was at a loss for words or reluctant to offend me.

'Why don't you try me once?' I said, jumping right ahead. 'Let's meet, go out for dinner, then come home with me and if you enjoy yourself, we can make it a regular thing.' I think she was rather knocked out by my candidness.

'Let me…let me think about it, Mr Godbole,' she finally replied after a longish pause.

'What's there to think? You can just tell me straight away if you don't have a good time. I won't mind,' I lied, for I really was quite lust-filled. After all, it was at least twenty years since the last time I had coitus.

'But Mr Godbole, it might not be a good idea after er... what we just did together,' Madhuri said uneasily.

'Oh, come on! Who's to know, except for the turtles?'

'Sundar for one...'

'Why should he have a problem? Did you two have an affair or something?' I asked.

'No...no, nothing like that.'

'Then what?'

She hesitated some more. 'Actually, Mr Godbole, I'm not very comfortable. Let's just have dinner.'

'Don't be silly! I'm too old to just have dinner with a pretty woman and go home alone.'

'But you are assuming...'

'I am assuming nothing, but I have more than dinner on my mind,' I said. 'No point just going out for dinner, if you have already made up your mind that dinner's as far as you are prepared to go.'

She went quiet again.

'Well?' I asked after a minute.

'I...I don't know, Mr Godbole.'

'What don't you know, Madhuri?' I asked. 'I have already made my dishonourable intentions clear. Most men don't. So what's the harm? Surely you are not a virgin still, so all you need to decide is whether you are open to the idea of sleeping with me. You might at least learn how well Viagra works.'

'Mr Godbole, aren't you being too direct? You are embarrassing me. Who talks like that?'

'Ah well! Beating around the bush is a waste of time at both my age and yours,' I said. 'I wish I'd had that epiphany long, long ago. So, what's it going to be, lovely, sexy Madhuri? What do you feel instinctively?'

She hesitated, then said in a nervous voice, 'Actually, Mr Godbole, I'm…I'm a little scared of you.'

'Really?' I exclaimed, thrilled to the core, flattered beyond measure. 'That's new to me, I'm afraid, but you needn't be scared at all, Madhuri. Much as I'd like to take you to bed, I know it takes two to tango and sizzle. I know it's my charm and not fear that might work. I also know you are quite capable of taking care of yourself, Madhuri.'

'Okay,' she said.

'Okay what?'

'Okay, Mr Godbole, I'll go for dinner with you…'

'And bed?'

'Maybe, although I don't promise.'

'Well, if you do, I promise you super, sublime sex,' I quipped, such was my confidence.

Why? you may ask. Well that's because it wasn't true that my last coitus was twenty years ago. I had had two fantastic rounds on Viagra just days ago, with guess who? Not Sushilabai, for heaven's sake!

Remember the girl, the night I had returned from hospital – my neighbour Mobin's girlfriend, when I had them turn down the music – yes, that one!

How? Well, that's a story for another day!

~

'How long since your wife died?' Madhuri asked. It was the morning after the dinner, and of course, we'd become lovers and Madhuri had stayed over. We had torrid sex twice the previous night, and I was good to go for a third time with the Viagra going strong, but Madhuri was too spent and content. Instead, we just finished doing it this morning. And with the effect of Viagra having worn off, now I was spent, and the tank was super empty.

'Oh, a few months ago, during COVID,' I replied, not happy to be reminded of Sumitra, after the exciting rides I'd just had.

'I bet you had a fantastic sex life,' Madhuri said.

'What fantastic?' I smirked. 'We didn't have one.'

'Why not?' Madhuri asked, turning to me and snuggling closer.

'Well, I wasn't the man I am today...and Sumitra was never much of a woman,' I replied to the splendid, ravishing woman lying naked next to me.

'What do you mean?'

'Let's say I didn't know how to live till COVID almost killed me. I survived and now I am a totally cool, different me.'

'And what was wrong with your wife?'

'Everything...Let's just say we were thoroughly mismatched, bonded together only by mutual dislike, which is the secret behind most long-lasting Indian marriages,' I replied.

Madhuri giggled, then looked serious. 'I know, ditto my parents. So sad.'

'Too bad! They around still?'

'No, both Aai-Baba are dead.'

'Good that they produced you anyway,' I replied, my hands fondling her at the right places. 'My sweet Madhuri, and so how have you enjoyed being with me so far? Satisfactory? Good? Excellent?'

She blushed and gave me a rap on my shoulders. 'It's been nice.'

'What does nice mean?' I asked. 'Am I charming or not?'

She nodded. 'Yes.'

'Witty? Made you laugh?'

She nodded again. 'A lot...'

'Interesting?'

'Very…'

'Macho?'

She giggled.

'Gave you mighty orgasms? Courtesy Viagra but nevertheless…'

She blushed again but nodded.

'Then? There's no option called "nice". Satisfactory, Good or Excellent?'

'Excellent,' she replied and began laughing.

I kissed her on the mouth and asked, 'So, do we have a deal?'

'What deal?'

'We sex-mates from now on?'

'Is that how you'd like to describe us?'

'How else? What would you prefer? Lovers? Girlfriend–boyfriend? Couple?' I asked amorously. 'We can call ourselves anything, as long as we don't forget the crux of it…'

'Hmm…Let's not make it a deal yet…'

'Okay. But we do continue meeting and mating, right?'

'You are such a crude man!'

'Just frank…Honest,' I replied. 'Anyway, what will you call me?'

'I don't know. Old boy, perhaps?' she teased.

'No way! Call me Viru…'

'Viru? Why Viru?'

'Short for virile…' I replied proudly. 'Suits me just perfect, right?'

Madhuri threw back her head and broke into a really hearty laugh, the sound of which was indescribably pleasant and infectious. Why hadn't this woman been born earlier and become my wife? I wouldn't have minded even if her name was Sumitra.

'Okay, Viru…' she said.

I was about to commence foreplay again when suddenly the doorbell pealed. Madhuri gave a little start. 'Who's that?'

I grunted with annoyance. 'It must be my cook-cum-maid, Sushilabai. She's perpetually late but today she had to come on time!'

Madhuri began scrambling out of bed.

'Hey, no need for that. I am just going to ignore her. Sushilabai will ring the bell a few times and leave,' I said. 'Come back to bed…'

She was looking so voluptuous, standing up, fully naked, that no one at the door – not even the world's most famous person – could have got me to open it.

The bell pealed again, accompanied by a thump, and I could hear Sushilabai's faint voice calling out for me.

'But isn't she here to cook your meals?' Madhuri said. 'I better get dressed.'

'No, no, the less meals I consume made by her, the longer I'll live, Madhuri. Wait.'

But Madhuri was looking at her watch and the bell rang again. 'I need to go in any case, Viru…I'm already late.'

I loved the way she slipped in the 'Viru'.

'Oh, come on, it's not that late. Let's at least have a quickie. Look, the doorbell's also stopped ringing. Sushilabai's gone away.'

'A quickie?' she exclaimed, strapping on her bra. 'You really are too much. Hasn't it already been one too many since last night?'

'No, no, I still have one quickie left in me, Madhuri, come on…' I implored her.

But she had pulled on her panties too. 'No, I really must get going. Come, I'll quickly make tea for both of us.'

'I've had tea all my life, Madhuri. It stopped exciting me a long time ago. Sex and revenge are the only two elixirs of my life now.'

She gave that ripple of a laugh again and continued getting dressed. 'Come, it's time to put your clothes on, Viru. If tea doesn't excite you, should I make coffee?'

'Not unless you can brew coffee from tea leaves,' I quipped, 'because there's no coffee powder at home.'

She laughed again, and I was pleased at how good I had become at these repartees. Where had this wit been all my life? Nor could I remember such pleasant female laughter ringing around the house ever. Not that I could joke with Sumitra or that she would have got them, let alone laugh like this. But then, like the chicken or the egg, who knows what comes first – the wit or the laughter!

21

THERAPY

Ten minutes later, I was sipping the tea Madhuri had made. 'Are you sure this is how tea tastes?' I asked.

'Of course. What do you mean? Not to your taste? Too strong? Too much ginger?' Madhuri queried.

'No, it's pretty good. I am just wondering what then was I swilling all my life?' I replied with a wink. 'Do you want a quickie with it?'

'Oh, come on, Viru, stop it…' she said with a coy smile.

'Sorry, that was a slip of tongue. I meant "cookie". Not "quickie". Do you want a cookie with it? Biscuits?'

She grinned. 'Naughty man you are. Yes, I wouldn't mind a cookie…'

'Quickie?'

'Cookie…'

'Okay,' I said, getting up and reaching out to grab a container. 'Here you go – biscuits and cookies…'

'Ah, you like Monaco too – I just love them…' Madhuri said and bit into one.

'Well, I actually like Krackjack the most – salty and sweet,' I said.

That's when I suddenly heard the front door open and Ravi's urgent voice calling out 'Kaka', followed by Sushilabai's plaintive cry of 'Saheb' alongside footsteps rushing in.

Madhuri's face had lit up with alarm, and I grunted, realizing what must've happened. 'I'm here in the kitchen, Ravi,' I hollered, and a moment later, the astonished and awkward faces of Ravi and Sushilabai were staring at Madhuri and me. There was a pregnant pause all around.

'Thank…thank God, you are okay,' Ravi finally spoke. 'Sushilabai called me in a panic, said that you were not opening the door…That's why I rushed over.'

'As you can see, I'm perfectly fine, Ravi. Why did you needlessly bother him, Sushilabai? Why didn't you call me on my phone first?' I said with irritation.

Sushilabai's eyes, which were entirely riveted on Madhuri, turned to me finally. 'I thought since you were not opening the door, something had happened to you, saheb. Weren't you home? I mean were you out elsewhere? Taking a walk or something? Because I asked the watchman and he said he had not seen you this morning.'

Madhuri was looking at me guardedly, a little embarrassed by the whole situation obviously, with both Ravi and Sushilabai training their gazes on her.

I was itching to say something that would scandalize Sushilabai, but then Ravi was there too so I kept it mild. 'Your concern for me is really touching, Sushilabai, but you can't assume I'm dead every time I don't open the door. Neither should you get alarmed, Ravi,' I said. 'Anyway, this is Madhuri Awati…'

They waited for me to elaborate but when I didn't, Sushilabai nodded at her, curiosity unsatiated, while Ravi said, 'Hello…'

He shuffled awkwardly then very politely asked, 'And what do you do, Ms Awati?'

'She's my therapist…' I replied quickly before Madhuri could.

Madhuri's eyes darted at me, and she smiled.

'Therapist? What kind of therapy, Kaka?'

'General well-being, very holistic,' I replied. 'Madhuri is very good.'

'I see,' Ravi said, though he clearly did not and had more questions.

Sushilabai was still goggling at Madhuri.

'Get on with your duties, Sushilabai. What are you cooking for me today?' I said and Sushilabai's face soured. 'Let me see, saheb.'

Meanwhile, Madhuri had scrambled to her feet. 'I also need to get going. Er…Mr Godbole, I need to collect my things.' She bit her lips as she said that, realizing that all her things were still in the bedroom and collecting them would be a dead giveaway.

'Can you also collect that book you had so kindly lent me? I have finished it. It's in my room, if you don't mind, lying on the table next to my bed,' I butted in, coming to her rescue. 'Just so that I don't have to get up.'

She smiled at me gratefully. 'Oh sure, Mr Godbole. Did you enjoy it?'

'Oh, it was so enjoyable – one of the few books one can read again and again,' I replied, sounding lascivious even to my own ears.

I could see Madhuri trying to suppress a nervous giggle, as she quickly said 'goodbye' and slipped past Ravi into the bedroom down the passage.

Ravi's puzzled eyes followed her, then involuntarily exchanged a brief glance with Sushilabai who, although standing at the kitchen platform, had still not started any preparations for cooking.

'Sweet girl,' I said to Ravi. 'Come, sit, do you want some tea?'

'No, no…Kaka, I must get going too,' Ravi replied.

'No, hang on. I need to speak to you for a moment…'

'What?'

I gazed sternly at Sushilabai and back at Ravi, then whispered, 'After the lady leaves…'

A minute followed then another and I enjoyed the discomfort of both Ravi and Sushilabai. Finally, we heard Madhuri shuffle out, open the main door and shut it after her.

'Okay,' I said to both. 'Sushilabai, you have to stop making a nuisance of yourself, and Ravi, you have to stop Trupti or Sushilabai or anyone else turning you into a damned rescue squad.'

'But, saheb.'

'What "but, saheb"! So what if I didn't answer the bell? I could've been doing anything – bathing, potty-ing, sleeping, meditating, listening to rock music.'

Ravi scowled. 'You are right, Kaka. I guess I overreacted. I feel very responsible for you.'

My nephew was really a good soul. 'I know, Ravi. I know… But you don't have to worry so much or scramble.'

'But where were you, saheb?' Sushilabai blurted out, still dogged in wanting to get to the bottom of the mystery.

'Here. Where else? Engaged in intercourse with Madhuri,' I said, unable to resist the urge to shock my audience.

'What?' Ravi exclaimed as if he'd been shot.

Sushilabai seemed to have lost her power of speech and had almost jumped up on the kitchen platform. I found a strange satisfaction in their reactions.

'Spiritual intercourse. Discourse. Therapy,' I said with a straight face.

'Therapy?' Ravi echoed.

'Therapy!'

'And you both didn't hear the two–three bells Sushilabai rang?'

'We were deep into the…er…therapy.'

'Oh!' Ravi said doubtfully, wondering how to delicately enquire further. 'Exactly what does she make you do, Kaka? Meditation of some kind?'

I smiled. 'Fornication!' I wanted to say and could think of many factual, ribald answers, but was searching for the right euphemism.

'Conversation, role-play, vitality exercises – it's tailored for widowers to overcome spousal loss,' I said solemnly.

Ravi's expression immediately cleared of all doubt. 'That actually seems like a very good idea, Kaka. Hope it's helping you.'

'Oh definitely. She's very good. I'm going to do many more sessions with her,' I responded.

Ravi nodded. 'Okay, Kaka, that's great. I'm going now… Take care!' he said, bade me goodbye and left.

My nephew had appeared convinced. But Sushilabai still didn't seem to be having any of it. She was looking at me like she'd seen through me and knew exactly what was going on.

'You are going to have these sessions everyday, saheb, at this time only?' she asked me suspiciously.

'Why are you asking?'

'I mean, you might as well then keep the door open for me, if you are going to be deep in therapy.'

'Why don't you start coming an hour later?' I shot back. 'Anyway you are always late…except for today…'

Sushilabai bristled. 'Not always. Sumitra Madam never asked me to change my timings ever…' she said, drawing herself up.

'Well then, wait outside till the session gets over and I open the door.'

Sushilabai wasn't amused one bit. She made a face. 'I can't wait. If it starts happening frequently, then I'll have to tell Trupti tai when she calls me next that I might not be able to continue…'

So that was her gambit. Subtle blackmail.

'Is this how you treat an old man who's just lost his wife?' I said and gave her a pained look. 'You can't adjust even a little?'

Sushilabai gave me a vexed glance. 'But I have other work in the neighbourhood too, no, saheb…' she replied slyly. 'Why can't that lady therapist come at a different time?'

'I'm like a patient, she's like a doctor. How can a patient dictate a doctor?' I asked, looking aggrieved.

Sushilabai was silent for a while as she kneaded the dough. 'I haven't even received a wage raise for a long time. After Sumitra Madam's demise, I'm doing so much more around the house, saheb.'

The liar! 'I can consider that, if you are willing to adjust your timings as and when needed…' I replied.

Her eyes brightened. 'How much?'

We haggled a bit and agreed on a figure. Having successfully concluded negotiations, I began to leave the room when Sushilabai spoke again, in an incredulously innocent tone. 'Who made the tea, saheb? The lady?'

What a nosy, wily woman she was, and I almost chuckled.

'I did.'

Sushilabai did not believe me at all. She fluttered her eyes. 'Never seen you make tea before.'

'One of my many hidden talents, Sushilabai.'

'She must be Trupti tai's age, right? Is she Trupti tai's friend?' Sushilabai was unwilling to let go. She probably had instinctively figured out everything. Or was the busybody reminding me that Madhuri was my daughter's age?

I sensed an opportunity for mischief. 'No, Trupti's father-in-law, Swanand Saheb's father recommended her,' I said with a straight face.

'But isn't he a widower?' she asked, puzzled.

'Yes, but his wife's not keeping too well. Maybe he is preparing for life after,' I quipped and made my exit from the kitchen.

~

The next few weeks were perhaps the best of my life hitherto. I was in my element; Madhuri and I met and mated regularly; Nandu's travails and troubles continued; and Sundar had been neutralized for good.

I ate well and slept well and felt healthier and chirpier than ever before. I did as I pleased and developed an inner swagger and aplomb that convinced me I would live to be a hundred, without aging a day more. All the more reason to make it my mission to hunt down my tormentors.

So far, I had fixed Sundar and Nandu. I still wasn't done with them but then revenge was not just a dish best served cold, but also to be partaken bite by bite, to really savour it – a hundred bites. Nandu and Sundar would have more coming their way, but a little later.

Therefore, all my thoughts had already started turning to my other tormentors, on whom I hadn't started as yet. Who was I to go after next?

I didn't need to mull over it too much. It would either have to be my loathsome ex-boss of many long years, Kamal Kishore Puri; or the woman responsible for the biggest humiliation of my life – Geeta Hirway née Divte. A toss-up was the best way forward. Heads – Kamal Kishore. Tails – Geeta Hirway.

I flipped the coin one morning – Tails. Geeta it was going to be!

GEETA HIRWAY NÉE DIVTE

22

BRISK BETROTHAL

1980. Six months earlier, my parents had started looking for a bride for me in earnest.

There was nothing special about Geeta Divte. She was as plain and pimpled as they come. She wasn't very fair or striking in any way, nor particularly bosomy. Neither was she chatty or charming or blessed with a good voice. Even the mandatory poha, tea and ambawadi that was credited to her, prepared for us when my parents took me to 'see' Geeta as a prospective bride, wasn't lip-smacking in taste. She wasn't a vision at all as she stood before me, playing coy.

The only thing that could be said about her was that she didn't have buckteeth or a squint. And that was probably all one could expect of a possible bride for someone who fell into my category as a prospective bridegroom. I mean, I was just a graduate, with a job as a clerk, drawing a monthly salary of 350 rupees, which wasn't really much of a catch even as far back as 1980. Of course, I too didn't have buckteeth or a squint, nor was I going bald. So, Geeta and I were sort of evenly matched.

I had seen three other girls earlier in this match-making spree and even though some had made better poha and tea, my parents had rejected the first two, as a matter of form or superstition. On my part, I could have agreed to anyone, given I was almost twenty-eight and had no chance of getting hitched to a Cleopatra.

But even I baulked at the third candidate and put my foot down, refusing to even eat the poha. No doubt all those three must've got married to some weary man or the other, sent specially into the world for them. For even men and women with buckteeth, squints and sundry other shortcomings do finally get married to someone. Don't they? And live unhappily ever after, just like all the others.

Well, anyway, Geeta Divte was therefore girl number four. I can't say I liked her or anything about her. But I didn't mind her. I was already bored of the rigmarole, because all the proposals coming my way were plain Janes, with nothing much to distinguish in their looks, personalities, backgrounds, education, or skills.

So when a day later my parents told me they were in favour of clinching the deal – especially with horoscopes matching and Geeta's parents offering a rather bigger dowry than others, I just gave my assent. I mean, Geeta wasn't exactly a dream girl, but she was a girl nevertheless and would do, I guessed; since marriages were rumoured to be made in heaven, as per received wisdom.

Things moved fast, and soon Geeta and I were to be formally engaged, which was the first time we met again, by the way. There wasn't much scope for any real interaction or even getting a better look at this girl that I had agreed to marry. But that's the way it was in those days for conservative, lower middle-class denizens and perhaps is even now. Still, I had to make some attempt to break the ice, didn't I, as the man?

'Psst…' I said when we were briefly posited next to each other in the chaos of the ceremony. 'You…you are looking good.' Geeta didn't look or respond. 'Psst…' I said again. No response and I wondered if not having buckteeth or a squint, didn't still leave open the possibility of Geeta being deaf or hard of hearing. A panic seized me, but how was one to ascertain? Of course, I was being foolish, I realized, since Geeta had replied to a few questions thrown at her by my parents and me, in the first meeting.

I was going to make another valiant attempt at conversation with a louder 'Psst…' when she stole an appraising glance at me and whispered, 'You don't have any defects, right?'

It was as if someone had rudely poked me in the ribs. It was rather indelicate coming from a woman, or so I thought. I mean what was I? A product to have defects?

I was speechless and just gave her a startled gape and looked away.

'Yes or no?' I heard her whisper again.

'No…' I whispered back.

'Sure?'

'Yes.'

No further whisperings ensued for some time as we got drawn into ceremonial inanities again. Then ten minutes later, I heard Geeta hiss again. 'Why didn't you ask for a meeting with me before the engagement?'

Again, I was at a loss for words. 'Why didn't you?' I finally replied.

'It's a man's job,' she retorted. I couldn't think of a comeback, so I stayed quiet.

'Ask for one now…in a day or two…' she whispered again.

'Okay,' I replied.

Our unofficial tête-à-tête for the day was over. My first conversation with Geeta Divte was far from what I had expected, and it left me unsettled. The only other connection we had that day was when I slipped the engagement ring on her finger and she gave me a rather doubtful look, as if she were thinking of asking me whether it had any defects.

Well, it all weighed on my mind and the very next day I asked my parents, that now that the engagement ceremony was done, could I ask Geeta out? My parents, who had never ever looked not grave, gave me another grim look.

'Out? Where?' my father asked, as if he knew no places where a fiancé could meet his fiancée without causing scandal.

'A café, cinema or even a park,' I replied.

'Alone?'

'Yes, just the two of us.'

'It might be inappropriate,' my father remarked, continuing to look grave.

'Nothing inappropriate. We are engaged to be married.'

My father sighed grimly and looked at my mother, who too sighed grimly. 'It might appear like showing unseemly haste.'

'Why? Geeta and I haven't even been properly introduced yet.'

My father gave me a bewildered look. 'Well, you know her name, how she looks, cooks, talks and walks.' My mother nodded in agreement.

'But that can't be all,' I said. 'In today's times...'

My father sighed again. 'Okay. I'll send a message to her father.'

~

'No, I neither like coffee nor dosa,' Geeta Divte said.

'Then why didn't you order something else?' I asked, taken aback.

The meeting had materialized. Geeta's parents had immediately acceded to me asking her out, even beamed happily as we left. Her father gently told me to deposit her back by 7.30 p.m.

I had brought her to the famed Vaishali Restaurant on Fergusson College Road, which was the go-to place for everyone in Pune.

'Like what?'

I felt rattled. 'There are so many other items on the menu. How about batata vada or sabudana vada and some juice instead?'

She made a face. 'Nah! It's okay, I thought you might take me to Café Goodluck or something.'

My heart did a double take. Café Goodluck? The den of non-vegetarian food, run by Irani owners, less than 300 metres away! How could a good, lower middle-class Brahmin girl suggest something so outrageous?

'What?' I stuttered. 'Café Goodluck?'

'Can we cancel the order here and go there instead?' Geeta asked wistfully.

'But…but…it serves only non-vegetarian dishes…' I stuttered.

'Yes, mostly, I know…' Geeta said and there was something in her eyes, which made me fear the worst.

'You've been to Goodluck? You…you…you've tasted non-vegetarian?' I asked, hardly able to keep the horror from my tone.

Geeta giggled, her pimpled face sly. 'Haven't you?'

My head was spinning. 'No…I…I haven't…'

'Then, come no, let's go there. You can have bun-maska. That's not non-veg…' Geeta chirruped. 'And I'll have an egg-pudding.'

I think I got indigestion and a couple of ulcers by just hearing those words. 'No, no. I can't take you to Goodluck and let you have egg-pudding. What…what will your parents say?'

'Why would they know unless you tell them?'

I was flabbergasted. 'But someone might see us, or tell your parents or even mine…It'll scandalize them, perhaps kill one of them.'

Geeta frowned, pouted, then frowned again. 'Nobody has ever spotted me and my friend before, even while we were having chicken.'

I thought the earth was going to open up and swallow me. Was I engaged to be married to a full-fledged carnivore and bring home to my parents a meat-eating daughter-in-law?

'Chicken?'

'Yes, it's so delicious.'

'With a friend? What friend?'

'College friend.'

'You mean a boy-friend or a girl-friend?' I asked, now wary of another bombshell coming my way.

'No, no. Noorie Joseph, we went to college together.'

'Noorie Joseph? She's a Christian?'

'Half Christian and half Muslim,' Geeta said. 'She's the one who introduced me to Café Goodluck.'

Our coffee and dosas arrived. I made a stern face. 'My family is pure vegetarian, so is yours, Geeta. You can't go to Goodluck and have non-vegetarian food after marriage.'

'Says who?' Geeta said, giving me an unpleasant look, while scrunching her dosa.

It's not that I had recovered from all the things that she had hit me with so far, but I had to do something to assert myself. 'I do. We are engaged to be married. I am going to be your husband.'

She stared at me and bit into a morsel of dosa with such ferocity as if she was taking a bite of me. 'Why did you say yes to marrying me?'

I crunched on my dosa too, though I had lost all appetite. It was a good question for which I had no good answer. Why had I said yes, God alone knows. 'I…I liked you obviously,' I replied.

'Liked what?'

I took a sip of coffee to buy time and in the process got my tongue scalded. Geeta offered no sympathy.

'Liked what about me?' she repeated.

'Everything,' I said defensively. 'Why? Didn't you also say yes because you liked me?'

She gave me a ruminative look and said nothing for a long time, then spoke, 'My parents took the decision…'

'Without asking you?' I queried, concerned.

She was again quiet for some time. 'Kind of! Took me for granted.'

My perturbance increased. 'Taken for granted? Means what?'

She blew on her coffee, as if silently showing me how to not scald one's tongue. 'You were the first one to say "yes" after seven or eight boys. That's why. Where was pimply, plain, poor me going to find anyone better?'

I winced at the rather non-flattering comment – or, rather, was it a lament! Even Vaishali's heavenly chutney and sambhar had lost their flavour for me. We were both silent for a while. I could hear her scrunching her dosa, and she could hear me sip my coffee.

'Look, is there a problem?' I finally asked anxiously.

Geeta looked away for a bit at other people on other tables. 'You don't want me to go to Goodluck and eat non-vegetarian food. Is there anything else you or your family don't want your wife to do?'

'Like what?' I asked, my throat dry.

How was I to supply a list of forbidden things, if I didn't know the kind of forbidden things she liked doing? I mean, who in their wildest lower middle-class imagination, in those days, would have thought a girl like Geeta Divte would develop a craving for non-vegetarian food at Café Goodluck? God knows what other social taboos she might or might not have a thing for.

She said nothing and the silence prompted me to speak. 'I mean we are a normal conservative Brahmin family.'

'So, anything non-conservative would be frowned upon,' she exclaimed.

'Well…I mean…Anything your family minds, my family might mind too,' I replied, trying to sound practical and reasonable in this difficult conversation.

Geeta sighed. 'My family has an objection to everything, even breathing through my mouth instead of my nose, as I tend to.'

A wretched silence fell between us again, broken by the waiter asking if we'd like to order anything else. I told him to get the bill.

'Are you asking me about objections because you would want to work after marriage or something?' I asked with trepidation, as the thought suddenly struck me. Many women had started working full-time in the seventies and eighties, preferring not to remain just housewives, creating marital flashpoints, with in-laws and men objecting.

'What?' she asked distractedly. 'No no, I don't want to look for jobs.'

I felt relieved and intrigued at the same time. 'Then? Then what is it?'

'Fun!' she said. 'I want to have fun. My family hates having fun.'

'Mine too!' I blurted out and bit my tongue. It had flown out of my mouth spontaneously.

'Oh my God!' she said, putting her face into her palms for a few moments, then looked up at me again as the waiter brought the bill. I quickly paid and he went away to get change.

'And you?' Geeta asked me. 'Do you also hate fun?'

'Me? No, no,' I replied. It was a question I hadn't even thought of really. What kind of fun was she talking about anyway? 'I try to have fun when I can.'

'What fun do you have?'

I cleared my throat, grateful that the waiter was back with the change. I collected it and decided to leave a small tip – two rupees, may be three...

Geeta was watching me, waiting for an answer. 'Like going to a vegetarian restaurant or a movie...or a play or a picnic to Lonavala sometimes,' I replied, then quickly added, 'things within my means.'

Her expression had changed to dismay. 'That's it?'

'Yes,' I said, rather alarmed and annoyed now. 'What else?'

She didn't reply but looked away again. We sat like that for five minutes – me looking at her now and then, while she looked into the distance. Then I shot a glance at my wristwatch.

'It's past 7 p.m. I need to get you home,' I said apologetically. 'Your father...'

'I know,' she said and picked up her purse, as we both got up from the table.

Outside, we caught an autorickshaw and the only talking during the ten-minute ride was done by the auto-driver. As we alighted in the lane leading to her house, I asked, 'Er...Geeta, did you have some fun at all today?'

'We didn't go to Goodluck, did we?' she replied, and I didn't have any stomach left for further conversation that evening.

23

FREAKY FIANCÉE

For two days, I brooded over the conversation I'd had with my fiancée. And the more I thought about it, the more uneasy it made me. I had no one to really talk to or seek advice from. In lower middle-class, Puneri parlance, the word 'fun' had an ominous ring to it, as it is. And the way Geeta Divte had said it not only seemed to hint at forbidden things, but also filled me with foreboding.

I had to talk to her again for the sake of my peace of mind. Therefore, I called her father directly from a public phone and put in a request that I'd like to take Geeta out again on Sunday for a little longer, maybe even to a movie. Her father dithered a bit and pondered whether twice in a week was inappropriate, but eventually agreed, probably not wishing to offend me – his future son-in-law.

'If not to Goodluck, let's at least go to Poona Coffee House…' Geeta said to me breathlessly, as soon as we had we left her house on Sunday. 'You don't have an objection to that, do you?'

Poona Coffee House was a restaurant in the Deccan Gymkhana area again, with a kind of bohemian reputation – a hangout for hep folk and artists, writers, painters, the English-speaking young crowd and so on. I hadn't really been there either, but it wasn't a strict 'no-no'.

'Sure,' I said. 'We can go there.'

Geeta looked relieved. 'And we are going to a movie too after that…right?'

'Yes, we are, we can catch the 3.30 show…' I replied, as I hailed an auto.

I cleared my throat in the autorickshaw a couple of times but was still deciding whether to first ask her which movie to go to or to broach the topic about what her hobbies were.

'Er…' I began finally.

'Don't you smoke?' Geeta beat me to the opening volley.

I swallowed back my question and served up a reply instead. 'No…I don't smoke.'

'Why not?' she asked, like I wasn't normal.

'It's a bad habit and injurious to health,' I said virtuously.

She seemed disappointed by my reply. 'It's so stylish. Haven't you ever tried a cigarette?'

I shook my head and anticipated with horror what she was going to say next.

'I have,' she said with a superior smile. My heart missed several beats. I just stared, speechless, as she continued. 'Wills Navy Cut.'

'Once?' I asked with a hiccough.

She looked at me and shrugged. 'More than once.'

'Where? How?'

She didn't reply for a few seconds, then said, 'It was fun!'

There was that word again – fun!

We'd reached Poona Coffee House by now and alighted. An excited smile was playing on Geeta's face as we walked into the crowded restaurant and looked around for a place. Music was playing and there was loud chatter and laughter all over. It was a crowd in which I immediately felt like a fish out of water – people with sideburns, flashy clothes and goggles, men with their shirt buttons open, displaying chest hair, bold girls wearing bell bottoms and clingy T-shirts and air thick with smoke.

'See, so many men smoke,' Geeta remarked, as if I suffered from a deficiency that needed to be urgently rectified.

I wanted to walk out of the place, but how could I? Instead, I spotted an empty table for two and pointed at it. 'Let's take that,' I said over the din.

'No, no, we need a table for three,' Geeta replied.

'Three? Why three?'

'I've invited Noorie to join us,' Geeta replied shortly.

I quivered with indignation. 'What? Why?'

'Because she's my friend and I wanted her to meet you,' Geeta replied nonchalantly. 'Let's sit there.'

She moved to a table that was just being vacated by some people. I followed and plonked down grumpily. I wasn't liking this at all.

'Why didn't you ask me before?' I said with heat.

Geeta gave me a cool look. 'I've to take your permission even to introduce you to my best friend?'

'No…no…that's not what I am saying…But…but…but…' I said, spluttering angrily.

'You want to fight with me on just our second outing?' Geeta said accusingly. 'Just because I'm making you meet my best friend who couldn't make it to the engagement?'

Of course she succeeded in immediately putting me on the backfoot. 'No…no, not like that,' I grumbled. 'But would you have liked it if I got a friend to join us without telling you?'

'I bet you don't even have a friend in the first place,' Geeta said sharply. 'Because friends are fun and you don't like fun.'

I felt I had been kicked in the stomach. This was the girl I was set to marry? Who was already firing at me with whatever little ammunition she had gathered?

Before I could think of a rejoinder, someone walked into my field of vision and two voices shrieked with joy.

'Geeta.'

'Noorie.'

A busty girl, dressed in a bust-hugging T-shirt and jeans hugged Geeta and sat next to her, then held out her manicured hand to me.

'Hello, Geeta weds Gajanan. I'm Noorie,' she said with a toothy grin.

I don't think I had ever shaken hands with a girl or a lady before. 'Hello,' I said, feeling even more self-conscious than usual. I took her hand briefly and let go hastily, as if I had been caught doing something naughty.

Noorie Joseph was gazing at me quite uninhibitedly, as if appraising me with her kohl-enhanced eyes. She was quite ordinary looking, wearing Zeenat Aman–type big-framed spectacles that were in vogue, which she removed now. Her long hair was let loose, cascading all the way down, while her bright red lipstick and nail paint were matched with her heeled sandals. She had a hip air to her, which made me most uncomfortable.

She turned to Geeta, and said in what seemed to my sensitive ears a sarcastic tone, 'So, congratulations, Geeta.'

In response, Geeta slapped her arm. 'I'm so glad you came,' she giggled.

Noorie turned to me again. 'So you are going to be Geeta Gajanan Godbole,' she said, the ironical tone deepening. 'When's the wedding date?'

Geeta pinched her arm this time. 'Ouch,' Noorie shouted.

'Why are you in such a hurry?' Geeta squealed.

'That hurt, yaar,' Noorie retorted, rubbing the pinched spot on her arm. She turned to me again, as if waiting for the answer to her question.

'Around two months from now,' I replied. 'The…the elders will soon decide a date.'

'I see…So exciting…' Noorie said and winked at Geeta.

'Shall we order something?' I asked.

But they were not paying attention to me because Geeta was busy whispering into Noorie's ear. 'Really?' Noorie said and gave me another shrewd, amused glance. 'You've never tasted non-vegetarian food or smoked a cigarette so far, Gajanan?'

I felt myself turn red in the face. What girl mocked her fiancé like that? 'No,' I said hoarsely.

Both the girls burst into giggles and I found myself turning hotter under the collar. I wanted to just stand up and stomp away that very moment.

'So, I guess beer or whiskey would also be out of the question,' Noorie said, between their guffaws.

I stiffened. There was no reason for me to allow them to ridicule me like that. 'What…what's so funny about that?' I finally croaked, trying to contain my anger.

'No, no…I'm just teasing you, Gajanan,' Noorie said, trying to stifle her laughter. 'But as they say, bad habits maketh a man!'

'What? Who says? I…I…I don't understand,' I replied. 'Let's order.' I gave Geeta an angry look, but she didn't seem to care. Noorie, meanwhile, had opened the menu card and peered through it, humming and hawing. It took us five minutes to order. Just as I was beginning to think I had managed to convey my displeasure to Geeta and her friend to stop needling me, Noorie spoke again.

'So, Gajanan, did you have a girlfriend before?' There was a mischievous glint in her eyes.

'What? No!' I said.

'No?' Noorie exchanged a glance with Geeta. 'That means you have never done it before?'

'Done what?' I asked. She was really getting under my skin.

'You know, hanky-panky with a girl?' Noorie said, biting her lip and smiling suggestively.

This was too much. 'Of course not,' I snapped. 'How... how...how can you talk like that?'

I was shaking now. What was wrong with these two? How could any fiancée allow her friend to talk dirty with her fiancé like that? But all my outrage was lost on Geeta and Noorie, who had dissolved into laughter.

'No, no...Gajanan, please don't mind our girlish silliness! In fact, Geeta, I must congratulate you for finding yourself such a virtuous man, with no vices whatsoever,' Noorie remarked, trying to sound sincere, even though mirth still danced in her eyes. Geeta too had stopped laughing, though her expressions were indecipherable. She first looked at Noorie, then me and back towards her friend again.

Our food arrived. 'Let's hurry, Geeta. I still have to stand in the queue for the tickets. Today's Sunday,' I said shortly.

'Noorie's coming with us too,' Geeta replied.

'What?' I said, now completely infuriated. 'You...you can't just decide on your own.'

Geeta wasn't bothered in the least. 'Why can't Noorie come with us?'

My exasperation was beyond my control now. 'Look, you can go with your friend. I'll go home,' I replied tersely.

'Okay,' Geeta retorted. 'Anyway she's much more fun than you are.'

I was aghast at how easily she was ready to put me down.

'No...no...Geeta,' Noorie spoke before I could get up and leave the table. 'Gajanan is right. He's your fiancé, and he wants to spend time with you alone, naturally. I think you both should go to the movie. Anyway, I was not planning to accompany you and become a kebab-mein-haddi.'

'But why?' Geeta asked her.

'No...no, it's your evening together. Count me out. Listen to me,' Noorie said quickly. Geeta slapped her arm again and frowned at me darkly. We ate our dishes in silence.

'Which movie are you taking her to, Gajanan?' Noorie asked, probably to relieve the awkwardness that had descended.

'*Do Premi*,' I said, 'Rishi Kapoor and Moushumi...It's running at Rahul.'

'I don't want to watch that movie,' Geeta said promptly. 'Let's go to an English film.'

'What?' I asked.

'Let's go to that James Bond movie at Alka Talkies...' Geeta said.

'James Bond?' I said, my heart sinking again. 'But what will your parents say? It's...it's an "A" movie, Geeta.'

'I am an adult. Aren't you?'

'Of course I am,' I replied. 'But...but...your father might not like it if I took you to a movie with "adult" scenes.'

'You don't have to tell them the truth, do you, Gajanan!' It was Noorie who had spoken. 'Just tell them you watched *Do Premi*. Although if you ask me, that title might shock them more.'

I hadn't quite thought of it like that.

'Are we going to watch James Bond or not?' Geeta asked me peremptorily.

'Okay,' I said.

'Great!' Noorie exclaimed and winked at me this time. 'Have you at least watched a James Bond movie before, Gajanan?'

'Of course...I have...' I lied quickly.

24

THE BOND FIASCO

I had looked around nervously a goodish deal when we entered the theatre, terrified that I might bump into someone I knew. Exactly why I was so apprehensive I'm not sure, for anyone familiar I would run into would be equally guilty of the same depravity of watching a 'Bond' film, which I was indulging in.

What was also galling was that apart from a handful of couples and a small group of college boys and girls, the audience was packed with men. From what I'd heard, the real attraction of English films, particularly Bond movies for the 1970s and 80s urban Indian man, lay in the promise of getting an eyeful of cleavage, the odd 'bedroom' scene, passionate kisses and shower sequences. If only you'd been born in my era, would you understand the extent of my acute embarrassment and anxiety. Geeta, on the other hand, appeared unabashedly excited and unbothered.

'I like Roger Moore. He's so handsome,' Geeta said, as we waited for the lights to dim and the movie to begin.

I was about to ask who she was talking about, then realized it must be the actor playing James Bond. 'Yes,' I replied. 'He's okay.'

She fixed me with a scornful look, as if I were an ugly frog compared to the prince, Roger Moore. Mercifully, the trailers began and for Geeta, I think I soon ceased to exist. Ten minutes later the film began. While my self-consciousness did slip away, it re-asserted itself every time James Bond got cosy with some stunning lady, all too ready to slip out of her clothes.

What made it worse were Geeta's uninhibited gasps as she leaned forward in her seat. Every now and then she would half turn to me during such scenes and ask, 'What did he say?' Her eyes would, of course, swivel back to the screen instantly, and I didn't really need to reply.

The lights finally came on for the interval and she glanced at me doubtfully, as if she'd found another flaw in me. 'Don't you understand English dialogues?'

'I do, but sometimes it's difficult. They speak so fast,' I replied defensively.

She appeared to disbelieve me. 'Aren't you getting any snacks for us?'

'Oh, of course, sorry! What would you like? Popcorn, wafers?'

'Samosas and a Gold Spot,' she replied, as if I were a waiter. I promptly got up and rushed out, for I knew samosas generally got over quickly. Fortunately for me, I got the last samosa. But Gold Spot wasn't available, so I grabbed a bottle of Limca.

By the time I got back, the film had started again. I stepped on legs, tripped, shuffled and finally reached our seats.

'Here,' I said, handing her the samosa on a paper plate. 'Sorry, there was no Gold Spot, so I got Limca.'

'I don't like Limca,' she said, eyes rivetted on Roger Moore, who had just removed his shirt. The scene changed and she turned to me in a vexed voice, 'There's no chutney with the samosa. How am I supposed to eat it?'

'Sorry, they didn't have any.'

'Hrmph,' she muttered, as if it was all my fault, then began eating it. 'This samosa is stale.'

It pissed me off. For a moment I felt like yelling at her to go tell Roger Moore to fetch her a samosa. But, of course, I said nothing to this gripe-mouth of a girl beside me. I heard her munch the samosa and slurp the Limca, without so much as offering a bite or a sip to me.

By now, Bond was into action sequences and during one of these Geeta spoke. 'You haven't even tried to hold my hand.'

It was probably loud enough for the person next to me to hear, for the man darted a quick look in my direction.

'Shhh,' I whispered apologetically to Geeta. 'I was not sure…'

'Of what?'

'That you would've liked me to do so in public,' I replied, my middle-class prudishness active and alive.

'Why come to a dark theatre if you don't have the nerve to even hold hands?' Geeta said, still at the same volume.

'Shhh…' I shushed again and groped to clasp her hand, found it and held it.

We sat like that for five minutes, then she complained again. 'You are not doing anything.'

Again, the man next to me looked at me.

'Shhh…Means what?'

She clicked her tongue and said, 'What kind of a man are you?' She pulled her hand away from mine.

Bond, meanwhile, had again started seducing another Bond girl, mouthing some corny dialogue, which of course I didn't follow. His hand was sliding up the girl's thigh and a passionate kiss had commenced. Indian censors, of course, knew how to nip it all in the bud, and the scene changed abruptly with Bond again slipping back into action mode.

'Kiss me,' I heard Geeta say.

I froze. 'What?' I asked after my vocal cords unentangled.

'Kiss me, like James Bond does...' she said, moving closer, her face turned towards me.

'What? Here? Are you crazy?' I said, panicked.

'Oh, come on, everybody does it.'

'No...no...I haven't seen anyone.'

'No one's watching. Quick.'

My vocal cords got locked up again as I stared at this girl. Where did she think we were? In America? In the free love premises of the Rajneesh Ashram in Pune? We were in Alka Talkies, two minutes away from the peths of Pune. And who did she think I was? Roger Moore? No! I was Gajanan Godbole, totally unequipped, in fact positively handicapped by my cloistered upbringing to even think of kissing a girl, even my fiancée, that too in a theatre.

'I can't do that,' I said as Geeta looked sternly at me to do her bidding.

'Hurrmph...What a sissy!' she scoffed and turned away. The man next to me was by now way more interested in what was unfolding between us than on screen. A minute later, he also looked away, probably disappointed.

I sat petrified through the rest of the film, my heart thudding and shame suffusing me with every breath I took. The auto-ride back to Geeta's home was made in complete silence – Geeta throwing me a dirty look every now and then, as if I had outraged her modesty. I was feeling too beleaguered and dazed to attempt any rapprochement or even utter another word. This time, the auto-guy wasn't talkative either, so it was as sombre a fifteen minutes as I had ever experienced in my life.

'Are you sure you don't have a problem of some kind?' Geeta remarked scathingly, as we drew near her house.

'What? What problem?'

She turned away and said nothing. I asked the auto to halt as we reached.

'I should've gone with Noorie only. You are no fun…' she snapped, before alighting and skipping away swiftly, without even a backward glance.

25

BELOW THE BELT

A storm raged through my mind for the next few days. What kind of a hole had I dug for myself by getting engaged to Geeta Divte? How was I going to climb out of it? If whatever little I had seen of her was any indication to go by, how was I ever going to be able to marry and live with Geeta? It was unimaginable and I was gripped by terrible misgivings. What was I to do? Whom was I to tell? How was this to be resolved?

As these thoughts rocked my mind, the final blow with all its humiliations arrived at my doorstep, mid-week, in the form of the matchmaker who'd got the marriage proposal in the first place.

'Ahem,' he said, clearing his throat, as if imitating the sound of a car that wouldn't start. He began sipping the tea my mother had made for him. 'There has been…er…a complication.'

'What complication?' my father asked with concern.

The matchmaker glanced at me and in a flash, I had a foreboding. 'It's delicate, mind you. I am just the messenger.'

My mother was alarmed. 'What's the matter?'

I knew. I just knew even before he spoke. 'The…The girl's side…er…is regretful that it has to call off the wedding.'

'What?' My parents spoke in one breath, as they'd never done before. They stared at the matchmaker, bewildered, then looked at me.

'Why? How dare they?' my mother said indignantly. 'How can they do that?' my father piped in.

The matchmaker again glanced at me. 'I was shocked too. I gave them a proper piece of my mind, but they said they had a genuine reason…'

'What genuine reason do they have that's suddenly come up after the engagement?' my father demanded. 'We hadn't approached them, they sent the proposal through you, offered higher dowry, chased us and now this! Who do they think they are?' He glanced at the matchmaker angrily. 'How could you allow this to happen? I will file a police complaint against them…'

I had never seen my father so riled up.

'I totally understand your anger, Godbole Saheb, but believe me there was nothing I could do. They…they were also very apologetic.'

'But what has happened? They are the ones who wanted the engagement done quickly. They rushed through it and then they commit this outrage! What "genuine reason"?' my mother lambasted him.

The matchmaker glanced at me again. I was speechless, dumbstruck, only apprehensive about what that girl, Geeta, had said or alleged.

'Godbole Saheb, I hate to say this but the girl said something is wrong with your son,' he finally replied.

'Wrong with my son? What utter nonsense are they blabbering? Who does the girl think she is? I demand to know what canards she's spreading,' my father said, quite incensed now.

The matchmaker hesitated. 'You should ask your son,' he said.

I was jolted out of my stupor as all eyes turned to me. 'Ask me what? I know nothing. That…that girl behaved so… oddly…both times we met that…I…I don't know what to do or say.'

The matchmaker frowned, then shrugged. 'The girl says you told her that you don't like women…and that you…you… well…are not interested in conjugal relations because… well…you have performance problems.'

'What?' I shouted.

And that, you see – these rumours of my impotency and disinterest in women – knocked me out of the marriage market for over two more years, courtesy Geeta Divte, who eventually became Geeta Hirway.

Only I know how I lived with the humiliation of this word of mouth, perpetrated by Geeta. It delayed my marriage by three years, and I ended up with Sumitra. The story of my life!

26

TRAIN ENCOUNTER

Geeta Hirway now lived in Thane, which was allergic to being called a suburb of Mumbai, or even a satellite town. It was another matter that except for true-blue Maharashtrians, everyone else considered Thane so, unable to distinguish it from the swathe of other suburbs of India's best-known metropolis.

Geeta had landed up in Thane after being hitched to Dinesh Hirway, a mathematics schoolteacher and a recently bereaved widower back then, since a Pune bridegroom was an impossibility after our betrothal was called off. Her parents had moved smartly to proposals outside Pune and got her married off within six months thereafter.

How did I know? Not because I kept a watch, but because it's a small world and almost ten years later, I bumped into Noorie Joseph on a train journey to Mumbai.

One moment I was engrossed in a newspaper and the next, someone plonked themselves next to me, and a female voice asked, 'Aren't you Gajanan Godbole?'

I looked up timidly, as used to be my default reaction to life. Not instantly, but it didn't take me more than a minute to recognize the gaudy woman seated next to me, although her name eluded me.

'Noorie Joseph…Geeta's friend. Poona Coffee House. Remember?' she said, giving me a hearty grin.

'Yes…' I said awkwardly.

'Oh, sorry. I know it might not be the most pleasant memory for you after what happened later,' she had the grace to say, although still beaming. 'But how are you?'

'Fine…' I replied, uneasily as the realization crept on me that she would be giving me company for the next few hours.

'Married, I hope?'

'Of course,' I said defensively.

'Good! Children?'

'One daughter.'

'Ah! Now planning another one, a son?'

The woman had appalled me back then and she appalled me now. Who was she to ask me such intimate questions? I shrugged and cleared my throat with dignity. 'How…how are you?'

'I'm great! I am Noorie Athlye now. I stay in the US with my husband…No kids yet, but that's not for lack of trying,' she said and burst into ribald giggles.

'Athlye, did you say?'

'Yes! Shocked?'

'No…No…' I said quickly.

'Well, I neither wanted to marry a Christian like my Dad, nor a Muslim like my Mom…' she chattered on blithely. 'Didn't meet a Sikh and didn't fancy any Parsis. So, a Hindu it was.'

'I see…I see…So, you arc here on a trip?'

'Yes…yes. In fact, I'm just going to meet Geeta today,' she replied. 'She lives in Thane, no!'

And with that, she gave me all the information that I didn't really want. Geeta had been married off to a widowed mathematics teacher, Dinesh Hirway, who had obviously started taking tuitions on the side. Something clicked and soon he had a flourishing business of maths coaching classes in Thane, raking in plenty. Geeta had two kids – a son and a daughter, and how well all was with her. Blah! Blah! Blah! I wished she would stop, but Noorie didn't. Except at Karjat junction, where she asked me if I cared for batata vadas. She merrily got some from a vendor and claimed to have no change, so I had to pay for it.

After she gobbled and washed it down with tea, she gave me a long, reflective stare. 'You know, Geeta shouldn't have done what she did to you,' she remarked.

I felt gratified and irked at the same moment. I said nothing and looked out of the train window.

'I feel sorry I might have inadvertently played a part in it,' she continued.

I looked at her and frowned. 'What? How?'

Noorie smiled enigmatically but it wasn't a derisive smile. 'You wouldn't understand. Anyway, the good thing is it's all in the past and she's happily married and so are you.'

I bridled and looked out of the window again.

'You are happy, right, Gajanan?'

'Much happier than I would've been with Geeta at least,' I snapped back, in a rare instance of sharpness for the Gajanan Godbole I was back then.

'That's the spirit!' Noorie Athlye said and beamed.

~

Over the years I needed to make a couple of visits to Thane – once or twice, for work. On these occasions I did happen to notice signboards of 'Hirway Maths Coaching Class' at some prominent locations in town. Obviously, her husband's business was thriving. Casual conversations with a couple of acquaintances also confirmed that Hirway's coaching classes had a reputation. Naturally, I wasn't too happy with the fact that she'd done well for herself by marrying this successful Joe, after her skulduggery with me.

Then some seven to eight years earlier, Sumitra had dragged me to a wedding all the way in Thane. And that is eventually where I set my eyes upon Geeta Hirway née Divte again. She was decked with jewellery and an air of well-being, all smiles. She and her husband – who else could it be – seemed to be treated like royalty, not only by the host, but also the other guests.

The worst part is, I had recognized her instantly but she didn't recognize me at all when her eyes rested on me briefly in the gathering. Pretty depressing that a woman who nearly ruined my life with brazen lies, not only had benefitted from her disgraceful actions, but had also blissfully forgotten the face of the man she had treated so shabbily. Weren't old sins supposed to cast long shadows? Weren't sinners supposed to be guilt-ridden enough to recognize the person they had sinned against? Apparently not in the case of a deplorable sinner like Geeta Hirway.

Well, of course, I chafed a bit and then let it go, as I had done all my life as the original Gajanan Godbole.

A few years later, I learnt her husband had passed away, but even though I could gain some satisfaction in that, she'd still had thirty-five years of marriage and prosperity. So it wasn't much of a triumph that she'd been widowed finally at around sixty. In fact, women probably have the best chance of finding happiness and becoming merry widows at that age.

That was the last I'd heard about Geeta, so now it was time to pick up the thread and deliver the retribution she had escaped so far. And so, I made my preparations and landed up in Thane to confront her.

27

BAITING GEETA

In an otherwise happy life, Geeta Hirway, it seems had one problem. Her son apparently suffered from bouts of depression. And when he did, he would make himself scarce for a month or two. Where he went was a mystery, but it was rumoured he went to some godman's ashram to seek solace, while others believed he actually went to a psychiatric therapy centre, away from the city.

How did I know? Ah well, the distant relatives to whose daughter's wedding Sumitra had dragged me several years ago, supplied me with this information. They had called me to offer their condolences after learning of Sumitra's demise, and I had spoken to them perfunctorily in my role as a grieving widower.

Now, a couple of days before I left for Thane, I had called them up and mentioned I was coming to their city and would they mind if I dropped by? The poor dears were probably astonished at why somebody who'd never shown much enthusiasm for them earlier, now wanted to visit them at home. But they were an old couple and probably lonely too, so they welcomed me and then in the course of our conversation, gave me the inside story on Geeta Hirway's son. Even better, as luck would have it, it seemed the boy had gone missing again about two weeks ago.

It then fell to Geeta and her daughter-in-law to handle the affairs of various family businesses while he was away. The daughter-in-law, well-qualified herself, oversaw matters at the coaching centres, which now included MBA entrance coaching too, spread across four to five locations in Thane and nearby Kalyan. Geeta, on the other hand, supervised the Titan franchise they had and another Hidesign showroom.

COVID apparently had also hit their fortunes and the Hirways had had to shut down or sell off two other establishments that they had owned earlier. They couldn't afford more losses, hence the women had to chip in, whenever the son absconded, for a couple of months.

All this was music to my ears, of course, that all was not as well as it had once seemed. Geeta deserved some more pain, and I was quite keen on inflicting it.

I first visited the Hidesign outlet as a customer and made enquiries about various high-end handbags, which of course was just a ruse. That the boutique belonged to Geeta was confirmed, as also that she came along there every day around 5 p.m. I said I was an old acquaintance and might drop by the next day, so that I could get to meet her. Next, I tootled over to the Titan showroom, which was in another part of the city. I looked at watches, then made enquiries about Geeta and was told that she was expected there any minute. Most importantly, there was a small cabin at the back of the store, where it seems she sat when she was present.

I realized I would have to come back when she was already ensconced in the cabin. So that I could corner her inside it, for there was no knowing what her reaction would be if we first met right in front of her employees, in the display area. Just then, the employee got a phone call. She listened and said,

'Yes, madam.' Once the call got over, she turned to the cashier and said, 'Madam is going to be late. She'll be here around 1.30 p.m.'

I smiled. I wouldn't have to wait till tomorrow. I could just return a little while later today. I wove my story about being Geeta's acquaintance again, and that I would return a little later so that I could get to meet her too. Out I went, and had a leisurely bite of lunch, rubbing my hands with glee in anticipation of how the woman who'd handed me the worst and most unfair humiliation of my life would receive the worst shock of her existence.

When I returned to the shop, the employees gave me a wide smile. I was a genuine buyer after all, they must've thought, not one of those people who never came back.

'Is your Geeta Madam here?' I asked.

'Yes, sir…' the employee who had attended me earlier said. 'But she's busy with the cashier.'

'I see,' I said as the employee again led me to the watches I had shortlisted. 'So which one do you want to finalize for your wife, sir?'

'They are all so attractive,' I grinned and began pretending to pointlessly fret over them again.

Just then, I noticed the cashier walk back to his counter, probably to fetch something Geeta might've asked for. This was my chance and I quickly grabbed it.

'I'll just say hello to Mrs Hirway,' I said to the saleswoman and before she could object, I rushed towards the cabin, opened it and stood facing a startled Geeta Hirway.

'Hello, Geeta,' I said, grinning widely. Forty-two years older since we had last met, Geeta Hirway had plumped and gaudied up and gotten grey-haired; yet even without pimples, her face had retained that look of callous sourness.

'Yes, please?' she said, frowning.

She had not recognized me, obviously mistaking me for some customer who'd had the temerity to barge in.

'It's been such a long, long time yet it's so unpleasant to see you again,' I replied.

'What?'

The saleswoman had by now reached and stood behind me, at the open door of the cabin, trying to peer in.

'Madam,' she said apologetically, 'this gentleman said… he…he…knew you…'

Geeta threw her an annoyed look, then glared back at me. 'I'm sorry, I don't recognize…'

'Poona Coffee House, James Bond, Noorie Joseph,' I remarked with a chuckle.

Geeta's face fell almost instantly, and she looked speechless. 'You…you are…Gajanan Godbole?' she finally said, as recognition slammed through her.

'Correct,' I said in a ringing voice, then looked at the saleswoman. 'There, you see. Go, run along, let two old friends talk.'

The saleswoman hesitated, looked at Geeta, who sort of gave her a distracted nod of dismissal. She faded away and I let the cabin door shut. I settled down in a chair, facing Geeta, who was now looking at me with a foul expression that looked exactly like the ones she'd thrown at me during our meetings back then.

'Why are you here?'

'To blackmail you with the passionate letters you wrote to me,' I stage-whispered.

'What?'

I chortled, enjoying all this greatly. 'Relax,' I said, 'I just thought it was a good time to catch up with you in the winter of our lives.'

She looked at me uneasily, with that trademark nasty glint in her eyes. 'Catch up?'

'Yes, Geeta. I can't let bygones be bygones you see. It's time to settle scores with you for what you did!'

Geeta stiffened. 'I don't know what you are talking about. I didn't do anything.'

I sneered. 'You've remained a sneaky little liar, haven't you, Geeta! You lied that I told you I didn't like girls and that I was impotent! And your filthy lies made a laughing stock out of me. It took three long years to put that humiliation behind me.'

She flinched. I could sense my eyes and expression suffused with the cold fury I suddenly felt. 'I…I don't know who told you that. I completely deny all this,' Geeta bluffed.

'Ah! Really! So the matchmaker made up this story, I suppose?'

'Yes…yes…not me…'

'Oh, how I misjudged you, sweet Geeta,' I said, my tone soft, my eyes hard, my heart harder. 'But you did break the engagement or was that the matchmaker's idea too?'

I watched the cunning, calculative look settling back in her eyes, after the initial shake-up. She sighed, then fluttered her eyelids. 'Look, Gajanan. You don't know the half of it…it…it was actually my father's idea and the matchmaker's, because you see they wanted me to marry my late husband.'

The woman's insidiousness took my breath away. How smoothly she had shifted the blame to her father and the matchmaker – who were both dead by now, and thus, beyond the pale of truth-telling. Moreover, even her husband was no more.

'Go on…' I said.

'You see, my late husband had visited about three to four days before you and your parents had come to see me and… and his "yes" to the proposal came by post a few days after our engagement…' Geeta got into her stride, weaving her fake tale, '...which...which my father felt...not me...my father felt was more suitable for me...Also, because my late husband didn't want any dowry...so...so they hit upon this plan to break the engagement by claiming...that you had told me all those things. Believe me, Gajanan...I had no role to play. I...I was just a puppet.'

I could have rolled with laughter at the lies that rolled so easily from her tongue – at her sheer brazenness. It was clear her crooked soul had remained bent. People rarely changed, except for me, of course.

'You expect me to believe all this soap opera crap, Geeta? That your father and the matchmaker were the villains of the piece and you the naïve, innocent fall-girl?'

She immediately switched gears to being the poor, helpless, remorseful woman, 'Believe me, Gajanan. I know...it was terribly, terribly wrong. I was shocked when I learnt what they had claimed as me having said. I am so sorry for all that you had to undergo. May Lord forgive my dear father and that matchmaker. I really, really apologize on their behalf! Forgive me too, Gajanan, although I swear on my late husband's soul. I had no role whatsoever.'

I watched, fascinated. Diabolical this woman was; I wondered what she must've been as a wife to the late Dinesh Hirway, the mathematics teacher. I smirked and shook my head. 'You think an apology is enough for the damage done to me? After all these years!'

'No, no...I know it's not enough. But what else can I do, Gajanan? It was all so long ago. I was a victim too, you know? I wasn't to blame. You think I was keen on marrying a person almost twelve years elder than me, that too a widower, in... in comparison to you?' Geeta said. 'Why would I do it? Why would I lie and say you said such things and try to break off the engagement? I mean, I liked you. I told you that...remember?'

Of course, she had said no such thing, and she knew that! But the cheek of the woman to falsify history was no less astonishingly blatant than politicians of a particular ideology.

'Geeta, you are lying through your false teeth, dear,' I replied. 'I know the truth.'

'I'm not lying...and I don't have false teeth,' she said, annoyed that I didn't seem to be buying into her story.

My eyes twinkled with amusement. How did I know? I could see myself in the reflection of a framed painting behind her. 'You see, Noorie Joseph told me all...'

Geeta's face fell several storeys, like an elevator that snaps. She suddenly looked like a hunted animal seeking cover.

'What do you mean? What did Noorie say?'

I grinned and leaned forward. 'At first I thought you did what you did because you probably had a boyfriend, whom you wanted to marry and thus, needed to break off the engagement with me,' I said, talking slowly, as if chewing thirty-six times to enjoy the flavour. 'But then I realized, your boyfriend wasn't a boy at all...It was Noorie Joseph!'

Geeta's face had blanched. It was like one of those death row execution scenes in Hollywood films, in which the prisoner is given the fatal injection and the victim's families watch him die. Of course, Geeta seemed to be only figuratively dead, but her expressions were a virtual confession of the truth. Noorie Joseph had told me nothing. But while planning my vengeance, when I had recalled all that had transpired back then, I'd come to realize that there had been some queer and kinky vibes between the two girls. Something that in 1980 had been an almost completely unknown phenomenon or possibility to have struck the mind of an average Indian of my background.

But now, in hindsight, it seemed to me as the most likely explanation. To add to it, why had Noorie said she felt guilty about what happened to me and that she might have been inadvertently responsible? It had still been an intuitive surmise, but Geeta had just confirmed it by her reaction. Not that the girls might have been lesbians, but probably given those times, for a girl like Geeta, fun and sexuality of some kind might have been possible to experience only in the company of another girl – Noorie.

Geeta's eyes finally rose and met mine, then they fell again. 'Not true. I…I got married within six months…So why would I…if what you say was true…?' she replied without conviction.

'Well, you still got six more months with Noorie, and could continue meeting her whenever you came to Pune, couldn't you?' I replied. 'Which I seemed likely to forbid…'

Geeta retreated into a furtive silence, then asked, 'What do you want, Gajanan? I've already apologized abjectly to you, I'll apologize again.'

I didn't feel one bit sorry for her. When cornered, everyone whines and tries to cut a sorry figure. She might have been wretchedly and miserably bewitched with Noorie back then; she might've been a poor, repressed girl but that hadn't stopped her from wrecking my life with what she knew were blatant lies.

'An apology does nothing, Geeta. It's too light a punishment for the kind of damage done,' I said. 'For my trauma to heal, you must undo what you did!'

'Undo? How?'

'Well, your dear husband is no more, and my darling wife is dead too,' I said, prefacing my deliciously wicked plan. 'So what could be a better happy ending than two old flames reuniting in holy matrimony?'

'What?' Geeta sat up in her chair as if she were the pilot of a plane going down, about to eject.

'Yes, ugly, pimply Geeta, it's engagement time once again!' I said. 'That's the only way to make amends. Announce to the world that you are re-uniting with your first love…me…and have decided to live happily ever after with Gajanan Godbole.'

The shock and horror on her face made her look uglier than she did even in her youth. 'Are you crazy?' she asked in a choked voice.

'About you!' I said, blowing her kisses and rumbling with laughter. 'Don't worry, Geeta…The engagement will last only for a short while. I have no flickering flame for you. Nor any urge to marry or make love to you. It would be just for a few days and this time I'll break the engagement thereafter! Fair enough?'

'But…but…but you can't be serious! At this age. I can't do that. What will people say?' she cried.

'As my favourite superstar Rajesh Khanna put it, in *Amar Prem*, "Kuch to log kahenge, logon ka kaam hai kehna," my dear Geeta,' I replied.

'No…no…please have mercy, Gajanan. What will my family feel? I've got grown up children, their spouses…even a grandchild…I'll…I'll die of embarrassment. It would be so shameful,' Geeta said, now totally shaken.

'But that's the whole point of your punishment – shame and embarrassment – just a fraction of what you subjected me to,' I said. 'Three months compared to three years! Promise! After three months, I'll break it. Deal? Just a little tat for your tit, oh sorry, no pun intended, sweety. Tit for tat, I mean!'

She suddenly had tears in her eyes, looking at me soulfully, without any semblance of a soul though. Obviously I didn't melt, for I no longer was the melting kind. She sniffed and said a few minutes later, 'Don't do this to me please, Gajanan, I beg you. I know I did wrong but please, surely you are bigger than that!'

'I assure you I'm not. I'm as petty and low as I would like to go,' I replied. 'But there's no question of force. I have an alternative too! Want to hear it?'

'What?' she asked eagerly.

I wished I had a keychain in my hand that I could twirl around my index finger as the villain Pran did, in one of his films, as he blackmailed the heroine. But never mind, I knew I had enough to chill Geeta, even without it.

'I know about your son's depression. So how about I drive him over the edge by informing him and all of Thane about your lesbian shenanigans of yore and youth with Noorie Joseph? Who knows better than you the power of a little rumour-mongering in destroying reputations?'

Geeta's eyes were back to being saucers, fear competing with shame in them.

'Think about it. No hurry. Let me know in a week, okay! Now you'll know how much fun I really am…' I said and left her stunned in her seat.

28

BLACKMAIL

I let Geeta simmer for a week. She made dozens of calls to my mobile, left text messages asking me to 'Please call back.' But I didn't reply for several days.

Then one day I responded. 'Were you trying to reach me?'

Five minutes later my mobile buzzed.

'Gajanan,' she said breathlessly, as soon as I took the call. 'Look…look…We need to talk…'

'About what?'

'About what you said, of course,' she replied.

'Hmm…Come over to Pune, Geeta. I can't hear too well on the phone,' I said.

'What? When?'

'Any day, tomorrow or the day after.'

'But why?'

'Didn't you just say you wanted to talk?'

'Yes…but…'

'Tell you what…There's a treat in store for you, if you come,' I said. 'We can meet at…Guess where…?'

'Where?'

'Café Goodluck, my dear. The place you so yearned to go to on our first date…It's still standing where it was,' I replied, totally thrilled at this sudden inspiration that had struck me. 'I love non-vegetarian food now, you know. I hope you haven't given it up.'

'But, Gajanan, can't we just talk on the phone?'

'Okay, see you in Pune. Call me the day you are coming,' I said, cutting her short and hanging up.

She frantically tried calling me a few times more, but I didn't pick up.

~

Two days later we were seated at Café Goodluck, the Irani restaurant that had enjoyed an almost iconic status for over eighty years; although its charm now was not quite the same. Even film star and matinee idol Dev Anand would eat here, way back in the 1940s, when he first started out as a newbie at the iconic Prabhat Studios, which was now the Film and Television Institute of India.

Located at the junction of Pune's once famous Deccan Gymkhana area, Bhandarkar Road and Fergusson College Road, it was the place where thousands of generations of Punekars lost their vegetarian virginity, succumbing to the temptations of non-vegetarian food and consummating their desires.

'Here we are!' I said brightly. 'You do look exceedingly more of an eyesore every time I see you, Geeta.' She gave me her sour look and threw an uneasy glance around. She had come alone. Not that I had expected her to bring someone in tow, for whom could she confide in really?

'What would you like to have, Geeta? You can order all the non-vegetarian stuff you want today. My treat!'

'Actually…actually, can't we go elsewhere…I…I… can't…I don't…' she said and hesitated.

'You don't eat non-veg?' I completed the sentence for her. 'What a pity! Why?'

'Our household was…is…totally vegetarian.'

'You mean because your late husband was strictly vegetarian?'

She nodded.

'Well, your future husband loves non-vegetarian food…So that will have to change, Geeta,' I said cheekily. 'Not only will you have to eat but also cook chicken and fish.'

Geeta baulked. 'Look, Gajanan, please…please…I…I can't do it.'

'You mean you can't eat it or cook it?'

'No, no. I mean I can't do what you are asking me to do, get engaged to you and all that. Please…it's impossible. It will create all sorts of problems for me…It'll devastate my son. I can't do it, please. You have to have mercy on me,' she pleaded.

'Hmm…I see,' I said. 'Do you want a cream roll and tea?'

'What?'

I smiled, hailed a waiter and ordered.

When he was gone, Geeta spoke again, 'Please, Gajanan. Please, I am truly sorry for what I did back then, but don't… don't do this to me. I beg you…'

'Well, Geeta, it really is disappointing. I mean, I was so looking forward to embarrassing you and then breaking off the engagement…' I said, drawing my eyebrows close. 'But… if that's not going to happen, then I'll go ahead with the alternative – revealing your scandalous secrets with Noorie Joseph to your son and everyone in Thane.'

'No, no, Gajanan…Come on, that will harm my son and family beyond repair too…' Geeta said, wringing her hands. 'Please…please find some kindness in your heart and spare me. In any case, what Noorie Joseph told you is not true…She probably told you out of spite after we had a bad falling out, some years ago. Otherwise, I would have confronted her for telling you such rot. But, please, Gajanan. I'm sorry for what happened. Have mercy.'

She had fully switched on her grovelling – I'm a poor woman – mode.

The waiter was back and laid out the egg pudding for her, and the tea and cream roll in front of me. Geeta recoiled. I sneered then switched our dishes. I dug into my egg pudding and tasted a morsel.

'Umm, delicious,' I said. 'Want to taste?'

She shook her head, tense and waiting for my response.

'Well, if you take a bite, I might reconsider,' I said wickedly.

'What?' She grimaced. 'Really?'

'Yes, if you taste it, I'm willing to give you a third alternative.'

'What's that?'

'Eat the pudding first, dear. Come on, you might actually like it,' I said, thrusting a spoon towards her.

She made a face again but then gingerly dug a spoon into the pudding and scooped a tiny morsel and put it in her mouth as if it was violating her in some way! The drama queen, who'd mocked me for not having non-veg once.

'Good, no?' I winked.

She didn't react, then asked, 'So, what…what is the third alternative?'

I ate a few bites of my egg pudding, then said, 'I want you to do something for me.'

'What?' she asked warily, licking her lips.

I looked at her strung up demeanour. 'Something fun!'

'Fun?'

'Yes, remember you said you like to have fun?'

'I don't understand.'

I smiled and ate some more of my egg pudding. She still hadn't touched her cream roll and tea.

'You still like James Bond movies?' I asked.

'Yes?' she replied in a guarded tone.

'Did you watch *Casino Royale*?'

She nodded and gulped.

'Remember a lady brings Daniel Craig a drink at the card table. Bond has it…and nearly dies of poisoning?'

Geeta nodded again, totally bewildered as to where all this was leading.

'So, you are going to be the lady who hands over a drink, bottle gourd juice, to someone I want dead,' I finished smoothly.

She appeared dumbstruck, and seemed to have ceased breathing. For a moment I thought she was either going to scream or swoon, but neither happened. 'Murder?' she asked finally.

'Correct. I need you to help me murder someone I hate. You don't know the person; you don't stay in Pune, so no one will ever suspect you. My work gets done and you would've made amends for the wrong you did me…win-win for all! Very simple, nothing complicated…'

She stared at me with disbelief, blinking, baulking, breathing heavily. But I knew instinctively she would agree to it for I had recognized that aptitude in her – the willingness and lack of compunction to harm others.

29

PLOTTING MURDER

Back in 2018, paging through the newspaper, I had come across a startling local news report chronicling the death of a forty-one year old woman jogger after consuming bottle gourd juice. A couple of follow-up articles in the next few days explained that bottle gourd belonged to the Cucurbitaceae family of fruits and vegetables that included others like cucumber, pumpkin and melon. Apparently, a tight concentration of cucurbitacin compounds could not only make bottle gourd bitter but also toxic enough to be fatal. Of course, this occurred rarely but there had been a few such deaths over the years in the country, which had forced authorities to take notice.

Four years was a long time I reckoned, for a second such instance to happen in Pune and this time the victim would be known to me – my old bench mate Nandu Khandagale. Frankly, I wasn't relying on the cucurbitacin in bottle gourd juice. The poison would have to be one of the more dependable ones, but at least prima facie it would be considered a case of juice poisoning. Diabolical, no?

Well, I had carefully pondered the poisons too – cyanide perhaps from a helpful, friendly jeweller, but then I didn't know one; or thallium, which I'd heard was undetectable, something an enterprising young man from Delhi had ordered online to help eliminate his wife's entire family, by feeding them fish curry. But I wasn't dumb enough to purchase it online, and I knew no other way to source it. So it would have to be something else.

'Madhuri sweetie,' I said, nibbling her ear, after we lay back, exhausted, one night.

'What, Viru?' she mumbled sleepily.

'As an animal welfare officer, I guess you know some snake-catchers?'

'Yes, why?' she asked, then looked over her shoulder at me curiously, suddenly wide awake.

'Oh nothing…always wanted to meet one,' I said nonchalantly.

The frown on her face deepened and she turned to face me fully. 'You aren't up to something, are you?'

'Up to something? Like what, honey-bunny?' I said, looking as innocent as I possibly could.

'Like plotting Nandu's or Sundar's murder by snakebite or something?' Madhuri asked forthrightly, raising herself on her elbow and scowling sternly.

She was one hell of a sharp lass, I had to admit. 'Murder by snakebite? You mean like that Kerala fellow, who got rid of his wife by getting her bitten by a cobra?' I asked, attempting unsuccessfully to sound incredulous.

'Precisely!' Madhuri said. 'Why else would you be asking me about snake-catchers?'

I guffawed. 'Sweetie, you think I want to get hold of a snake-catcher through your connections to procure a trained serpent that I can let into Nandu or Sundar's house?' I remarked. 'You honestly think I am daft enough to try such a lame murder?'

Madhuri looked at me for a few moments then said, 'Well, the reason you gave is no less lame.'

'You cut me short before I could explain, darling.'

'I didn't...You said the reason is that you've always wanted to meet a snake-catcher.'

'That's true. But you didn't let me come to the real reason.'

'And what's that?'

'Actually, I was asking for Ravi, my nephew...' I replied. 'His friend owns an old bungalow by the hillside, and a couple of snakes were spotted in the garden.'

Madhuri kept eyeing me, totally unconvinced. 'Well, ask him to search Google for snake-catchers in Pune. He'll find plenty...' she replied.

So that conversation put paid to the possibility of procuring snake venom on the sly for plotting Nandu's assassination. It made me move to the next alternative – something more domestic, a pesticide maybe or other, over the counter stuff for rodent disposal, crushed sleeping pills or expired medicines perhaps. And then, inspiration struck me – how about dead lizards and their droppings?

Amazingly, I had to thank my late wife Sumitra for this electrifying flashbulb moment. Throughout our married life, Sumitra had been paranoid about leaving milk uncovered while boiling or even otherwise. The reason, she had told me, was the death of some near relative many decades ago because of consuming milk from a vessel into which a dead lizard and its droppings had fallen, discovered after the relative had kicked the bucket.

So, had I struck gold? There were at least a few geckos in my house, and I would notice them or their droppings every once in a while. Would all that was required be to kill a couple, mash them up, mix them with their droppings and pour the concoction into a bottle of home-made bottle gourd juice? But how was I to know the efficacy? How many lizards and their droppings did it require to ensure enough poison?

I needed to verify all these doubts on Google, but without using my own computer or phone. But then, whose phone or computer was easily accessible to me? The answer was obvious – my darling Madhuri's or my dear nephew Ravi's. I concluded that doing my research on Ravi's computer would be better, given Madhuri's suspicious reaction to our recent 'snake-catcher' conversation. Besides, Ravi would ask no questions, nor have any reason for his suspicions to be aroused.

It went like a breeze. Ravi put his laptop at my disposal when I asked him if I could have it for a few hours, since I wanted to browse a few destinations to retreat to for some Ayurvedic treatment or Vipassana kind of a camp.

My hopes came crashing down when I realized that dead lizards and their droppings did not cause death or even guarantee severe illness. It was an exaggeration – a remote possibility that couldn't be engineered, because, apparently, geckos are not toxic by themselves, rather their skins might carry salmonella, which could cause poisoning in rare cases that might or might not be fatal. So how in the world was I going to ensure my house lizards had salmonella on their skins, that too of the fatal variety?

But even as I was crestfallen for a moment, my brain conjured up, out of nowhere, one word – datura. The common plant one could find all over the place, if you knew where to look; whose seeds, leaves, roots, and milky white discharge – were all poisonous as hell.

Half an hour of browsing later, I was convinced I had the perfect poison – a plant extract to mix with another plant extract, bottle gourd. Moreover, a vegetarian poison to the hilt, so as to make it a perfect fit in new India. Forensically speaking too, it would be ideal to stump doctors, I guessed.

I took another thirty minutes to jot down copious, handwritten notes, and then deleted the search history. For a few more minutes, thereafter, I aimlessly browsed, checking random alternative medicines and therapy retreats as well as pilgrimage destinations, just in case Ravi was curious to see what I had been up to. Then I shut the computer and began preparations for executing Nandu Khandagale.

~

Geeta Hirway gazed at the shapely 200 ml glass bottle I had placed before her, full of the parrot green liquid. The glass was transparent and clean, neatly labelled, sporting the logo of a locally well-known Ayurvedic products brand, with the words 'Bottle Gourd Juice' printed on it in English and Marathi. The words 'Pure' and 'Fresh' were prominent too, as was the best before date – five days from now. In short, it looked like any other retail juice or health drink bottle.

I was proud of the effort that had gone into creating five such labels – contributing to the overall authenticity of the product. Yet Geeta's face had doubt written all over it.

'It…it looks like a local home-made product,' she remarked.

'It's meant to,' I replied. 'The labels are supposed to make it appear hygienic and good quality.'

'They look tacky…Hand pasted.'

'They don't,' I contested hotly, 'at least, not enough to arouse suspicion.'

Geeta gave me a frown then looked away. 'Why will he take the juice from me when he has it at his regular counter every day?' she asked.

'Because no one refuses a free sample in India,' I asserted. 'All you have to do is to catch hold of him as he completes his walk and reaches his car, make your sales pitch. If he shows any sales resistance, pull out the impoverished middle-class widow card, appeal to him and offer him a free sample.'

'But won't he find it suspicious, I am selling it only to him and no one else?' Geeta asked. 'Or what if some other walker also wants to buy or asks for a free sample? Then what do I do?'

'Well, you give them a free sample too.'

'What?' she looked aghast. 'What if the other person dies too?'

'No danger of that, only one bottle contains the poison,' I replied, irritated.

'But how am I to distinguish which bottle?' Geeta panicked.

'You just keep it apart from the others, you dodo. I am going to give you a plastic basket to carry the bottles. You keep that one bottle with poison separately and give it to Nandu.'

Geeta shook her head. 'A plastic basket won't do. I'll get confused about which bottle is the right one…which side it is on.'

'Okay, okay. We'll figure it out so that you can easily identify the bottle,' I replied. 'Calm down.'

She, of course, didn't calm down. 'But won't my fingerprints remain on the bottle? When they realize that's what killed him?'

'Relax, Geeta. Unless you have a criminal history or police record, they won't be able to trace you with any fingerprints, because they have nothing to match it with.'

'But what if they trace me through Aadhar biometrics?' she asked me.

'No. The police are not allowed to do that,' I replied.

'No, no. I'll wear gloves.'

'Don't be silly. You'll look suspicious if you do,' I stated vehemently.

'Then I won't do it at all,' Geeta declared. 'I don't want to leave my fingerprints behind on the bottle that poisons him.'

'All right, we'll get you gloves,' I conceded.

'I feel sick,' she responded. 'Why are you making me do this?'

'Will you stop moaning, Geeta!' I snapped. 'It's payback time for what you did to me, and all I am asking you to do is to hand over a bottle to a man. It is so bloody simple! Nobody's forcing you. If you don't want to do it, just walk away, but then you should be prepared for the consequences…Karma!'

Geeta was quiet for a few minutes, fidgeting, cornered and probably trying to work out the possibility of defying me. Then she sighed. 'And if…if I do this, how do I know you'll leave me alone after that?'

I grunted. 'Of course, I will, Geeta. Why won't I? What will I gain troubling you thereafter? After this, we'll be partners-in-crime, won't we? I would have a stake in your well-being, won't I?'

She looked at me uneasily. 'Why do you want to kill that man, anyway?'

'The less you know the better, Geeta.' I smirked. 'Just do what I've told you to.'

Geeta gave a little shudder, and I felt the thrill of power run through me.

30

DOUBLE STRIKE

Did I mention to you that Nandu Khandagale had stopped going to Vetal Tekdi for his walk? I guess I didn't. You see, following his arrest for turtle smuggling and his reputation getting tarnished after the scandal, Nandu had probably thought it prudent to avoid going to public places that he was known to frequent. Instead, he had started going to a public park, which also had a walking track, a few kilometres away from his house, where it would be unlikely for him to be recognized.

I had stumbled upon this fact when conducting a recce two weeks earlier, prior to putting 'Operation Bottle Gourd' into action. To my delight, it would prove a far more convenient location than Vetal Tekdi. It was bang in the middle of the city, not on a hillside, so it solved the problem of having to arrange a prompt getaway afterwards for Geeta. It would be far easier for her to pose as a random woman distributing samples, without being particularly noticed. She could approach Nandu and disappear after doing the task, simply by walking some distance, and then hailing an autorickshaw.

Also, although there were some regular stalls catering to joggers and walkers, no one seemed to be offering bottle gourd juice. Nor did Nandu seem to stop at any counter on a regular basis, as he had done at Vetal Tekdi.

All in all, it was good news, especially because it would also make my task easier to keep a watch and supervise the assassination plan without being conspicuous. I put Geeta through a dry run two days before, mainly so that she could get a good look at Nandu and the overall scene of the walking track at that hour. And today, hopefully if all went well, was the day Nandu Khandagale would finally pay with his life, for wronging me all those years ago. I chuckled silently to myself as I watched him circling the walking track.

Geeta was also in position, dressed in a neat but faded saree, looking like a middle-class widow fallen upon hard times. She was moving around listlessly, offering samples desultorily to walkers and joggers who entered or exited the entrance to the track. Nobody seemed to take even cursory interest. Indeed, who would be interested in a bottle of bottle gourd juice, I thought wryly.

Nandu was expected to exit the track any time now. I could see Geeta suddenly get restless, then look this way and that with distress. What was happening, I wondered. Was the cow losing her nerve? I suddenly saw her glance in my direction, then stop a walker and ask her something. The other woman pointed towards the track as if giving her directions. Geeta gave her a nod and hastened inside. I felt alarmed. What the hell was she doing? This was not part of the plan! Had she suddenly lost patience and decided to approach Nandu on the track, rather than wait for him to exit?

A chill ran down my spine along with a flush of fury. If that bitch was going to do something stupid and ruin the plan then…I was too speechless with anger, even to complete the sentence in my own mind.

Baffled and fuming impotently, I waited, only to see Nandu walking out of the exit after about ten minutes. He headed to his car but didn't seem to be holding anything in his hand, so clearly Geeta had either not approached him at all or hadn't been able to persuade him to take the sample of bottle gourd juice. Either way, it meant my plan was going nowhere.

Where the hell was Geeta anyway, I thought, my fury getting the better of me. And, just as Nandu reached his car, to my astonishment, I saw Geeta bolt out of the track exit and scurry hurriedly towards him. She was, of course, no spring chicken so I was quite doubtful whether she would reach him before he could start the car and drive away. But somehow, she miraculously did and struck up a conversation with him. A throb of thrill ran through me as I saw Geeta earnestly offer him the sample. Nandu looked at the bottle, then put on his spectacles and read the label.

Would he accept it or return the sample to Geeta, who had started throwing nervous glances around? Then Nandu nodded at her, started shaking the bottle, as people tend to do, prior to opening and drinking it.

Now, was Nandu actually going to give me the pleasure of watching him seal his own fate by tasting the juice right there and then? I waited in tense anticipation. Geeta, on the other hand, seemed to give a little jerk and lurched away from the car. I couldn't blame her for having no appetite to watch Nandu consume the poison from close quarters, but hoped her reaction wouldn't alert Nandu that something was wrong.

By now, Nandu had unscrewed the bottle cap; another second and he would put it to his lips. Instead, he paused to first sniff at the contents, as some of us do. 'Go ahead, gulp it, stop wasting my time,' I found myself murmuring under my breath, all excited.

As if heeding my urging, Nandu put the bottle to his lips and took a swig. My throat suddenly felt parched, for now was the moment of reckoning. Would Nandu find something odd with the smell or taste, or simply not like it and stop after one sip? It was quite possible with a drink as foul as bottle gourd juice for even a regular drinker to find it unpalatable after a gap.

I thought or imagined Nandu grimace. Was he going to put the cap back on, deciding he didn't like the sample? In which case, I was afraid, just one sip might not be enough to kill him. Perhaps it might just upset his stomach or make him throw up after some time. But, much to my relief, Nandu took another gulp, and then another.

'Bottoms up,' I hissed with glee. My retribution was on track. Nandu was downing the poison. The datura would soon be in his bloodstream and with luck, he would be dead in a while from now, after perhaps throwing up and collapsing.

I threw a sweeping glance around, to check if Geeta was anywhere in sight. It looked as if she had managed to scramble and disappear. My eyes swivelled back towards Nandu. He had finished the juice and was once again looking at the label. He glanced outside then stepped out of the car, looking around in all directions. It struck me, he was probably looking for Geeta, perhaps to take a few more samples or purchase them. He had probably liked the taste. Nandu took a few more steps to see if he could spot Geeta somewhere then looked at the bottle in his hand again and threw it in a dustbin.

This was an unexpected bonus. Nandu wouldn't be carrying any physical evidence with him, with which the police could attempt to trace the source of his poisoning, after his death was reported.

He got back into the car, strapped on the seat belt, and soon drove away. My heart went wild with joy. Nandu Khandagale would soon be history. I looked forward to getting a confirmation in the news by late evening.

~

'Is…is he dead?' was the first question Geeta asked me, as soon as we were face to face.

'Should be,' I replied, 'if you gave him the right bottle.'

Where could an old man kill an old woman without hindrance, and get away with it? And how? I had pondered both the questions for long.

'Of course I did,' Geeta asserted. 'So here, take the remaining bottles with you.' She pointed at the basket and shuddered, as if it contained vials of some deadly virus.

'Sure, I'll get rid of them,' I said. 'When I saw you talk to that woman and then rush inside towards the walking track, I was wondering what you were up to…'

An awkward expression spread on Geeta's face. 'I…I had to empty my bladder. The toilet was inside.'

Ah, so that explained why she had deserted her post so frantically. Nature's call. 'Your first murder…nervous, I guess,' I said understandingly.

Outdoors was too risky and things could go wrong. There could be a struggle and screaming – someone would see or hear perhaps. Killing her at my place would mean too much work afterwards – cleaning, disposing off the body, destroying any evidence. Plus, of course, nosy neighbours, who might see me, or her, or us together. So, it had to be at her spinster sister's place in Pune, where I just needed to catch her unawares, send her to her maker and flee, unobserved, as far as possible.

'Did you see him drink it?' Geeta asked.

'Oh, yes. He finished the bottle.'

Her eyes widened. 'Oh my God! And then?'

'Well, Nandu drove away.'

Her mouth was dry. 'So, you don't know yet if it even made him sick, let alone kill him. What happens if he is okay?'

'Ah, in that case you'll have to go through the whole thing again. Make another attempt.'

'What?' She was aghast. 'No...I'm not going to do that... no way.'

I smiled, delighted to see her rattled. 'Relax. I'm sure he's gone, the stuff I gave him was super deadly...'

'So, you won't bother or blackmail me again, ever...and won't disclose anything to my son or my family?' she asked.

'Don't worry, Geeta. I've given you my word. This is our last meeting,' I said, keeping a straight face.

People never think someone's going to kill them in their own homes, you know, or familiar places. They think they are safe. That's why Geeta had immediately agreed that we should meet at her sister's Pune flat – to collect the bottles and basket, and discuss what to do if we ever came under suspicion for Nandu Khandagale's murder. I had suggested it beforehand, and as luck would have it, her sister was going outstation for a couple of days.

I got up now and reached into my trouser pocket. The moment had come. 'You didn't offer me tea or anything, but that's okay,' I said with a smile. 'Can I at least have some water before I leave?'

Geeta looked at me distastefully, as if I had demanded alcohol or something, then nodded and turned as she went into the kitchen.

I quickly removed the coil of plastic nylon rope I was carrying in my pocket, unrolled it and held it in my left hand, which I put behind my back. I unscrewed the spray cap of the small bottle I had in my front shirt pocket.

Geeta returned with the water. I drank a few gulps and put the glass down on the teapoy by the side.

'I've got a small parting gift for you – a farewell token.'

'What?' she asked, frowning, eyes wary.

I reached into my front pocket and removed the small bottle. 'A bottle of perfume,' I said, holding it out and moving it closer towards her. Then I pressed the pepper spray twice, in quick succession. It stung Geeta's eyes and she gave a little cry, ducking to one side, her hands trying to cover her face and rub her burning eyes at the same time. I had already pocketed the bottle and swiftly put the nylon rope around her throat and yanked, then wound loops around her neck and began squeezing.

Geeta started thrashing about and grappling in sheer terror. I held on as she lost her balance and fell forward. I lurched forward with her, then lowered myself while pressing my knee into her back, pulling and squeezing, as she choked and clawed at the rope loops, trying to scream and loosen my hold – neither of which she had any chance of succeeding in.

The nylon plastic rope began to bite into my palms, but I clung on even as the intense scuffle took my breath away too. The muscles all over my body, and especially in my back, shoulders and neck, felt as if they would snap or tear by the time Geeta finally succumbed.

Yet, it was amazingly exhilarating and exciting, as the realization grew that I was actually close to fulfilling my long-cherished urge to kill another human being with my own hands. And what better choice of victim could there have been than Geeta Hirway? I could hear her guttural groans and gurgles and grunts.

I wanted to jump with joy and pump my hands in the air – it was such a sublime experience for a man who, for much of his life, had been treated like a worm. The worm had turned! I swear, it was a grand catharsis. So much so, that it took me a while to realize that Geeta had stopped moving and was probably dead now.

There was no harm in squeezing some more to be absolutely sure, so I did so, for another few minutes. When I finally slackened the rope, I was bathed in sweat and my heart was pounding like an African drumbeat. As I tried to stand up, my body let me know that I had multiple sprains in my back and an almighty crick in my neck and shoulder area. My palms were not bleeding, but the nylon had tattooed its indentations into the skin and grated some of it, turning the flesh a deep beetroot-red. My fingers ached like hell, and my hands had a burning sensation all over.

But the triumph racing through my being was like a super balm that made me want to beat my chest and let out a war cry, like one of those tribal warriors or Red Indians one sees in films. I perched on the sofa for a few minutes, just staring at Geeta Hirway's corpse. My heart heaved with pride at the comeuppance I had just delivered this obnoxious woman. Whatever they might say about revenge, it was fantastic and deeply satisfying. Two tormentors dispatched in a day – Nandu Khandagale and now, Geeta Hirway. I deserved to gloat a bit!

Another ten minutes and I had regained my overall composure. I was ready to move on. I double-checked Geeta was dead, then began picking up things that needed to be removed – the nylon plastic rope, the bottle of pepper spray, the basket, and the bottles. No doubt I must've left my fingerprints, DNA and lots of other stuff for forensics to try and decipher, but that really wasn't a big concern for me. I just looked around to make sure I had not dropped any of my belongings inadvertently – my watch, my keys, my wallet, my mobile – anything that could directly be identified as mine.

Next, I wiped the glass with my handkerchief and put it in the kitchen sink. Finally, I looked for Geeta's mobile – that ultimate tracker of our lives these days. If the screen had been locked, I wouldn't have bothered. But since it wasn't, I quickly checked if she'd saved me as a contact, first and foremost. Mercifully, she hadn't, as I had instructed her. Next, I scrolled through the call details with my number and text messages, and I was glad that she had promptly deleted all text messages that we exchanged and the last call between us had been two days ago. So, no immediate connection could be made with me. Finally, I looked through various files – if she had made any recordings of our calls and saved them. That didn't seem to be the case either. So, all in all, it would be best to leave the phone here, since there was nothing really incriminating me on it. I wiped the phone with my handkerchief and left it back where I had found it.

Nobody had seen me come, and I wanted to ensure nobody would see me leaving the flat now either. I looked through the eyehole. There seemed to be no one around. It was time to exit the crime scene. I was 99 per cent sure that no one would see me and even if someone did, who would notice or remember or be able to describe a nondescript old man – a stranger; especially since Geeta's body was unlikely to be found for at least a day or two.

I opened the door and swiftly stepped out, closed it without hesitating or looking here or there furtively, and took the steps down the landing. I passed no one on my way three storeys down. Luck seemed to be with me so far.

I now only had to pass under the lone CCTV camera over the gate, making myself as little visible as possible. The best way to do that was to pretend I was talking on the phone, which is exactly what I had done while walking in earlier. All unnecessary as it turned out. Apparently, as I read in a news report later, the damn thing hadn't even been working.

31

NATUROPATHY

Nandu did not die instantly. He succumbed ten hours later in hospital, after a great deal of distress and unpleasantness. Don't ask me why. Maybe the poison quantity was a drop or two less than the ideal fatal dose – after all, it was my first time. It could also be that Nandu had the constitution of a horse or an ox or an elephant, or perhaps the doctors tried a little too hard to save him. All I can say is that in the end it only prolonged his agony, which was a kind of unexpected bonus. So, you could say, fate too contributed its two bits to my vengeance.

'Did you have anything to do with this?' Madhuri asked me when she finally responded to my dozen missed calls that evening.

I was just resting my aching bones and muscles in my room at the Spiritual Santulan and Ayurveda Village near Karjat, about two hours from Pune, where I had retreated to after sending Nandu and Geeta to their maker.

Remember I had looked for pilgrimages and alternative therapy retreats on Ravi's computer, while Googling poisons? Well, I had figured that if I booked myself at a place like this for a ten-day course, it would serve as the perfect alibi and hideaway. I mean, which murderer checks into a spiritual and medicinal spa right after committing murder? Conversely, which man who checks into an Ayurveda healing centre of all places, could be suspected of murder! Chuckle! Chuckle! Lol!

'Anything to do with what, my darling Madhuri?' I cooed to her.

She didn't coo back. In fact, there was an uneasy silence before she spoke again. 'This news about Nandu?'

'What news, honeypot?' I asked, sounding as innocent as a babe. 'There's no TV, no internet here for the entire duration of the course, darling. I am cut off from the world since I arrived this afternoon.'

'I don't believe you! What a coincidence that…that… Nandu…' she spluttered.

'What, Madhuri, what?' I asked, sensing she would be reluctant to say words like murder or poison or even Nandu's full name over the phone, for you never knew who was listening in these days. 'I can't understand a word of what you are saying.'

I was right. More silence followed.

'Sundar's right,' she said. 'He or I could be next. You… you…'

I cursed Sundar. I murdered him in my mind. The bastard! 'Madhuri, my love, calm down! Why are you speaking in riddles? I swear on you…'

I heard an abrupt click. She had cut the call. I grunted with annoyance and dialled her number a couple of times. The calls went unanswered.

Ah well, I thought philosophically, murder took some time getting used to. She would eventually come around to accept that killing was quite a reasonable, legitimate means of expression in the repertoire of human behaviour. Murder had never gone out of fashion in the history of mankind. Men had always killed. They still do. Governments all over the world killed people, didn't they – enemy soldiers, terrorists, criminals, dissidents, opponents, innocents – for all kinds of punitive reasons. All of it really was part of that much revered, age-old human right to revenge for any harm done! Oh, Madhuri would definitely come around!

On the other hand, it was quite possible she or Sundar would anonymously tip off the police about me. Or maybe even turn approver, spilling the beans on the Olive Ridley turtles and how I nursed a grudge against Nandu! But I didn't see that happening, because it involved too much self-incrimination for them. Yet, it was a possibility I had to watch out for and pre-empt.

In any case, Sundar had polluted the planet Earth for too long, so I owed it to the environment to get rid of him. I would, the moment I figured out how. I certainly hoped all the Ayurveda and spirituality over the next ten days would inspire me to think of some bright idea.

Meanwhile, I still had no news about Geeta. Had her body been discovered? So, I stepped outside my room to go check. You see, it wasn't strictly true that we were cut off from the rest of the world. There were no TVs in our rooms, nor any Wi-Fi, and the mobile internet signals were terribly weak. But there was a common hall with a TV.

Every inch of my body ached like hell – I was stiff; I had cricks and sprains and pulls in every possible muscle. Indeed, Geeta's murder would remain a muscle memory forever, in that sense.

The television room was full of other old fogeys, who'd come for the course that was to begin the next day. I realized it wasn't just a TV room, but a kind of entertainment centre. Some people were playing carrom at a table, another set was playing cards, while the largest group sat like zombies, watching some television serial. Now, how the hell was I going to make them switch channels, and turn on the news? Not a chance!

The old Gajanan would have slunk away without saying a word, but the new one was a different kettle of fish, as I knew by now. I simply went up to the TV watchers and said loudly for all to hear, 'Folks, you have been watching the serial for some time. Let's switch channels and catch up with the news for a few minutes, please.'

A dozen displeased faces turned to me. 'We are in the middle of an episode. Wait for some time,' a prim old lady said.

'I have already waited for long,' I retorted.

'I just saw you walk in…you weren't waiting…' another man observed.

'You need to get your eyes tested,' I replied unkindly.

'Shhh…' someone hissed. 'I can't hear what's happening in the scene.'

'Okay, listen. I am going to give you all ten more minutes,' I said, raising my voice. 'After that I am going to damn well put on the news. Is that clear?'

A few grumbles and murmurs of outrage followed and several zombies threw me nasty looks, but no one challenged me.

'Ten minutes,' I repeated, then began walking away when I suddenly heard someone call out my name.

'Gajanan?'

I swivelled in the direction of the voice. First my jaw dropped and then readjusted itself to fit into the devilish grin that was now spreading across my face. For whom should I see waving at me diffidently from the cards table, but my very next quarry on the list – Kamal Kishore Puri, my evil ex-boss, with whom I had an axe to grind.

'Arre, KK Sir, what a surprise!' I responded cordially, moving towards the cards table. If this was not divine intervention, then what was!

What made it even more delightful was that old age had turned this man, who had once been a six-foot, oily-haired, pan- and tobacco-chewing, foul-mouthed bully into a balding, toothless, unimposing, cane-holding codger. And yet, I felt almost fond of him right now, while responding to his oddly affectionate, even ingratiating call out to me. As if I were not an underling he'd harassed once, but a long-lost friendly acquaintance.

An epiphany moment if there were any – perhaps, we miss and love our enemies the most, for hatred is as deeply passionate as sex, I guess!

KAMAL KISHORE PURI

32

MOGAMBO

Kamal Kishore Puri scared the shit out of me, right from the day he was unleashed upon our branch office in 1986. Even though I still had the cushion of a supervisor above me and hence did not directly report to him, I lived in dread of what might happen once Ranadive, my supervisor, retired in two years.

His surname and typical north Indian aggressive manner, which we mild Marathi folk were intimidated by, often made me wonder if Kamal Kishore Puri was the youngest brother of screen villains Madan and Amrish Puri. In fact, half the office thought so too, for he was promptly nicknamed 'Mogambo' after the iconic baddie Amrish Puri played in the blockbuster film *Mr. India*, which released soon after, in 1987.

Of course, Kamal Kishore wasn't blonde-haired like Mogambo, but long years of henna use had turned his hair almost beetroot with shades of orange, which added more mirth to the comparison. Obviously, the nickname 'Mogambo' never escaped my lips, for I was too terrified of being overheard and hardly aspired to be an office wisecrack.

I generally kept my head down, held my breath and tried to turn invisible like Mr India, whenever Kamal Kishore was lurking outside his cabin or striding across the office to holler at someone. I don't think he even noticed me in the first year. I was just a part of the landscape. And even when he came to bark at Ranadive, once in a while, he ignored us lowly minions, except to look us up and down, as if we offended him by merely breathing the same air.

Alas! That changed one afternoon, when I was alone in our department, sipping the 4 p.m. cuppa. It was a Saturday and just ninety minutes were left before everyone would start exiting the office for the weekend. All of a sudden, there was a buzz, a thudding of footsteps and before I knew it, Kamal Kishore flamed into the enclosure like one of those commandos who break into an enemy hideout and start firing around. I, on the other hand, was like one of those poor soldiers whose only job was to get startled and then shot.

'Where's Ranadive?' Kamal Kishore asked, scowling at me.

My reflex action, when he burst in, was to bolt up from my seated position. His question unnerved me further and I reacted by hastily trying to lay down my teacup, which in my agitated state, I only managed to overturn and spill. The puddle of spilled tea quickly formed two or three tributaries, running in different directions, sloping across the table, and soaking the papers and documents that were spread all over.

'Idiot,' Kamal Kishore growled. 'Dimwit! Look at the mess. What's your name?'

I goggled at him, terrified, unsure of my name, horrified that the tea was soaking the documents. What was I to do first? Answer the big man or rescue the documents from the tea?

'Sorry, sir,' I blurted out, taking out my handkerchief and staunching the flow of tea on the table, cursing myself. 'I'm… I'm Gajanan Godbole, sir.'

'Godbole,' he said, smirking. 'What kind of clumsy sons of the soil has the company hired! Where's Ranadive?'

I was already shaking like a leaf. I shook some more. 'I…I really don't know, sir. Ranadive Sir didn't tell me.'

Kamal Kishore bristled and I swear his hair turned redder. 'Go find him for me then, you fool, get him right away!'

I cast a helpless glance at the table, the tea and the soaked documents, then scrambled away as I caught Kamal Kishore's eye again.

I looked hither and thither and yonder – all over the office, in the corridors, in the canteen, at the paan-shop below – every place I could think of. But Ranadive Sir was nowhere to be found.

There were no mobile phones back then or at least hadn't made their way to India, so you couldn't just locate someone by calling them up. It had been fifteen minutes since I had started looking, and I reckoned it was time to return and report to Kamal Kishore that Ranadive Sir was missing.

I baulked at the thought, especially because a sinking feeling grew in me that perhaps Ranadive had already left for the day, as he slyly did sometimes. Bad things happened to people who brought bad news, I knew from films and life; Kamal Kishore was like a ticking time bomb, and I was going to die in the ensuing explosion, for I would be the one setting it off, when I went back to report.

'Sir…' I knocked on his cabin door feeling like one of those luckless simpletons sent by the villagers to be devoured by the presiding demon.

'Come in,' Kamal Kishore ordered peremptorily.

I opened the door and blinked at Mogambo in his lair. His mood seemed fouler than it was fifteen minutes ago.

'You again? Where's Ranadive?'

'I…I don't know, sir. I looked everywhere,' I stuttered.

'What?' He glared at me as if he suspected me of somehow making Ranadive disappear through sorcery. I half expected Kamal Kishore to whip out a revolver at this juncture and shoot me. But instead, his eyes left my face and strayed to the right, over my shoulder.

'Ranadive! Where in the hell were you?' he roared.

I recoiled, only to discover Ranadive Sir had just ambled into the cabin and was standing next to me now. The defining feature of Ranadive Sir was his complete nonchalance and unruffled demeanour.

'Here only, sir,' he replied.

'Don't bluff. This nincompoop assistant of yours said he looked for you everywhere,' Kamal Kishore thundered.

Ranadive Sir kept a straight face and said, 'He forgot to look in the toilet, sir. I was there. You know my problem, sir… irritable bowel…'

'You and your bloody bowel…' Kamal Kishore grumbled. Then he looked at me and said, 'Get out. Go and clean the mess on your table. And I'll skin you alive if I see you having tea at your table again.'

I nodded weakly and staggered out of the cabin a wreck. Thus ended my first bruising encounter with Puri. More devastating ones were to follow!

33

LOLLIPOP

Encounter number two occurred a few months later. The 1987 Cricket World Cup fever consumed us all. An offshoot was the sprouting of inter-office and inter-branch cricket tournaments all over.

While I loved cricket, I had no pretensions about playing it at any level. Yet, I suddenly found myself on the office cricket team. No one was more bewildered than me. I had not volunteered, and why would anyone suggest my inclusion, since I had neither claimed nor displayed any skill at cricket?

When I finally asked my boss, Ranadive Sir, he guffawed. 'They needed four extras, since all teams had to send fifteen-member squads for the tournament.'

'But, sir. I…I neither bat nor bowl well,' I said wretchedly.

'Don't worry, Gajanan. You won't even play. You just have to turn up on match days…'

But Ranadive Sir was wrong. The first two matches were uneventful. I was just a general dogsbody, expected to carry kits and run in with drinks or the batsman's gloves or even the groin guard at times.

Kamal Kishore Puri was by default the captain of our team, but he hadn't been able to make it to the first two matches. At the third match, however, he appeared and by a remarkably odd coincidence, three other teammates skipped the match, all mysteriously indisposed. The real reason, someone told me, was not wanting to play alongside Puri, who, apparently, was no different on the cricket field than at office.

I was at first elated to know that I was still only the twelfth man, safe from Kamal Kishore's wrath, who wasn't pleased to see me at all. 'You are that tea-spiller, right? Ranadive's assistant!' he had rasped.

'Yes…yes, sir…' I confessed, wildly hoping he'd tell me to get out of his sight and go home.

'Hmm…You bat or bowl?'

'He's not in the eleven, sir,' the vice-captain said quickly, without elaborating. He knew I was just a filler.

Kamal Kishore instantly lost interest in me and I breathed easy for a minute.

The game started and Puri lost the toss, so we had to bowl. All I had to do now was not spill water, or whatever it is that I was called upon to take in as the twelfth man.

And then disaster struck. In the twenty-first over of the match, one of our players got injured. Since he was to open our innings, Kamal Kishore promptly dispatched him off the field to apply some ice and nurse the injury. My heart sank when I was asked to field as his substitute. Only four overs and a couple of balls were left, but I was convinced I was going to make a damn fool of myself. My moment of reckoning had arrived. My legs wobbled as I stepped on to the field.

'Hurry up. Run!' I heard Kamal Kishore bark.

I began running in his direction.

'What was your name, again?' he asked tersely, as I came within earshot.

'Gajanan Godbole, sir.'

'Don't you dare mis-field. Go to third man,' Kamal Kishore said.

'Yes, sir,' I replied, even more jittery, and began jogging away in some direction.

'Where the hell are you going, you idiot! Third man, I said,' Kamal Kishore hollered out. It is not that I didn't know where the third man position was – I really did, but I was disoriented as hell. Mercifully for me, a teammate quickly pointed me to the right spot.

Once there, I began praying to all the gods I knew, to keep the ball away from me at all costs. I suddenly hated cricket, for even as I prayed, I was filled with fear that the ball was now going to start chasing me around; every ball was going to be hit in my direction, and I was going to let each and every one of them race to the boundary.

But the whole over passed without any mishap, then two more, and I began to feel a little better. No batsman seemed interested in edging, cutting, or hitting the ball towards the third man. The wicketkeeper too had not let any byes through. So far so good, and I prayed for it to remain so.

Kamal Kishore was now involved in a long discussion with two other teammates, gesticulating here and there. Then suddenly he took the ball, removed his cap, and handed it over to the umpire. The pot-bellied, red-haired marvel had decided to turn his arm over and bowl the penultimate over. God alone knew why, for he had been clobbered all over the ground in the lone over that he had bowled earlier in the innings. Yet, who could stop the captain?

He began shuffling the field again and I found him waving at me. 'Quick, come here to mid-wicket,' his voice boomed.

My mouth ran dry again as I trotted towards him, trying frantically to remember where mid-wicket was. As I passed him, he glowered at me and stabbed his fingers at the exact position he wanted me in. Then he continued instructing and placing other fielders, as if setting up the perfect trap for the batsman.

Once he was done, he strutted to the top of his short run-up, twirling the ball in his hands, and bowled the first delivery. The batsman whacked it away over Puri's own head, all the way for 4 runs. The next 4 balls yielded one 6, one more boundary and two singles.

Again, my fielding skills remained untested, and I thought my prayers were working. Kamal Kishore Puri's over had already cost 16 runs and I could hear low sniggers from some fielders, who were at a safe distance. Puri shuffled the field again, then shouted to no one in particular, 'Watch out for a catch, boys.'

He twirled the ball again as if he were a gifted spinner, about to slip in a gem of a delivery. The next thing I remember was the sound of the bat hitting the ball and the red cherry gently being lofted in my direction. It wasn't travelling fast, and I didn't need to move an inch. All that was required for me to do was to cup my hands and receive the ball as it dropped into my palms.

It was, what was then called a 'lolly', which any half-wit should have caught. But that was not to be for I, Gajanan Godbole, managed to drop the 'lolly'. One moment it was in my hands and the next it had popped out and landed on the ground.

I heard the mother of all howls, and then a torrent of recriminating abuse sprang forth from Kamal Kishore's mouth. As he went hammer and tongs at me, my disgrace was complete and I wished the earth would open up and swallow him preferably, but if not, then me.

'Mother-f*****r, sister-f****r, arsehole, father's cock-s****r, you animal fornicator…' Kamal Kishore breathed fire, as if he were a zamindar of yore and I, some low-caste serf.

I think that's when he turned totally anti-me!

34

MURPHY'S LAW

But my persecution really started after my third encounter with Kamal Kishore Puri. This was in 1988. Ranadive had retired, and no one had been appointed in his place. In fact, the department itself was merged with another. And now, in addition to our normal duties, we were expected to also handle any general admin duties that were delegated to us.

I continued to try and stay below the radar, hastening to duck out of sight when Kamal Kishore was stomping around, biting people's head off. I was mortally terrified of him, as I was of just about anybody big or aggressive or north Indian. And Kamal Kishore happened to be all three!

Moreover, despite our branch office having around 35–40 staff members, somehow, I sensed Kamal Kishore had taken a special dislike to me. Every time he spotted me, his lips would curl up, his scowl would become darker, and he would throw me a look that felt as if he was just awaiting a chance to sack me. Of course, sacking was easier said than done in those days, but he could always make an exception, couldn't he!

One of my colleagues, Mohan, was going on his annual Earned Leave for about a week. He had availed Leave Travel Concession and during his absence, his duties were assigned to me. One of the antiquities of the time, which our office still used in place of photocopying, was a process called cyclostyling for internal and external notices, circulars, or communiques for our staff, as well as commission agents, and dealers of our region.

Mohan's job was to get the draft of the document to be cyclostyled made, take an approval from the concerned department and Kamal Kishore, then have the requisite number of copies cyclostyled. Simple enough. I had seen him get it done. A peon doubled as the cyclostyle operator. There was also a servicing person one could call if there were problems with the cyclostyle machine.

But I guess, Murphy's first law – if anything is to go wrong, it definitely will – seemed to always apply to me when Kamal Kishore came into the picture.

An important notice needed to be circulated to all our agents in the Pune region with regard to change in commission rates for our different schemes. Kamal Kishore Puri had just been promoted and had got himself a brand new secretary, after his earlier one had proceeded on maternity leave. He had nothing to do with that, mind you!

Sapna was easier on the eye and buxomer than the one who had gone on maternity leave, but far sloppier, overbearing and sharp-tongued, as if she embodied Kamal Kishore himself. She also insisted on being called 'Sapna Madam' by the staff.

She handed me the typed version of the notice with the modified rates of commission marked by hand on the existing charts. Then I got the modifications made, formatted the commission charts and notice for cyclostyling, and handed these back to Sapna Madam, for checking and Kamal Kishore's approval, along with the original documents she had given to me.

It was a Friday afternoon and the circulars had to be released and dispatched to agents and dealers by Monday. Therefore, I needed to get the cyclostyling done by Saturday. When Sapna Madam hadn't summoned me even by 5 p.m., I got panicky. I needed the go-ahead since the peon had told me he was needed for some other duties after lunch on Saturday, assigned by the other senior manager of the branch.

'Hello…' I said, when Sapna finally picked up the intercom, 'did you get the cyclostyling approval?'

'I would've called you, no?' Sapna snapped at me high-handedly. 'Don't eat my head.'

'But Sapna Madam, it will get delayed…' I said anxiously.

'You don't understand or what, Godbole? He's busy…' she replied dismissively and cut the call.

I sighed and waited. As always, talking to her had left a bad taste in my mouth. How did Mohan manage to deal with Sapna, I wondered, for she was always playful and smiling with him. One and a half hours later, I was still waiting past office hours. I was getting really tensed, so I called her again.

'Yes? What?' she said.

'Er…the cyclostyling?'

'You come here and take his approval on your own. I am leaving,' she replied.

'But…?'

'What "but"? If you are in such a hurry, you ask him yourself, no? Or wait till tomorrow morning,' Sapna replied in her usual abrasive way.

I had no desire to stand in front of Kamal Kishore Puri and get fired at. Yet, I resented having to listen to his two-bit secretary talk like that. There was not much difference in our staff grades, and she was also a new employee.

'You are his secretary, not I…' I blurted out, 'and urgent approval is required. The cyclostyling peon is only available tomorrow morning, not later.'

In response, she just slammed the phone. I had already started regretting what I had said and waited uneasily for fifteen minutes more. Restless, I got up from my seat and tiptoed across the office to check if Sapna was still at her desk, only to run into a peon.

'Is Puri Saheb still there?' I asked nervously.

He nodded sagely.

'And Sapna Madam?'

'She just left,' he replied laconically.

'What? How long ago?'

'Two minutes.'

I was just about to ask the peon to run down the stairs and stop her when the buzzer outside Kamal Kishore's cabin rang.

'Puri Saheb is calling,' the peon said and instantly set off to attend to the big boss, while I was left standing there, fidgeting with my crotch, wondering whether I should gather my nerve and follow the peon into Kamal Kishore's cabin and remind him directly about the approval for cyclostyling.

But my nerves knew what was good for them, and no amount of crotch-scratching could persuade them. So I decided to go home too. I mean, it wasn't my fault that Kamal Kishore or his secretary hadn't given me the approval so far. Perhaps there were last-minute changes to be made or the circular was to be delayed a little later than its originally scheduled time. Who was I to follow up with the mighty Mogambo?

But the next morning sent me into a fresh tizzy. Even an hour after regular office time began, I still had no word from

Sapna. I had decided to wait for her to get in touch, but there had been complete radio silence from her end.

Just as I was getting increasingly frantic, Kamal Kishore's peon walked up to me. 'Sapna Madam asked me to give these to you,' he said, handing over the papers.

'Where is saheb's approval?' I asked, looking at the papers.

'Sapna Madam called, instructed me to remove these papers from her drawer, and hand them over to you. She says Puri Saheb wants copies by afternoon,' the peon replied.

'Called you? What do you mean? Sapna Madam hasn't come to office!'

'She's taken a casual leave today.'

'What? Then why didn't she give me these papers last evening before leaving?' I asked, agitated.

The peon shrugged. 'No idea, maybe Puri Saheb left them in her drawer late evening and spoke to Sapna Madam this morning.'

But somehow, I was sure Sapna had deliberately delayed sending them to me, out of sheer spite. She was just the kind. She knew she was going to be on leave today and what could have been passed on to me last evening, just before she left office, she had delayed to this morning. So that I would have to sweat quite a bit to get the damn thing cyclostyled and delivered in time or risk the wrath of the boss.

'Did she tell you if Puri Saheb has approved it without corrections?' I asked cagily.

'No, she just said to give it to you. Why don't you ask Puri Saheb directly if you have any doubt,' the peon advised me.

'No…no…' I replied hastily.

The peon gave me a bemused, patronizing smile. 'Come on. Puri Saheb won't eat you. Look at me, I go in there several times a day and come out alive,' he said, then guffawed.

I gave him an annoyed look but snapping at sneering peons was also not my forte. 'Do you have Sapna Madam's home number?'

'No. Sarita Madam, our receptionist will have it,' he said and began walking away, now visibly bored with our conversation.

As I was furiously debating whether to approach the receptionist to try calling Sapna at her residence, the cyclostyle peon, Balu, materialized next to me.

'Godbole Saheb, is the cyclostyling to be done? I told you that I have to go with Wagle Saheb in the afternoon,' Balu said. This Wagle Saheb was an equally senior manager in our branch office, so Kamal Kishore's work could not be prioritized over his. I knew there was no time now.

'Yes, yes. I was just coming. Here, you can take this and start the job – 250 copies,' I said to Balu and handed him the three-page communique that had to be duplicated.

Balu rushed off. Cyclostyling was a fairly messy process – cutting the stencils and then making copies by inking and duplicating. There was always the possibility of smudging or unequal impressions. Unfortunately, since we still had the machine, we had to keep using it. Although photocopying services were available in the market. Then, there was the whole bogey of confidentiality, as if we issued top-secret circulars, instead of fairly routine office stuff. The long and short of it was that in-house cyclostyling was something unavoidable.

Proverbially and literally therefore, the die was now cast for Kamal Kishore to start baying for my blood. For, need I repeat, Murphy's first law kicked in with vengeance! Take a look at what all went wrong. First, there were glaring errors in the circular because the agent commission percentage for one particular scheme, which should have read as 1.75 per cent was printed as 7.15 per cent. A similar mistake in figures was made for one more scheme. If that was not big enough, Kamal Kishore, who had recently been promoted to the post of 'Senior Regional Manager', was incensed to find that the circular still carried his old designation of 'Regional Manager'. This was compounded by the appearance of an extra 'K' in his initials, which read as 'KKK Puri' instead of 'KK Puri'.

'You incompetent fool, you imbecilic son of an unwed mother, I had pointed out these very errors,' he yelled at me, rage-filled, shaking his fist. 'Didn't you see? Are you blind? Should I have sent you corrections in braille?'

If no words came out of my mouth immediately, it was probably because I had swallowed my tongue.

Meanwhile, Kamal Kishore continued railing at me. 'Are you the general manager to turn 1.75 per cent to 7.15 per cent commission? You bloody clerk!' he said, raining some spittle on me in the process as he expostulated. 'And don't you know my designation is "Senior Regional Manager" now? Also, how dare you add an extra K to my initials?'

'I…I…Sir…Sapna…'

'Don't blame someone else for your mistakes, Godbole,' Kamal Kishore continued, foaming at the mouth. 'Were you unaware of my new designation? Are you going to feign ignorance of my initials?'

He had picked the weakest spots in my defence. How could I really not have noticed the designation error on my own? And I simply had no clue how that extra 'K' had slipped in and escaped my eye. It was totally baffling, for it wasn't even there in the cyclostyled format that I had submitted for approval – as if some supernatural phenomena or the office ghost had inserted it.

'Sorry, sir. I am really sorry,' I blurted out, for I was feeling too wretched and beleaguered for having overlooked the two errors.

But Kamal Kishore wasn't the kind of boss to be easily assuaged. 'Sorry is not going to save you this time, you Marathi moron. Do you know how much damage it would have caused, if that faulty circular had been sent out to our agents and dealers? Who would've paid for the fiasco?'

I was not expected to answer of course, but to just stand there, hanging my head in shame, whimpering, till his fury was spent and dressing down complete.

'Don't just stand there now,' Kamal Kishore thundered. 'I want the corrections made and fresh cyclostyled copies ready overnight. Get out, before I chop you into pieces!'

I scrambled out of his cabin with my tail between my legs, relieved I had made it out alive. Little was I to know that my cup of woe was still to overflow. For, it transpired that the cyclostyling machine had gone kaput and the authorized service technician was no longer contactable, for his office had closed for the weekend.

Needless to say, short of tarring me with feathers, Kamal Kishore Puri did everything he could to make me wish I had never been born. Apart from several more public roastings, I was made to run helter-skelter all over town all of Sunday, to locate the elusive technician. Since Mohan too wasn't reachable, and nobody else knew where the technician lived, I was ordered to search high and low and find some other technician to get the machine repaired pronto.

When Balu and I did manage to get hold of a seedy-looking cyclostyle machine mechanic, not only was he unable to identify the problem but also managed to break a part, as a bonus. More opprobrium followed, with Kamal Kishore now accusing me of sabotage. He would probably have had me shot at sunrise, if that had been within his powers.

The suggestion for having photocopies made of the circular, was met with the rhetorical question: 'Is company money your father's property, Godbole? Or are you going to pay for it from your own pocket?' Kamal Kishore was enraged. His eyes were bulging from their sockets, and I was sure any moment beams would shoot out of them and incinerate me on the spot.

'Sorry, sir,' I said for the thousandth time, I think.

'Then, shut up!' he bellowed.

Monday morning brought more grief when the authorized technician finally responded and took a look at the cyclostyle machine. He declared major repairs were required since the seedy guy had broken an important part. If the spare part was available in the Pune warehouse, he'd get it done by the evening, but if it was to be ordered from Bombay (as Mumbai was known then), it would take up to two days.

I groaned and faced another barrage of invectives from Kamal Kishore. But Mohan was now back from his leave, and so things finally got done a day or two later. However, Puri was not done yet. I was issued a scathing memo and for a week my fate hung in balance. It was touch and go. Zonal Office probably didn't think termination or suspension of my service was to be recommended.

Nevertheless, that only meant I now firmly occupied the position of Kamal Kishore's favourite whipping boy henceforth for all time to come.

35

SON OF THE SOIL

Mogambo spared no opportunity to get after me for the slightest of reasons. Every little day-to-day matter was blown way out of proportion and got me a fresh blasting, every few days. I swear bosses could be blatant jerks in those days, if they wished to, for offices hadn't yet acquired the veneer of corporate sophistication.

It was as if Kamal Kishore had taken an intense dislike to me and was determined to make a scapegoat of me, or make life so difficult that I would eventually quit on my own. Six months passed, then a year, but he simply wouldn't ease off.

With Sumitra at home and Kamal Kishore in office, my life became one long tale of harangue. And one day, I just burst into tears, right at my desk, in the middle of my department, with most of my colleagues around. I had just been subject to another petty, snarky remark, this time from Sapna, on behalf of her boss, over the intercom.

There was a stunned, awkward silence as everyone around watched me sob and sniff. Nobody spoke a word for a few minutes even as I was acutely aware of how I had embarrassed myself again. Then my erstwhile boss, Srinivasan Sir, came up to me and asked perfunctorily, 'Are you okay, Godbole? What happened? Some bad news?'

I just shook my head, desperately trying to stop sobbing more.

'Some family problem?' my boss asked again.

'No, sir…' I replied wretchedly.

He stood for a few minutes, unsure of what to do next. Then he said to no one in particular, 'Fetch a glass of water and a cup of tea for Godbole.'

A glass of water was promptly placed on my table by someone. Srinivasan Sir, who thought he had done all he could, then said, 'You can take the rest of the day off if you want, Godbole.'

I am sure he knew what was going on, for there was a hint of kindness in his tone, but there was nothing he really could do to protect me from Kamal Kishore's petty wrath. Times were different then, as I said.

'No, no, sir. I am okay now. Thank you,' I said.

The tea arrived. 'Here, have some chai, you'll feel better! You drink too little tea. It's the key to survive in office,' he joked, then patted me on the back and walked away.

I looked at the cup of tea. If Kamal Kishore happened to walk in just then and saw it on my table…I quickly shifted it to the windowsill, by my side. One by one, colleagues began coming up to me, exchanging a word, or making a gesture to express sympathy and cheer me up. I was petrified that word would get around the office soon that Godbole had broken down, for someone was bound to gossip.

That evening, when I left office, Mohan was waiting for me at a tea stall nearby. He waved at me to join him. I really was in no mood, but didn't want to be rude, because he was one of the few colleagues who didn't pick on me.

'Look, I know what's going on,' he said without beating around the bush. 'If you want the harassment to stop, the only way is to write to the Zonal Office with a complaint against him.'

'What? Lodge an official complaint? Are you crazy, Mohan? Who…who complains against a senior RM? Why would Zonal Office listen? Instead, I'll be sacked,' I said, shaken even by the very idea.

'Not if you play it right,' Mohan said, lighting a cigarette.

'I…I don't understand.'

He blew out smoke. 'Allege discrimination and that he regularly chides and harasses you – taunts you with anti-Marathi abuse! He does it often enough, doesn't he…?'

I nodded slowly. 'But…how can I? I mean no one would take cognizance at Zonal Office.'

'Of course they will have to take serious cognizance, Gajanan. Here in Pune, the heart of Maharashtra, how can they ignore a complaint of this nature?' Mohan said. 'A north Indian boss has no business targeting a Marathi subordinate in this manner. Not just that, he uses profanities openly and humiliates you continuously, correct?'

'Yes…he does…' I replied, a lump rising in my throat again.

'Your increments have been blocked, right? You were also due for change of grade this year, no? I hear that too has been stopped?' Mohan observed, pulling on his cigarette.

I nodded, almost near tears again.

'Well, then, unless you do something about it, he won't rest till he has you dismissed or terminated,' Mohan warned me direly.

A chill ran through me as I heard Mohan's words. I was shit scared of losing my job, and I was shit scared of also turning up at my job every morning. I had to do something to protect myself or perish. And that's how timid little me, ended up writing to the Zonal Office against Kamal Kishore Puri, alleging discrimination and harassment for being a Marathi native. I also sent a copy to the Head Office.

~

My very own David vs Goliath story unfortunately did not end up felling Goliath Puri, nor did underdog David Godbole emerge even mildly victorious.

No doubt Kamal Kishore got the initial sock in the jaw, when Zonal Office notified him about my complaint, for he had never expected a worm like me to turn and put on boxing gloves. But then faced with the disgrace of having to defend himself against allegations made by a lowly clerk like myself, Puri did what all unscrupulous higher-ups do.

He breathed fire and pulled two rabbits out of his hat – fictitious complaints made by two local 'Marathi' vendors against me, claiming that I had sought bribes from them. In his version of events, he had upbraided me a few times, only because of verbal bribery complaints that he had received and other disciplinary issues, including misbehaviour with his secretary, Sapna. Not to mention the previously issued memo for gross incompetence during the cyclostyling episode. And that I was vengefully getting back at him through these motivated and baseless allegations of being anti-Marathi and harassment. He dared me to produce a single witness who would buttress my claims against him.

And therein lay the nub. For when Zonal Office asked me to produce witnesses, I obviously couldn't, for who would risk crossing paths with a senior official like Puri, in support of an inconsequential colleague? Not even Mohan, who had put me up to it in the first place. I suddenly realized how big a hole I had dug for myself. What was I to do now? Why had I not thought this through? Why had I picked up a skirmish? I had neither the weapons nor the heart to fight.

Just as I was wallowing in despair, for I dared not even tell Sumitra about it, a most unexpected guest turned up at my house on a Sunday. I had just returned after dropping Sumitra and my four-year-old daughter, Trupti, at my in-laws' place, when I found my old retired boss, Ranadive Sir, sitting nonchalantly on his parked scooter, below the tenement building I lived in.

'Ah, there you are, Gajanan!' Ranadive Sir said, skilfully unloading the tobacco plug from his mouth to the ground.

'Ranadive Sir…How come?' I said, taken aback.

'What kerfuffle have you got yourself into, Gajanan,' Ranadive Sir said. 'Do you have a nut loose?'

It took a few minutes for it to dawn on me what he was talking about. 'You mean, sir, that you know?'

'Yes, of course I know what's happening in office even if I am retired,' he replied matter-of-factly. 'I have been requested to drive some sense into you.'

'But, sir, what could I do? Puri has made my life hell,' I said helplessly. 'I thought…I thought…'

'…that a complaint against Puri would work,' Ranadive Sir completed the sentence for me. 'What a naïve fellow you are. That's not how the cookie crumbles. Anyway, what's done is done. Now, what are you going to do if no one's backing you up?'

My shoulders were slumped, and I was sure I would begin sobbing any time. 'I don't know, sir. I really don't…'

'Alright, take my advice then! Withdraw the complaint against Puri.'

'What? But…but, sir…How can I do that? I'll be accused of cooking up a false complaint and action might be taken against me. I could be terminated,' I wailed.

Ranadive Sir chewed on his tobacco, while regarding me thoughtfully. 'Listen to me, Gajanan. You withdraw your allegation against Puri. He will withdraw the bribery allegations against you. Time to call a truce and end the matter.'

I stared at him, then blinked. 'But my allegations against Puri are true. His bribery allegations are utterly false,' I protested.

'You chump, he can produce witnesses, by hook or crook – those vendors. You can't, can you?' Ranadive Sir said, clicking his tongue impatiently. 'Understand your position. He holds the aces.'

'But what if I withdraw and he doesn't?'

'He will! He will! Trust me. It's my assurance. That's why I have come here to offer you a way out,' Ranadive Sir said sagely.

'You mean to say Puri Sir sent you?'

He nodded benignly. Chewing his tobacco, looking as unruffled as ever. I looked disbelievingly, but then why would Ranadive Sir be lying? He had long retired.

'What if the office decides to take disciplinary action against me for…for…all that has happened?' I said, ready to clutch at straws, but still scared.

'Nothing will happen, Gajanan! I am telling you, no? Everyone wants the matter settled,' Ranadive Sir replied. 'I'm the discreet, unofficial peacemaker.'

What choice had I but to trust him and accept the proposition? I had been so stressed out and fearful in the last few weeks, living in dread of losing my job. I had lost weight, a bunch of hair, my appetite and my sleep. I suppose I could have asked for my increment and grade change to be unblocked as part of the deal, but did not possess the presence of mind to do so.

On Monday, I wrote to Zonal Office and withdrew my complaint against Puri, just as Ranadive Sir had advised me to. In fact, he had also dictated to me the exact wording to be used before he had left the previous day. As promised, two days later, Kamal Kishore wrote to withdraw the counter charges against me. I heaved a sigh of relief but I should have known that Puri would have the last laugh and make me pay, despite what Ranadive Sir had assured.

This sting in the tail came in the form of my transfer orders two months later to a small town, Ichalkaranji, near Kolhapur. Kamal Kishore had taken his revenge by banishing me from Pune to what could be best described as a punishment posting.

I could see that gloating, vicious gleam in his eyes, when he passed me in office one day! The bastard!

36

BAFFLEMENT

The same obnoxious man was now clasping my hand like an old comrade, and beaming at me now, over three decades later. 'I…I wasn't sure it was you, Gajanan, the way you were ticking off those guys,' Kamal Kishore said with a meditative smile. 'You certainly have changed.'

Did I imagine a hint of wariness in those words under his smile? I responded with a phony, hearty chuckle that people like to display at such times. 'You were my inspiration, sir, so I decided to become like you.'

'Splendid! Splendid! You flatter me, Gajanan,' he cackled back at me, perhaps mistaking it for a real compliment.

'But I still remain Marathi, sir…that hasn't changed,' I remarked sardonically, looking him straight in the eye.

'Of course, of course!' Kamal Kishore now definitely looked embarrassed and licked his cracked lips.

'Some health problems? Is that why you are here for the course?' I queried, moving the conversation along, thrilled that fate had dropped him right into my spiderweb like that.

Kamal Kishore's face clouded. 'I underwent two angioplasties in the last eighteen months and have been recuperating. The cardiologist recommended this naturopathy course, so I said, "Let's try it."'

'Oh, I see...' I said, glad at what had inevitably befallen him. It was fascinating to observe that his hennaed hair had all but disappeared, leaving him over three-fourths bald. Whatever foliage remained – some of it was maroon brown and some of it was white.

'And you? Any ailments that you have come to treat?' he asked me hopefully, since I had not volunteered any information.

'Oh, I nearly died during the second wave of COVID, almost a year ago,' I replied. 'Took a heavy toll on me. That's why I am here.'

'Ah,' he said wistfully, as if he would have liked it better if I suffered from some heart disease, or cancer, or at the very least, diabetes. 'And, how's, er...your family?'

'Well, although I survived, my wife, Sumitra, died,' I replied, going back to playing the grieving widower.

'What? Sumitra...er...your wife's dead? My God!'

He looked truly and utterly shocked and seemed at a loss of words for a few seconds, then said, 'So sorry to hear this... my...my condolences, Gajanan! Sad!'

'Thank you, KK Sir,' I said. 'I hope your wife's hale and hearty?' That came out wrong, even though I hadn't meant it to sound sarcastic.

He nodded almost glumly, 'She's okay.' I swear I sensed a note of lament.

'And children, all well settled?' I asked.

'Yes, yes,' he said, brightening up a little. 'My son is abroad, in Australia, and my daughter is married to a well-to-do businessman in Chandigarh. You...you also had a daughter, right? Triveni...I think, her name was...'

'Trupti, sir…not Triveni,' I replied, yet I was surprised he'd almost got the name right. 'She's in Silicon Valley, sir, married to a top IT guy.' It grieved me to refer to Swanand as a top IT guy, but hey, what the hell – KK Puri did not need to know that he wasn't.

'Oh good! Good!'

A silence fell between us. As it often does when acquaintances meeting after a long time run out of things to say, after exchanging pleasantries and basic information.

'Well, sir…let me check out the news now,' I said. 'Looking forward to many chats and catching up with you in the next few days.'

'Sure, sure,' Kamal Kishore replied. 'I am so glad to have run into you here, Gajanan.'

We shook hands again, and I walked back to the TV area. I was elated that I had some time before confronting him in style, about all the ugly things he'd done to me, and demand an apology from him. I was excited to speculate on just how Kamal Kishore would react. He was no longer the Kamal Kishore of old. Life seemed to have reduced him to a mellow septuagenarian. So, would he squirm or turn belligerent or hum and haw? Express some token regret perhaps to avoid hostilities, now that he had had his angioplasties? I licked my lips in anticipation. It was going to be fun.

'Gentlemen,' I announced in an authoritarian voice to the serial watchers seated in front of the TV still, 'I am now turning on the news!'

People again gave me dirty looks, but no one protested as I changed channels. Some of them started to leave, now that I had got hold of the remote. Others stayed, probably ready to watch even the news, because they had nothing else to do and weren't sleepy yet. Overall, I loved the effect of my new personality on everyone.

I watched one news channel for about ten minutes, then another, then surfed other news channels too. While all carried news of Nandu's death, nowhere did I see any 'breaking news' or ticker mentioning that Geeta's body had been found. So, was she still lying there exactly as I had left her in the morning – a stiff corpse that still hadn't been discovered? Unbelievable and strange, but that's what seemed to be the only conclusion.

The image came back to my mind – my last glimpse of Geeta – her tongue sticking out; eyes bulging, the size of giant marbles; an expression of utter terror on her face; her legs splayed; her fingers still trying to pull at the rope around her throat; the nails bloodied by scratching desperately at her own skin. And yes, I remembered how exhilarating and awesome it had felt – my heart pumping like an oversized piston, the blood coursing through my veins as dopamine and adrenalin, and all kinds of happy chemicals, splashed about through my body, while I held Geeta down.

Oh please! I needed that sensation again so desperately. Would I get a chance to kill Kamal Kishore here? That would be so gratifying, so bloody blissful!

~

I had decided I would confront Kamal Kishore on the fourth or fifth day of the course, once we had 'bonded' a few more times. Once he had let his guard down, thinking I bore no grudge against him, I would take him by surprise and remind him that I hadn't forgotten his skulduggery.

But lo and behold! On the third evening, it was Kamal Kishore who bowled me a googly instead. 'Yaar, Gajanan, something has been weighing on my mind…' he said hesitantly, as we were walking back to our rooms, after dinner.

'It's...It's time I apologized to you for...for the way I treated... rather mistreated you all those years ago...'

I almost did a double take and stared aghast. What had I just heard? Kamal Kishore Puri offering me a voluntary apology even before I had demanded it? The devil quoting scriptures! Was I hallucinating or was this happening for real?

Kamal Kishore was looking at me anxiously. 'Look, Gajanan. I...I know my apology probably comes too late and hardly makes a real difference anymore. But believe me, it's heartfelt. I know how awful it was of me! I was spiteful, arrogant, drunk on my own ego and absolutely unfair. I am so ashamed that I literally harassed you, tried to fix you with false charges after you lodged a complaint, and then got you transferred to a godforsaken place far away from Pune and your er...family.'

I gasped with disbelief. Had Kamal Kishore's personality also undergone a drastic change after the angioplasties, as mine had after COVID? What else could explain such harsh self-indictment?

'Your conduct was horrible! Unforgivable!' I replied, in bewilderment rather than with vehemence.

Kamal Kishore flinched. 'Correct...Absolutely correct! My behaviour was unforgivable. That's why I wish to beg your forgiveness, Gajanan,' the man said, almost ready to weep. 'You know, for the last few years I have been a disciple of Vishwaguru Jaggu Sukhdev.'

'That fellow who murdered his wife?' I interjected.

Kamal Kishore looked pained. 'No no, that is calumny heaped by rivals on Vishwaguru Sukhdev. He's a great spiritual master and his teachings have finally brought me peace. After my angioplasties, he told me I need to seek forgiveness from all those I harmed or hurt with my ego, my temper and thoughtless arrogance. And so, my friend, my younger brother

Gajanan, I admit I caused you great distress, but please, please forgive me.'

Stunned though I was at this unexpected twist, I must admit, the man wasn't faking it. Kamal Kishore was being a 100 per cent sincere. There was genuine anguish in his demeanour and tone.

I had got what I wanted even without asking, and yet it felt as if he'd cheated me and stolen my thunder. This is not how it was supposed to play out. I was supposed to confront him – with him feeling affronted, then squirming, resisting, denying, and finally, grudgingly admitting to his chicanery. Even better would have been for him to refuse to apologize, so that I could take my grudge to the next level!

Kamal Kishore had taken all the fun out of the revenge I was entitled to and had looked forward to righteously enjoying. I found myself resenting it. And the worst part was that now that he had profusely apologized, I was obliged not to let my grudge fester further! I mean, what more could I ask of this old man? A public apology, as I had asked Nandu for, or a grovelling video apology, as I had made Sundar provide with the potential for embarrassment if I chose to post it on social media?

Well, Kamal Kishore hadn't turned out to be a cad like the other two, refusing to own up, so it didn't quite make sense. Yet, letting him off the hook just like that seemed too soft on him. After all, he had damaged me quite heinously at one time. Actually, Kamal Kishore really deserved to be murdered, not let off with a mere apology!

'Gajanan,' Kamal Kishore spoke again. 'Say something. Don't be quiet.'

'Well.' I shrugged with annoyance. 'Forgiving is not easy, KK Sir. After the kind of things you did to me…'

'I know…I understand that, Gajanan. I am genuinely sorry. Look, if there is anything else I can do to make it up to you, to somehow make amends, please let me know. I'll do whatever is possible – any gesture you want me to make, any favour, any little thing, within my power.'

'Okay, let me think about it,' I replied tersely, itching to ask him if he would be ready to cooperate in his own murder if I so requested.

'Meanwhile, once again, I am so sorry,' he repeated ingratiatingly.

We shook hands, said our 'goodnights' and parted ways to go to our respective rooms. I had scored a major victory over a man who had once wronged me, and I should have been happy, but I clearly wasn't! I felt the exact opposite of that. It was all very curious – his apology and my foul mood.

Could it be that only murder made me happy? Murder and sex? I was startled at this insight about the reborn Gajanan Godbole. Hmm…what a profound journey of self-discovery life was! I sighed to myself.

Sex had got me thinking of sweet Madhuri! I dialled her number, but the call went unanswered yet again. She hadn't picked up any of my calls for the last three days. I missed her, man!

37

TROUBLES COME CALLING

The shrill rings of my mobile phone woke me up, about half an hour later, just as I was nodding off. I grabbed the phone, expecting it to be Madhuri returning my call, having made peace with the possibility that she was enamoured by a murderer.

'Papa,' Trupti's voice assaulted my sleepy eardrums. 'How is the yoga camp going?'

I groaned inwardly and guessed that she must've learnt from Ravi that I was attending this health course. 'Naturopathy, not just yoga,' I replied. It was 11.30 p.m., but it probably didn't cross my daughter's self-absorbed mind, I could have been asleep here in India.

'What?'

'Naturopathy,' I repeated.

'Okay,' Trupti said, uninterested in facts. 'Any way, listen, Papa, we are coming to India the week after next.'

I groaned inwardly a second time. 'All three of you?'

'Only Swanand and me. Not Vihan,' she replied. 'I know you haven't seen him for a long time, but he can't come.' If she was trying to console me for my grandson's absence from their forthcoming trip, then it was unnecessary, for I was actually relieved.

Trupti and Swanand were bad enough to deal with, but my grandson, Vihan, was the kind of twerp who should have been smothered in his crib. Absolute gargoyle – let's leave it at that – having outgrown any cuteness as a teenager that might have once existed in him as a child.

'Okay,' I said. 'Will you be staying…er…with me or at your in-laws' place?'

'Papa, you know I cannot do without an air-conditioner in India,' Trupti whined. 'Then how can I stay with you? But don't worry, I am going to spend lots and lots of time with you. I have to sort out Mum's things too, don't I?'

'Yes, okay,' I replied without much enthusiasm.

I had rather hoped to woo Madhuri assiduously, as soon as I got back to Pune, after the course. Who knew how much time that would need. So, having Trupti parked in my apartment and monopolizing my time was not going to help.

I decided to wind her up a bit in return for putting a spanner in my works and disturbing my sleep. 'Trupti, I was wondering if…if I can accompany you back to the United States…' I said.

There followed a few seconds of telling silence. I could visualize Trupti getting irked and trying to think of a way to fob me off. 'You…you mean you want to come and stay with us for some time?' she asked finally.

'Yes…yes! Your mother's demise and my own illness have taken a heavy toll on me, you know? And I am also feeling very lonely, dear. I could really do with a change,' I said in my most poor, old father voice.

Trupti promptly began humming and hawing. 'I…I will have to check with Swanand, Papa. He's very busy these days and…and so is Vihan…with high school. Don't know how convenient it would be. Let me see. Also, I hear it's very difficult to get a visa appointment. There's a very long waiting time.'

'But our multiple entry visas were already done, Trupti, remember…mine and Sumitra's? Our trip got cancelled last time, but we had already got our visas. So that won't be a problem,' I pointed out.

A few years ago, Sumitra had wished that we visit our daughter, since we had never been there. Trupti had reluctantly acceded. And we both had gone through the long process of getting our US visas done, only for Trupti to call and ask us to postpone our visit by a few months, which eventually got cancelled because the pandemic struck.

'Okay, Papa! Let me talk to Swanand, because he was saying his parents might be planning to visit too,' Trupti said, buying time to think of better excuses.

I knew my daughter only too well, and so I thoroughly enjoyed her discomfiture. But that wasn't all. There was another reason why I had played this card. Shrewd, cunning me!

'Okay, Papa, see you in a few days. Take care,' Trupti signed off with the most bogus phrase ever invented and spoken by humankind.

I switched off the phone and knew sleep would take time to take over again. I wished the entertainment room had been open, but they usually closed it at 10 p.m. sharp. I wouldn't have minded watching some TV or playing a game of carrom by myself, for I felt restless.

Geeta's body had been found the very next day and the police had made just a bland statement to the media that investigations were on. I had been closely following the news every day. And in the last two days, there was no report of any connection having been established between Nandu and Geeta's murders. Except for one more statement from the police that leads were being pursued and breakthroughs could be expected soon, news channels had mainly focused on snippets about the victims. Additionally, random interviews of city folk talking about how Pune was becoming unsafe and crime prone, were telecast. But that was all.

As of now, nothing pointed even remotely in my direction. I ran through the murders in my mind again – in slow motion, admiring the way I had planned and executed them. Indeed, I, Gajanan Godbole, had done something to be really proud of. Not only did I have a flair for murder, but a certain finesse. Hmmm…the restlessness began ebbing away and ecstasy began flooding in as I relived those thrilling moments in my mind, when Nandu Khandagale and Geeta Hirway kicked the bucket.

Sleep stole over. All I needed now was a wet, wet dream to wake up next morning feeling wonderful again; and most importantly, to plan my next move. You remember that Pepsi advertisement slogan of the late nineties – *ye dil maange more* – something like that is how I felt!

~

The naturopathy course routine started getting on my nerves – all that yoga, meditation, Ayurvedic concoctions and cures, health food, spirituality lectures, every bit of it. Even worse was the company of the other oldies – boring washed-out folk, one and all – who could talk hours on end about their ailments, aches and afflictions.

Kamal Kishore seemed to get along with most of them. I had spent time brooding over his apology and whether I could do something milder to him than murder, like causing him to fall and break a hand or leg – some punishment in lieu of murder, which might quench my need for violent reprisal – than just letting him go scot-free.

But on the whole, I reckoned it would be wiser not to make haste, rather to wait and maybe take him up on his word later, in case I needed a favour. So, even though I had a great itch, I decided not to scratch it. Instead, I found out a little more about him, his family, his investments, and property, where exactly he lived in Pune, his daily routine and so on. Kamal Kishore was willing to talk, as if we were great buddies now.

However, overall, my patience with the naturopathy course was running out and I toyed with the idea of returning to Pune early, by skipping the last two days. My purpose had been served. I had gained a kind of solid alibi – I had been at the course from the day of the Nandu and Geeta murders. Not many murderers in the history of homicide could've fled to a naturopathy course after killing their victims. I was sure the police would consider giving me the benefit of doubt, if at all my name cropped up during the investigations, based on this innocent oddity alone.

Just when I had decided to skip the last two days, my phone rang. It was an unknown number.

'Hello,' I said, taking the call.

'Are you Mr Gajanan Godbole?' a dry, wry voice asked me from the other end.

'Yes. Who's calling?'

'Mr Godbole, I am Inspector Wakde from the Pune Crime Branch, and I need you to come to my office at Range Hills Road,' the man said.

My heartbeat quickened. So, did this mean the chase was on? Had I left a clue behind? Was there a witness? Had some connection been made, that I had not taken into account? Or had Sundar or Madhuri tipped off the police?

'But I am not in Pune, Wakde Saheb,' I replied, my voice icy calm.

'Oh, I see! Where are you then?' the officer asked.

'I am here, in Karjat, at the Spiritual Santulan and Ayurveda Village for a naturopathy course. It'll get over two days from now. Then I can come and meet you. But, what is this regarding?' I asked.

'Since when are you at Karjat?' Inspector Wakde asked. There was a subtle change in his tone already.

'Let me see. I have been here for the last seven to eight days. One loses count of time at my age,' I said with a kind of apologetic jollity in my voice, like senior citizens do.

'Okay. Did you know Mr Nandu Khandagale?' Inspector Wakde asked.

'Yes, I know him a little. We were in school together,' I replied, trying to sound casual. 'Poor fellow got implicated in that turtle smuggling case recently. Why do you ask?'

'Are you aware that he is no more?'

'What?' I said, expressing shock. 'No, I don't. What happened to him?'

'You don't know that Mr Nandu Khandagale was murdered? Don't you watch the news, Mr Godbole?' Inspector Wakde asked sharply.

'My God! No! During the course we have very little access to the TV or internet. In fact, there is only one common TV where people mostly go to watch serials, so I…I didn't know at all. This is shocking,' I said, patting myself on the back once again for this brilliant naturopathy course brainwave I had thought of.

'I see,' Inspector Wakde said. 'Anyway, the moment you come back to Pune, give me a call. I'd like to ask you a few questions, based on the information we have…'

'But…but…what could I possibly know about his murder, Inspector. I didn't know Nandu well. I'd like to help you so you can ask me questions right away.'

'No, let's talk when you come here,' Inspector Wakde said and hung up.

That could only mean that I was not one of the main suspects, or perhaps not even a suspect at all. Otherwise, Inspector Wakde wouldn't have been so laid back, and I would have been summoned back to Pune at once.

Interesting times lay ahead.

38

ALIBI

Three days later, I was seated across the desk from the officer, at the Pune Crime Branch. Inspector Wakde seemed more brawn than brain, but appearances could be deceptive.

He eyed me without much interest, as I tried to look as shrunk and shrivelled and senior citizen-ish as possible. He had probably checked with the management at Spiritual Santulan and Ayurveda Village about my attendance at the course – the date and possibly the exact time that I had reached at.

'Mr Godbole, we understand you bore ill-feeling towards Mr Nandu Khandagale. Is that true?' Inspector Wakde asked.

'Good God! Who…who told you this? Some member of his family?' I asked, looking upset and distressed.

'Never mind that, just answer the question.'

'Preposterous! I…I didn't even know Nandu that well. We had been classmates some fifty-five years ago. I wasn't his friend or regular acquaintance. Why should someone allege such things?'

'Exactly! Why would someone specifically point in your direction?' Inspector Wakde asked.

I shrugged and trembled a little. 'I am shocked. I am shocked! Maybe someone played a prank on you by dragging in my name.'

Inspector Wakde grunted. 'When was the last time you met Mr Khandagale, and did you get into some quarrel with him?'

I wondered if the cops knew about the meeting. If Sundar or Madhuri had given the police an anonymous tip and the police had checked with Khandagale's wife and watchman whether I had visited him, then perhaps they might've recollected and told the police about my argument with him.

I decided to stay close to the truth. 'Look, I had met him about eight months ago for a favour, because he was an ex-corporator. But Nandu refused to help! I was naturally disappointed and may have said a few unkind words in anger…But that's it,' I replied vaguely, then turned my voice shrill and agitated. 'On the basis of that are…are you accusing me of his murder? With due respect, Inspector, are you out of you mind?'

'Mr Godbole, calm down,' Inspector Wakde started.

'Calm down? No, you tell me first, are you accusing an old man like me of murder?' I said, raising my pitch melodramatically. 'A woman murdered him, right, according to news reports? Do…do…I look like a woman to you? Or someone who'll cross-dress like a woman to poison a man? Isn't it ridiculous?'

'Mr Godbole, please don't get so excited, I have not accused you of murder. It is our job to investigate various tips and information we receive, so don't jump to conclusions…'

'But what is the meaning of calling me for questioning then, Inspector? I am almost seventy. Do I look like someone who will want to murder another old man just because he refused to help me with something?' I said, continuing my tirade.

Inspector Wakde was now looking rather uncomfortable and fed up. 'Just tell me what favour you had asked Mr Nandu Khandagale for, which he refused to help with?'

'I...I just requested him to give me a letter. You see, my wife, Sumitra, died during the COVID second wave. She... she was cremated directly, as was the norm in force at that time, you remember?' I said, turning sad and emotional. 'I...I think there was considerable medical negligence behind my beloved wife's death.'

I stopped and sniffed as if overcome by tears. Inspector Wakde's discomfiture had increased and was clearly visible on his face. 'Do you want some water, Mr Godbole?'

I shook my head and continued. 'So...so I sought out, and requested Nandu to give me a letter, supporting my claim of negligence by the authorities and, therefore, an enhanced compensation for her death, because he was an ex-corporator and politically well connected. But he flatly refused. It... it really hurt me, and I admit I shouldn't have said things in anger.' I paused again, took out the handkerchief from my trouser pocket and blew my nose. 'You really think I would murder him for that...Wakde Saheb?'

'No...no, Mr Godbole, please compose yourself. I understand. Thank you for clarifying all this. You are free to go now,' Inspector Wakde said. 'I am sorry, but we have to follow all leads...'

Fifteen minutes later, after treating me to a samosa and tea, and helping me book a cab, Inspector Wakde had escorted me out.

What can I say, I had thoroughly enjoyed my experience as a murder suspect running rings around a policeman. Boy, this part of killing was fun too! But now, I needed to take some rearguard action, and find out how the police got wind of me.

What had led them to me? Who had squealed to them? My bet was on Sundar, but it could have been Madhuri too.

I had to ascertain for myself by meeting them, as I was sure they would give themselves away in a tête-à-tête. Sundar was anyway on my hit list, and my brain was already busy trying to draw up half a dozen, foolproof assassination plans for him.

Madhuri had steadfastly refrained from taking my calls. I had suddenly realized that I had no idea at all about where she lived. I had visited her workplace, but I was told she was on leave. Someone said they had heard that she had applied for a transfer out of Pune, although no one knew where or if the application had been accepted and processed. Anyway, who exactly was I to make these inquiries? So perhaps, it was time to shake it out of Sundar Nambiar now – the whereabouts of my beloved Madhuri. Trupti was going to be here soon, and then my movements were bound to be cramped by the presence of my daughter for several days.

Come on, I bloody well needed a chance to convince Madhuri with some smooth lies or half-truths, win my lady-lust back and, you know, have at least a couple of rolls in the hay. It was over a fortnight since we had last copulated, and I was horny as hell for her. Who knew if I'd be able to have her over at my apartment again, once Trupti was in town. To go another fortnight without some below the belt action, was expecting too much from the new me! Especially since I was planning to fly off to the US for a few months thereafter.

So, off I went to confront Sundar Nambiar, right at his doorstep. I clanged the doorbell and scurried around the corner to the stairs leading up to the landing, where I couldn't be seen through the eyehole, for if he saw me, perhaps he wouldn't open the door. It worked, as Sundar's puzzled face peeped out soon to check who had rung the bell.

'Hello, Sundar, old friend. It's swell to see you, buddy,' I said, springing out of my hiding place and greeting him with a wide grin.

He didn't reciprocate my warmth. In fact, he appeared to slip into thermal shock, as if he'd just taken the ice-bucket challenge belatedly. His thick lips first protruded, then retreated, and then opened. 'Godbole?' he said hoarsely. 'Why are you here?'

It was so good to see the fear in his eyes. I almost felt like the capo of a dreaded mafia. 'To shoot the breeze with you, my friend,' I replied. As you might've noticed, I was attempting to practice Americanisms – 'swell', 'buddy', 'shooting the breeze' – for I had booked my ticket to the US, you know.

'Why don't you leave me alone now? I did what you wanted,' Sundar pleaded, refusing to be infected by my jolly banter.

'Ah! But you aren't minding your business, are you, Sundar?' I admonished him lightly.

His bulbous eyes glanced away, wary of meeting mine. 'I don't know what you are talking about.'

'Come, we need to have a little chat, Sundar – inside your house or downstairs in your society's sorry patch of lawn. Your choice.'

He went pale. 'I…I need to put on something.'

'No, no, you look sensationally handsome in your lungi and t-shirt,' I said, steering him away.

He called out to his wife nervously, saying he was going down for a few minutes, then stared at me as if I was going to murder him in the lift. His next words confirmed that I was indeed a mind reader.

'Let's take the stairs.'

I let out a bemused chuckle. 'Okay, Sundar, no problem. Now tell me, I hear you are trying to poison my girlfriend's ears against me. Is that true?'

He froze, then unfroze in an instant and broke into a sweat. 'Not true…not true…! What poison? Whose ears?'

'Poisoning my lovely Madhuri's ears, that I poisoned Nandu.' I grinned, and put my hand around his shoulders as we climbed down.

'What…what…what…what?' he stuttered, trying to keep his panic in control and shrugging my hand away, as if I was a python about to coil around him. 'There is some misunderstanding…I…I have not even talked to Madhuri. Why should I say anything like that, Godbole?'

'But that's what she told me,' I said, as we reached the ground floor, and moved towards the sorry excuse of a lawn.

'That's totally false, she's making up tales…Believe me, Godbole,' Sundar said anxiously, his blood pressure probably soaring and coming dangerously close to triggering a stroke.

I didn't want him to suffer one right now. He was supposed to die a violent death at my hands. I frowned. 'I see. Do you know her whereabouts? Are you in touch with her?'

'Not at all, Godbole. I have no idea, I swear. She must be in Pune only, I guess. Why don't you check at her office?'

'I already have. Do you know where Madhuri stays?' I asked, my scowl deepening.

'No…no I don't have her home address. I promise!' Sundar said quickly.

'You are not lying, are you, Sundar?'

'No…no…no…no…'

He was so jittery and jumpy that he would probably have gone on repeating 'No' as if it was some magic syllable to escape my wrath.

'Hmm,' I said, putting my hands on my hips and looking at my companion, who stood quivering in his lungi. I wondered whether he was lying through his teeth, which I bet were chattering too. Then I pondered whether it would be a good idea to make him call up Madhuri, snatch the phone if she answered and talk to her. No point, I finally reasoned, for what was to stop her from cutting the call.

'So…if you didn't poison Madhuri's ears, was it you who anonymously tipped off the police that I might have something to do with Nandu's death?' I said, moving to the next question on my agenda.

Sundar's expression and demeanour were dead giveaways. He seemed to have momentarily stopped breathing, while his facial muscles sprang to life, twitching and ticking, 'What? No…no I didn't do that either, Godbole. Come on, please… don't get such things into your head…Why would you think so?'

'Maybe because you're such a good citizen, Sundar. Like how you reported me to the police last time, when that Borg incident happened,' I said, screwing with him some more.

'That…was different and I really shouldn't have. Look, I've not done anything,' he pleaded again.

I gave him another long, silent look that made him queasier, then said, 'All right, I'll take your word for it, Sundar. See you around. And do nothing that turns my attention to you, and shortens your life.'

He nodded, turning white two or three times over, I noted with satisfaction, as I walked away. The countdown to Sundar Nambiar's murder had begun!

39

SHOWDOWN

'Who's the young woman who comes here for your therapy and counselling sessions?' Trupti asked, pursing her lips primly after speaking. Her one eyebrow was slightly raised, and she looked the spitting image of her unpleasant mother.

Ah, so Sushilabai had probably told her about Madhuri! I cocked a rebellious eye at Trupti. 'What about her?'

My daughter un-pursed her lips. 'I'd like to meet her…'

'What for?' I asked, already fatigued by Trupti's presence, after a mere three days. It was as if Sumitra had never raised her to be my daughter, but rather as a replica of herself to harangue me.

'Just to make sure that she is not a con woman in the guise of a counsellor, Papa,' Trupti replied tartly.

I smirked. 'Her therapy is fantastic. It's done wonders for me. But she's out of town.'

Trupti looked sour. 'When will she be back? Or I can always speak to her on the phone, can't I?'

'No, you can't, because it's none of your business, Trupti,' I replied, in the kind of tone I had only dreamt of using with Sumitra and her for years. The impact was wonderfully gratifying. Trupti's mouth shot open, her eyes flashed, and her nostrils flared. She made a number of noises of feminine outrage.

'Papa, what's got into you?' she finally said, sounding super offended.

'Puberty!' I giggled. 'At the ripe old age of sixty-nine, my dear daughter…'

'Eeks,' she shrieked, putting her hands over her ears, 'Papa, stop this indecent talk.'

'Then don't ask me stupid, idiotic questions,' I retorted.

We glared at each other in a kind of Mexican stand-off, then Trupti said sullenly, 'I have to sort out mother's things. Give me the key to her almirah…'

'Ah!' I said and suddenly realized that I had still not recollected where the hiding place of the almirah key was. I hadn't so much as tried to remember or locate it. It had completely slipped my mind. And now that Trupti was asking for it, it felt like a blessing in disguise that I hadn't looked for it because I smelt an opportunity here.

'Hmmm…what have you decided about my US visit?' I asked Trupti.

'What? I told you, Papa. It is not convenient right now. Both Swanand and Vihan…' Trupti started saying.

'If I am not getting to travel to the US with you, you are not getting the key to that almirah, Trupti,' I interrupted her.

'What?'

'You aren't deaf, Trupti. You heard it right. If you want to access Sumitra's jewellery, and the other precious booty that she kept in the almirah, then you are taking me to the US with you,' I replied chirpily, looking at my daughter's eyes ablaze with the same spite that had animated her mother, while she was alive.

'But Mum's things belong to me now,' Trupti said, spluttering with fury. 'You have no right.'

'Who said so? Did she make a will, leaving it all to you?'

'She did not need to make a will. She told me.'

'Prove it then, daughter dearest. Until then, it all legally belongs to me, her bereaved husband,' I replied with a caustic smile. 'Who knows, I might leave it to Ravi's wife, Hema, or even to your stepmother.'

'Stepmother?' Trupti's voice shot through the roof.

'Yes, if I decide to marry again.'

'Marry again? Have you gone senile, Papa?'

'More like virile.'

Trupti goggled at me. 'You are out of your mind,' she shrieked.

'Well, I need someone to take care of me, don't I?' I said, chuckling to myself, mighty pleased at the meltdown I was witnessing. 'And if you are not going to do that, Trupti, then I have to arrange for company.'

My daughter glared at me, as if she might soon go up in flames through spontaneous combustion. 'It's that counsellor bitch, isn't it?'

I giggled. 'It could even be Sushilabai, you know.'

'Sushilabai?' Trupti screamed.

'Just joking, Trupti. Anyway, it's none of your business again. I will choose my bride.'

After simmering a while, Trupti finally capitulated. 'Okay, Papa.'

'Okay what?'

'Okay, you can come to the US with us,' she said, fuming. 'Now can I have the almirah key?'

'Not so fast, Trupti. I'm going to need that in writing. I also need you to upgrade the to and fro economy tickets that I have already booked to first class and reimburse me the earlier fare,' I said.

'You…you want me to pay for your first-class tickets?' Trupti asked, incensed again.

'Yes. Not just this trip. All trips from now on. You are getting the jewellery, aren't you?'

Trupti stared hard at me, then blinked. Game, set and match to me!

~

I owned and drove a car only for about eight or nine years in my mid-fifties and early sixties, when Sumitra had insisted that we needed one. My heart used to be in my mouth every time I drove. Then after a minor accident with an autorickshaw, whose uncouth driver proceeded to scare the living daylights out of me and extracted a hefty compensation on the spot, I decided to retire from driving altogether about five to six years ago.

This, of course, did not go down well with Sumitra, but it was one of the rare occasions when I stood my ground because I was more terrified of suffering or causing loss of life or limb, than of Sumitra's heckling. Ravi had helped me sell the car and that was that. Therefore, it was to him that I had turned a few days ago, now that I needed a car to re-learn driving.

'I think I need to start driving again, Ravi. Can I practise in your car?' I asked him a day or two before Trupti arrived.

'Of course, Kaka. You want me to come along for a few days?' he asked helpfully.

'No. I'll just take it during early mornings, when there's no traffic about,' I replied.

So, every morning, I'd take his car from his house, which was about twenty minutes away, and proceed to effectively shadow

Sundar, under the cover of practising driving. His morning walk route was still the same, with a few minor changes. The good thing was that he went out earlier than usual, while it was still a little dark and fewer people were around. I worked out all the patches where he was in the company of other walkers, and those where he was usually alone. There was one particular patch of lane, about 50 to 60 metres in length, which greatly interested me.

Sundar did notice me once or twice, but I pretended so hard to be focusing on re-learning driving, that although he shot me nervous glances, he didn't suspect that I was keeping a watch; anyway, we stayed in the same locality and thus, it was perfectly natural for me to practise driving hereabouts when there was low traffic.

After a few days of mounting my surveillance, I concluded that my plan was workable, and just needed a few finishing touches. There was a tree by the compound wall of a bungalow in the quiet 50-metre lane, which was the perfect spot for running a car into him at a speed of about 50 kms per hour. Since the tree was in the second half of the lane, from the side which I was planning to drive, I had enough space to accelerate at the entrance, and then ram into him at the right speed.

Sundar's back would be towards me, so that wasn't a problem. More so, because like most Indians he had the habit of walking on the left side of any road, rather than facing the traffic. This would work to my advantage. Secondly, there was a ditch next to the tree, left open when some pipeline repair work had been undertaken about a month ago. There were some cement blocks and construction material inside and around the ditch, kept haphazardly, and a portion of the pipe was also protruding out – so characteristic of our great country's cityscapes, courtesy responsible municipal corporations and other public works departments. Sundar was bound to fall into the ditch or on the paraphernalia when the car hit him, or even in the likelihood he realized he was about to be run over and tried to get out of the way, which is what made it such an ideal spot for my plan.

As soon as I had knocked him over, I'd drive away and disappear. Chances were high no one would witness the 'accident', it being so early in the morning and just a little dark. Even if someone did, no one might see the car number, which in any case I was planning to camouflage with some dirt and mud.

As regards the question of which car I was planning to use, I had another ace up my sleeve. It wasn't going to be Ravi's car for sure. Indeed, it was going to be a car that belonged to someone who owed me big time – someone who had recently said he would be more than willing to do me any favour. Yes! Kamal Kishore Puri would be the man whose car I was going to borrow, without him knowing what I was going to use it for, of course.

What's more, my getaway plan was also in place – flying off to the US with Trupti and Swanand, the very same evening, while the police were still groping for clues on Sundar's hit-and-run case.

I rang Kamal Kishore's doorbell now, ready to ask him for the promised favour!

~

Trupti was back two days later with a typed and notarized affidavit, committing to arrange for my travel and stay in the US every year for the next five years. She had also upgraded my tickets and brought cash to reimburse the fare that I had paid. An unsmiling Swanand had accompanied her this time.

'Okay, this will work for now, but once you have gone through all the contents of the almirah, make a list of all the jewellery and other stuff, so that it can be valued. Then, we'll make a formal legal agreement about this arrangement,' I said, beaming at the sour-looking couple.

My son-in-law shot me an ultra-hurt look. 'Don't you trust your own daughter, Baba?'

'No, I don't, Swanand,' I replied cheerfully. 'She's her mother's daughter, and neither really cared to do anything, except to dominate me.'

Trupti scowled. 'How can you think of me like that, Papa?'

'Prove me wrong, dear,' I replied. 'Let's see how you treat me here onwards, and at your home in the US.'

The couple exchanged glances. 'Where's the almirah key?' Trupti asked, switching topics.

'Oh, I can't for the life of me recollect where your mother kept it. You'll have to arrange for a locksmith or break it open,' I said with an impish grin, as their faces fell.

40

OUCH!

Later that day, Trupti and Swanand showed me the list of the booty.

I whistled, truly surprised at some of the stuff, which I couldn't even recollect buying for Sumitra. My late wife certainly seemed to have been adept at squirreling away, and investing in gold for herself.

'Not a bad haul for you, Trupti. Quite a collection of jewellery your mother seems to have amassed! All from my hard-earned money, I guess.'

Trupti's eyes glowed, and Swanand had gone back to being his smug self. It was decided that they would get a valuation done in the next few days, and we would then get the agreement done by a lawyer known to Ravi. Until then, the jewellery would remain in my cupboard, since the almirah's lock had had to be broken.

Both left, happy they had struck the bargain with me and not been eventually disappointed by the riches that the almirah had yielded. Of course, they hadn't bothered to clear the rest of the mess, including some papers and documents of Sumitra, which seemed unrelated to anything of value. How bloody typical of Swanand and Trupti! I had half a mind to just dump all the papers in the raddi, but decided to take a quick look to ensure that there were no papers or documents of consequence in the pile.

That's when an envelope caught my eye. It was a pink greeting card envelope, in vogue till social media and hyper connectivity virtually wiped out the concept of greeting cards for different occasions.

I didn't remember ever having given a greeting card to Sumitra. I had tried roses once, only to be rebuffed. Perhaps Trupti had sent her one sometime. I picked up the pink envelope and stared at it. There was nothing on the cover. I opened the flap and pulled out the greeting card.

On it was the image of a cartoon character doing a headstand and staring up with a goofy, starry-eyed look. A speech bubble emanated from the cartoon character's mouth, with the words 'I am head over heels…' The ellipsis clearly indicated opening the card to look overleaf for the punchline, which I proceeded to do.

Inside, in big, bold font, covering half the page, were printed the words completing the sentence '…IN LOVE WITH YOU!!!' The image of a red-coloured heart with a golden-coloured arrow piercing it, lay below the wording. And further down, with a ballpoint pen, were the handwritten words:

Darling SUMITRA
Happy Birthday!
Love
KK

My jaw dropped. Was I imagining things? A birthday card from my boss, Kamal Kishore Puri, to my wife, Sumitra! My mind boggled, trying to comprehend and wrap my head around this super corny, mind-altering discovery. Sumitra and KK? When? How? Why? Had that son of a scoundrel been cuckolding me?

I didn't have to look far for confirmation. There were two more envelopes Sumitra had kept all these years – another greeting card from Kamal Kishore and a letter. My eyes almost popped out of their sockets, as I read the letter in a kind of daze. Who could have thought an affair between Sumitra and KK possible? And the most baffling and unbelievable thing was how in the world had Sumitra incited such passion in anyone's heart? And yet, it all seemed to have happened over thirty years ago!

No wonder Kamal Kishore had appeared so apologetic at the naturopathy camp! Not just because he had ill-treated me as a boss, but basically because he had had a torrid affair with my wife. That was the real reason for all his guilt and remorse, which had left me so puzzled. Well now that the cat was out of the bag, it was time to make Kamal Kishore pay, I decided there and then!

The revenge that I had foregone, was now back on the cards again. All it needed was a slight change in plans!

41

HIT JOB

'What is it, Gajanan? Why did you want to talk to me in private?' Kamal Kishore Puri asked me as we sat at a café.

I had half a mind to pick up the hot coffee being served by the waiter on the table next to ours, and pour it on Kamal Kishore's groin. But his scalded crotch wasn't adequate enough to qualify as apt revenge or punishment for his crimes, so I desisted.

'Puri, you piece of turd, I know about you and Sumitra,' I said with a calm frostiness, calculated to chill him to the bone.

And Kamal Kishore did sit absolutely still for a few seconds – his expression frozen, as if I had shouted 'Statue' at him. Then he gave a glimpse of the original Kamal Kishore Puri of yore, as I had known him back then.

His face turned red and his temper flared. 'What nonsense, Gajanan! Mind your f...king tongue!'

My foot shot out under the table and landed a well-timed kick on his right shin.

'Ouch!' he yelped and the pain travelled all the way up, reflecting on his face.

'I am so sorry, Kamal Kishore,' I said cheekily. 'That kick was aimed at your balls, not your shin.'

'How dare you?' he said, still rubbing his shin, glowering at me.

In response, this time I landed a sharp, sweet kick on his other shin.

'Ow!' he cried out louder, and now the other people in the café also seemed to take notice as he ranted. 'You bastard, Gajanan.'

I grinned at him and all the other people staring at us. 'Folks, this is Kamal Kishore Puri, my former boss. I just learnt that he had an affair with my wife thirty years ago,' I said at the top of my voice.

Puri's face turned pathetic and redder still, but his tone suddenly changed. 'Shut up, Gajanan,' he implored me.

'Then admit it, Kamal Kishore, you scum,' I said, with vicious amusement.

Why did violence feel so invigorating and empowering? All Kamal Kishore had to do was show more defiance and I was raring to land a punch on his bespectacled, irksome face.

The café manager had rushed over by now. 'Sir, please take your fight outside,' he said pointedly. 'No brawling here…'

I smiled at him, then looked at Kamal Kishore. 'Come, KK, you heard what the gentleman said. Let's settle this in a civilized manner elsewhere…'

Puri gave me a wary look, then got up without a word. 'Good we didn't order anything,' I said, getting up too, 'or it would have gone waste, after paying for it.'

Both of us walked out of the café, with the other customers watching us leave. 'So where do you want to confess?' I enquired.

'Gajanan, have you got dementia or Alzheimer's or that kind of thing?' Kamal Kishore Puri hissed, clearly nervous. 'Nothing like this ever happened.'

'Puri, you don't want to be slapped in the middle of the road, do you?' I snarled, but politely. 'I found your greeting cards and letter to Sumitra, damn it....'

He went into an almighty wobble, even as we walked down the road in silence. Just then I spotted a bus stop with a proper, undamaged shade. No one was around or waiting for a bus.

'Let's talk here,' I said and sat Puri down.

He was quiet for a few more seconds, recovering his composure. Then the story tumbled out. When I was on the transfer posting at Ichalkaranji, Sumitra had gone to my office for some work that I had asked her to get done, related to an office loan I had applied for. My boss, Srinivasan, had said Kamal Kishore's approval was needed as part of the formalities and that's how Sumitra had met him.

'I...I know it was wrong, but I...I just couldn't get her out of my mind,' Kamal Kishore said in a wistful tone.

I stared at him, perplexed that he was actually talking about Sumitra. What exactly was it about her that had bewitched him so much, when she'd held no allure for me?

'So...on some pretext I...I got your home address and dropped in to meet her,' Kamal Kishore continued his odious love narrative, 'and I realized she...she felt something for me too. Believe me, Gajanan, we...didn't know what was happening but...but...'

It felt surreal to hear him speak about himself and Sumitra like that. And then, in a flash, it all suddenly made sense to me. Why I had not remembered buying some of the jewellery for Sumitra, which Trupti and Swanand found in the almirah.

'I'll tell you what happened, you arsehole,' I cut in sardonically. 'Kamal Kishore Puri, Senior Regional Manager, is smitten by a lowly clerk's wife. She's easy game and is flattered…You bring her expensive gifts, maybe even jewellery and she gets ready to be seduced, for her husband's got no prospects of buying such stuff for her. You see your chance of some lustful trysts and a kind of revenge against me, by cuckolding me. This continues for about two years. Then you get tired and decide to end it, couching it in terms of how you can't leave your wife, and she her husband? Isn't it? She's also had her romp and her booty, and you've had your grand seduction…Things cool down, I'm back, but perhaps every now and then she gets in touch, and you gift her jewellery to keep her quiet.'

Kamal Kishore showed signs of being incensed. But he probably suspected that I was quite capable of more assault on his person, so he whimpered, 'It wasn't like that, Gajanan… believe me…You make it sound so sordid…I don't know what came over us. We…we knew it wasn't right…So after some time we stopped it…'

'I see…' I said nastily. 'Tell me, did you do it at my own house, in my bed, with my baby daughter under the same roof, sound asleep in the other room?'

He cringed, looking scared and shamefaced. 'Not always…'

I could have strangled him right there, in the bus shelter, but it wouldn't have been wise. Besides, as I had already decided, I needed Kamal Kishore to do something very important for me. Not that I had cared for Sumitra. But now I knew why she had withdrawn all conjugal privileges from me, so early in our lives, or had been so frigid, so as to suck out any enjoyment from it. It was because of all the clandestine pleasure she had probably derived from her romance with Kamal Kishore Puri.

And that's probably why she'd been perpetually irritable, spitting fire and oppressive towards me, all our married life thereafter. Because of her lost love, which probably had meant something, for why else would she have kept Kamal Kishore's cards and letter otherwise!

'You bloody well ruined my married life,' I snarled at a cowering Kamal Kishore. 'Sumitra got away without paying a price, but you sure aren't.'

'Look, I am so…so…sorry, Gajanan. I really am! It's been on my conscience,' Kamal Kishore said, with all the genuine remorse he could summon.

'Sorry doesn't cut it, KK. I need much more than your sorry,' I said tersely.

'What's that, Gajanan?' he asked apprehensively.

'Well, you have promised to loan me your car day after tomorrow. Now, you will also be driving it,' I replied with a chuckle.

'Drive it? Where?'

'Over someone,' I said and grinned.

'What?'

'I was going to mow someone down with your car, and now you will be doing it for me,' I said and quickly proceeded to tell him of my plan to get rid of Sundar.

As he listened, Kamal Kishore Puri looked on with horror, as if I was disembowelling him. 'Are you…you…nuts? You want me to kill this fellow?'

'Correct, KK! But don't worry, it won't be murder, just a hit-and-run,' I said soothingly. 'All you have to say is that you lost control while driving on account of your advanced age. The maximum you will get is a two-year sentence for rash driving, and that too a good lawyer can get reduced to just one year by citing your age and spotless record as a citizen. Simple! I get my revenge on Sundar Nambiar, the man you are going to run over. And thus, you pay your debt to me. It is a win-win for all.'

'You are a raving lunatic, Gajanan,' Kamal Kishore Puri croaked. 'I…I won't do it. I can't do it…'

'Oh, come on, Puri, you blasted adulterer, do you know what I'll do if you don't knock off Sundar?' I said, at my gentle and persuasive best. 'I'll inform your entire family, your children's in-laws and relatives that you had an affair with my wife many, many years ago. I'll show them all the evidence – the greeting cards and the letter, all in your handwriting. Next, I will file a case against you since adultery was an offence in India when you indulged in it, and then demand a hefty compensation as a cheated husband.'

I let it sink in as his face contorted with the weight of the possible consequences, then I spoke again. 'And then, I've also got one last alternative. I might even think of killing you to exact my revenge, if you don't kill Sundar for me!'

'What?'

'Just like I am going to kill Sundar day after tomorrow, with or without you. Trust me.'

He stared at me for a minute, then threw in the towel. 'All right,' he said in a voice that seemed as if it came from a crypt.

'I knew you were a smart man, Kamal Kishore Puri. Now, let's do a recce and a dry run. Where's your car?'

~

Thirty-six hours later, we were in position, waiting for our rendezvous with Sundar Nambiar's death. It was 5.45 a.m. If all went well – and why wouldn't it – Sundar would be sleeping the big sleep under the car between 6.05 to 6.10 a.m. A thrill of anticipation ran through me. I felt like one of those underworld hitmen, lying in wait for their hapless victim.

My packing for the US was done too. Trupti, Swanand and I were going to leave for Mumbai International Airport just after lunch to catch the 10 p.m. flight.

Roping in Kamal Kishore Puri as an accomplice and henchman had been a terrific piece of luck, because it had greatly simplified my task. As the Marathi saying goes – always get a guest to kill the snake. That way, the snake dies, you are safe, and it's the guest who runs the danger of getting bitten, if at all. My role was now just going to be that of a director, shouting 'Action' and 'Cut'!

In a few minutes from now, I was going to alight from the car as soon as I saw Sundar turn into the lane. This would be the cue for KK to start the car and get ready. I would then discreetly watch Sundar make his way up the lane and signal KK, who would then put the car into gear, turn into the lane, accelerate, and drive straight into Sundar, at the spot by the tree next to the ditch – just the way I had showed him during the dry run.

And when that happened, all I needed to do was walk away, back home. Depending on the situation, Kamal Kishore was to either make his getaway if there was no one around who had seen the 'hit-and-run' or call the police, claim it was an accident and surrender, if a watchman or two from one of the buildings or bungalows appeared after the sound of the crash and thus became a witness. He would probably be out by evening or at most spend a day in custody, before being released after giving a statement, while I would be thousands of miles away.

But perhaps I had become smug too soon. Kamal Kishore had been showing signs of nerves, but I reckoned everyone gets stage fright. So I was sure he'd pull himself together when the time came. Instead, just as the time drew nearer, Kamal Kishore said, 'Gajanan, please don't make me do this. It's a sin to kill someone…I can't…I can't…please, please.'

While this eventuality had crossed my mind, of course, I was still annoyed. 'You dare not chicken out now, Kamal Kishore, or I swear I'll mow you down one day.'

'No, no, listen to me please, Gajanan. I am prepared to own up to the accident and take the punishment for it. I just don't want to do the actual killing,' KK said, his hands folded and a look of abject wretchedness on his face. 'You do that, you drive into the man and jump out later. I'll say I was driving. I swear, Gajanan.'

I regarded the trembling, pathetic creature who had once made me tremble in my boots. Sumitra should have seen him now and perhaps she wouldn't have been as enamoured. Time was ticking away. Just a few minutes were left before Sundar was expected. I had to make a quick decision. I ran the whole scenario through my mind.

'Okay, here's how we'll do it, Puri. I'll drive into Sundar, knock him dead. Then, I'll reverse the car a little, so that you get space to jump out of the passenger side and hop around to the driver's side, while I simply slide over to the passenger seat, without getting out. Okay? That way, even if anyone's around they'll only see you get out of the car and might not remember which side you got out from,' I said, improvising rather brilliantly, I thought. 'Then we drive away, and you drop me after some distance and report the accident. Understood!'

'Yes...yes...Okay, all right, thanks, Gajanan,' Kamal Kishore Puri said with palpable relief. And the fellow actually grasped my hands and kissed them, as if I was royalty, granting him clemency. 'You are very kind, Gajanan. Thank you for sparing me this.'

We swiftly exchanged seats and I revved up the engine, as I got into the driver's seat. I was now the director and the actor. The countdown in my head began and I focused hard. Sundar would come into sight any moment now. He was overdue. I had to rely entirely on my own judgement now; when to turn into the lane after he entered it, and of course, executing the hit-and-run to perfection – the right timing, the right speed, the right spot!

I was suddenly pepped up. Kamal Kishore had backed out, resulting in this last-minute change of plan, but it also sent my adrenalin soaring! How much more of a kick I would now get, crashing the car personally into Sundar and ending his debauched life – to glimpse the terrified look in his eyes, experience the impact of his body being hit, hear his bones crunch and watch his blood spill. Oh, wow, this was going to be a real treat!

I looked at my watch. Was he late? Had he simply decided to be lazy and skip his walk today? Why was he not showing up? 'Stay calm!' I told myself.

Two more tense minutes passed, and then suddenly Sundar came into sight, in his phosphorus green t-shirt that I had often seen him wear. Yes, this was it – the long-awaited moment had arrived. I suddenly sensed what thousands of assassins must've sensed, since times immemorial.

I waited for him to walk up the lane and quietly drove into it behind him. I threw a glance around to see if anyone was around, then began moving the car again.

'My God! Hei Ram, forgive me!' Kamal Kishore began muttering.

'Shut up, KK,' I snapped and accelerated, all pumped up to strike Sundar.

The car picked up speed, and I raced towards Sundar. I was just about 10 feet way from him, when he looked over his shoulder. His body stiffened and the muscles of his face split every which way, streaked with horror as I careened towards him.

I heard him scream, and felt the impact as the car bonnet made contact with his body. So far so good. But the best laid plans of mice and men often go awry, as they say. The car spun out of my control, as I failed to apply the brakes, and after knocking down Sundar, hit the tree, lurched forward, and crashed into the adjacent ditch.

My body convulsed and shuddered as the car thudded to a halt. Something big exploded in front of my face and pinned me to my seat, pressing against my body. Bloody hell, I hadn't reckoned with that pesky thing called an airbag.

Dazed, I tried taking stock. How was I supposed to move to the passenger seat? I tried to reach out and unbuckle my seat belt, but it wouldn't. 'KK,' I called out. 'Help me out of the driver's seat.'

There was no response. I looked sideways, pushing aside the airbag. Kamal Kishore was slumped forward against the dashboard, his body in a twisted, unnatural position, with no seat belt holding him in place. If there was supposed to be an airbag on his side, that had clearly not deployed. The windshield seemed to have cracked. I could also see some blood.

I had been aware of some voices in the distance. These were now nearer. I looked into the rear-view mirror. An old couple seemed to be gaping at something lying on the road, behind the car. Probably Sundar's body, I guessed.

Then someone knocked at the car window on my side. 'Are you okay?' a muffled voice asked me. 'Open the door.'

'My God,' someone else exclaimed. 'I think the old man in the passenger seat is badly injured.'

'And isn't this that fellow, Sundar Nambiar. I…I think he's dead.'

I nodded to the woman who had asked me if I was okay and tried to move, to open the door. Excruciating pain shot through my ribs. 'Ouch!' I said.

'Don't move, don't move,' someone advised.

'But what if the car catches fire…'

'That happens only in movies...'

'Call an ambulance...'

'Call the police...'

'Ambulance is 112, right?'

'No, it's 108 for ambulance, 112 for police.'

'Then what's 100?'

'Just call any of those numbers.'

'I don't carry my mobile on morning walks.' Those were the last words I heard before I passed out.

42

THE WORM TO SNAKE PARADIGM

When I regained consciousness, I was where I hadn't expected to be when I had planned it all – the hospital. Trupti and Swanand were regarding me vexedly, and I suddenly had the urge to stick out my tongue at them. I would've loved to see their reactions.

Ravi and his wife, Hema, were there too, and soon the room filled up with more people – a ward boy, a nurse, a doctor and yes, a policeman.

It seemed I had suffered two broken ribs and minor burns on the inside of my right forearm, caused by the airbag as it deployed. Sundar Nambiar was dead – I had managed to maul him beyond repair. And while I had aimed to commit only one murder, I was told I had managed to kill two, for Kamal Kishore Puri too had kicked the bucket – succumbing to his injuries and consequent cardiac complications. One plus one free! Bullseye!

The news perked me up a great deal and I felt as if I was on cloud nine, even though everyone else appeared sombre and seemed unlikely to share my ecstasy.

Of course, I had been booked for rash driving and for causing the deaths of two human beings. But hey, I had a good chance of getting away with murder. I played my part as a distressed old man, consumed by remorse at what had happened. The policeman listened intently as I gave my statement, describing how the accident had occurred.

'The man in the green t-shirt, he suddenly tried to cross the road unmindfully and…and…Oh my God, I couldn't hit the brakes in time,' I said, breaking down super convincingly. 'Forgive me, God. Punish me! It's my fault. I should've been more alert.'

The policeman looked sceptical, but assured me that I would not be taken into custody till I recovered and then, only if required.

Curtains fell on the momentous day. Although my original plan had indeed gone awry, and I had not been able to fly away to the USA after successful execution, the bonus of Kamal Kishore's death had more than made up for that. As one more Marathi saying about windfall gains goes, the blind man prays for the boon of one eye, God gives him two! It probably applies to murders too.

Trupti and Swanand departed two days later without me, leaving Ravi to take care of the mess and me. I didn't let them take Sumitra's gold though! My nephew, as always, the gem of a person he is, arranged for a lawyer, who said I had nothing to worry about. It was an accident, and we would plead my advanced age to get a minimum sentence, but all that would anyway take at least two years for the case to get to the trial stage. So there was no immediate danger of imprisonment. I was in a kind of sweet spot, for everything seemed to be working out well.

Trouble, however, began on the fourth day, when the policeman came back, this time accompanied by the crime branch officer, Inspector Wakde, who had so recently interrogated me. He eyed me rather critically, asked me to recount what happened, but didn't seem in the least to be taken in by my helpless senior citizen act this time.

'Interesting. Mr Godbole, we have fresh information that you nursed a grudge against Mr Sundar Nambiar, just as you did against Mr Nandu Khandagale earlier,' he said nastily, watching my reaction. 'That you staged this accident, but it was actually a murder.'

I put on a pained expression, giving nothing away. 'Who is spreading such baseless canards against me, Inspector, and why? What grudge? I didn't even know Mr Sundar Nambiar.'

'How could you not know Mr Sundar? Wasn't he the one who filed a complaint against you under the Cruelty to Animals provisions, about three years ago?' Wakde challenged me, his tone and tenor now quite offensive.

So, it had to be Madhuri who was his informant, not Sundar. I had been wrong.

I didn't reply. The police couldn't force one to self-incriminate, could they? They needed to have hard evidence.

'We understand you also hired a private detective to follow Sundar around a few months ago,' Inspector Wakde continued, staring at me with his beady eyes. 'The fellow told us all about it. Now why would you have him do that?'

Ah! I had to watch my step now. Wakde had started ferreting out some circumstantial evidence against me. Far from conclusive, but enough to make them start digging for more.

I stuck stoically to the policy of silence, but I could see from Ravi's expressions that he was shocked. He would have recollected the dog attack case and Sundar's involvement in it.

'You can remain silent till you are discharged from the hospital, Mr Godbole,' Wakde sneered, 'but not once the court grants us your custody on prima facie suspicion of murder, you crafty old man.'

'You are letting your imagination run away with you, Inspector. Who will believe that a seventy-year-old harmless man like me would be a killer?' I finally said. 'Now please let me rest and recuperate.'

Inspector Wakde gave me a grim smile and left with the other policeman.

A minute of pin-drop silence followed as Ravi gaped at me. 'Kaka, what's all this? I mean, should we get you a good lawyer who specializes in criminal cases not traffic offences?' the poor boy asked me. I nodded after a moment's hesitation.

Truth be told, it was kind of getting exciting!

~

Well, that conversation was about two months ago. Ravi has got me the best criminal lawyer in town, but I am still in jail, while Inspector Wakde tries to piece together enough evidence to file a chargesheet.

He has interrogated me about half a dozen times, and it tickles me pink that I always manage to tire him out. I must say, he is not doing a bad job. He found out that I was engaged to Geeta Hirway once upon a time and that I had visited her at her showroom in Thane some months ago. He told me he has also got forensic evidence to establish my presence in her sister's house and on her body, when I strangled her.

The indefatigable inspector also traced Kamal Kishore's letters to Sumitra during a search of my house and through advance IT history search, evidence of my looking up 'datura' poison on the internet on Ravi's laptop. Ah, well, he's still a long way from having clinching evidence that will stick that I committed the murders.

And then, my lawyer also told me it takes years for a murder trial to be started and completed – at least five to six. So, it's a long, long way to conviction, and I am bound to get bail at some point in time after three months. So I am waiting eagerly to walk free and murder again.

I still have one more name on the original grudge list – Srinivas Bapat – and I am going to pay him a visit once I am out of here on bail. I am sure the man will be more than happy to apologize, given the rockstar reputation I have acquired now, having my photo and name splashed sensationally across newspapers, TV and social media as the prime accused in four murders. And if he still doesn't, well what's a fifth murder for someone who has already committed four? I rub my hands with glee at the prospect.

Oh, and yes, I may add one more name to my grudge list – sweet Madhuri Awati. Honestly, my lust, maybe love, overpowers any grudge I feel against her for ratting on me. So, all will be forgiven if she agrees to consort with me again. Hell, I am even ready to propose marriage. But she's got to reach out to her Viru or embrace him when he comes calling, once he's out on bail. If that does not happen, well then, I will have to add her to my grudge list!

That's just the nature of things because, you see, when worms finally turn, they stay turned! They might even turn into snakes. They just can't go back to being worms!

ACKNOWLEDGEMENTS

I don't have a long list of people to thank. Only two individuals, whom I can't thank enough – Thomas Abraham, managing director, Hachette India, and Anupama Manral, my editor.

Being published by one of the best publishers worldwide is a dream come true, and it couldn't have been possible if they hadn't responded the way they did.

And then of course, I owe a great deal to the two places where I wrote this book – Pune, the city of my birth, and Gullkistan Residency, Laugarvatn, Iceland.

Salil Desai
Pune
November 2024